M000027971

Chained to the Streets

Lock Down Publications and
Ca$h Presents
Chained to the Streets
A Novel by **J-Blunt**

Chained to the Streets

Lock Down Publications
P.O. Box 870494
Mesquite, Tx 75187

Visit our website
www.lockdownpublications.com

Copyright 2020 by J-Blunt
Chained to the Streets

All rights reserved. No part of this book may be reproduced in any form or by electronic or mechanical means, including information storage and retrieval systems without permission in writing from the publisher, except by a reviewer who may quote brief passages in review. First Edition January 2020
Printed in the United States of America

This is a work of fiction. Names, characters, places, and incidents either are products of the author's imagination or are used fictitiously. Any similarity to actual events or locales or persons, living or dead, is entirely coincidental.

Lock Down Publications
Like our page on Facebook: Lock Down Publications @
www.facebook.com/lockdownpublications.ldp
Cover design and layout by: **Dynasty Cover Me**
Book interior design by: **Shawn Walker**
Edited by: **Jill Duska**

UF
I-Blunt

Stay Connected with Us!

Text **LOCKDOWN** to 22828 to stay up-to-date
with new releases, sneak peeks, contests and more…

Submission Guideline.

Submit the first three chapters of your completed manuscript to ldpsubmissions@gmail.com, subject line: Your book's title. The manuscript must be in a .doc file and sent as an attachment. The document should be in Times New Roman, double-spaced and in size 12 font. Also, provide your synopsis and full contact information. If sending multiple submissions, they must each be in a separate email.

Have a story but no way to send it electronically? You can still submit to LDP/Ca$h Presents. Send in the first three chapters, written or typed, of your completed manuscript to:

LDP: Submissions Dept
Po Box 870494
Mesquite, Tx 75187

DO NOT send original manuscript. Must be a duplicate.

Provide your synopsis and a cover letter containing your full contact information.

Thanks for considering LDP and Ca$h Presents.

J-Blunt

PROLOGUE

"You know how I get down, my nigga. Ain't nobody movin' me from 'round here. Fuck Wacco! Nigga don't put no fear in me. My heart don't pump Kool-Aid. Nigga bleeds just like us," Jay vented, running a hand across the bulge at his waist.

"I hear you, my nigga. But we gotta be on point. That nigga runnin' all these blocks 'cause niggas ain't standin' up. All them niggas wanna ride dicks and be his shooters. But I'm wit'chu, my nigga. My mama stay on the next block. I was raised over here. Ain't no nigga finna tell me I can't get money in the hood I grew up in. I been blazin' niggas on these corners since I was a pup," Maniac breathed, searching the dark streets for signs of movement.

They were standing on the porch of one of the many abandoned houses that littered the impoverished neighborhood. Maniac and Jay had been friends for as long as they could remember. They grew up and threw up in the ghetto. It was all they knew - where they got money, partied, and would probably die. The hood for them was 41st and Clarke. Dangerous with a capitol D. Eighty percent of the homicides that happened in Milwaukee were in a four mile radius on the North side. Clarke was right smack in the middle of that four mile zone. Here today, gone tomorrow, was more than a statement. It was a part of life. Like breathing, or taking your last breath.

"Who dat?" Jay squinted, ducking slightly and reaching under his shirt.

A red Chevy Malibu that had seen better days pulled up to the curb. When the driver's door opened, the interior lights came on, allowing the men on the porch to see the car's lone occupant.

"That's action. I got this one." Maniac smiled, his rail-thin 6'6" frame slithering from the porch like a snake. "Cookie! What's up, girl?"

"Hey, nephew. You working?" she asked, climbing from the car with a hopeful glee in her glossy yellow eyes. Life had been hard on the crack addict. The pock marks covering her face and purple-black gums empty of teeth testified to that. The small, emaciated woman wore a dingy gray T-shirt, dark pants, and cheap black shoes that curled at the toes. Hair matted and uncombed made her the picture-perfect dopefiend.

"You know I got that work. What'chu need?" he asked, making a fist, bringing it to his lips and spitting the rocks he had under his tongue into his palm.

Cookie used a finger to pick through the ten dollar bags, searching for the biggest one. "Can I get two for fifteen?"

"C'mon, Cookie. Why you always do this to me, baby? That short shit gettin' old."

She looked disappointed. "But Draco n'em gimme two for fifteen all day."

"You see Draco or them li'l hoe-ass niggas out here? You know them niggas' shit be stepped on like a mu'fucka. I got A-1."

Cookie hesitated, looking up on the porch to Jay, hoping he would intervene and hook her up. At that same moment, a black 1987 Monte Carlo SS on 28" chrome wheels turned onto the block. Jay and Maniac noticed the car at the same time.

"Here. Gimme the money. Here go two."

Cookie smiled as they exchanged money for product. "Good lookin', nephew. Y'all stay out here. I'ma be back in a - "

"What you niggas doin' out here?"

Cookie spun around at the sound of the new voice. The Monte Carlo had come to a stop in the middle of the street. A brown-skinned man with rainbow-dyed dreadlocks was hanging halfway out the passenger window.

"Fuck you mean, nigga? We posted," Jay spat, hand inching closer to the pistol tucked in his waistband.

"Y'all niggas know this my uncle shit. Wacco don't want nobody hustling out here that ain't wit' the squad. I fuck wit'chu, Jay, but you can't keep testing us, my nigga. Y'all can't get money over here no more. This CSG shit. Only Clarke Street Goons gettin' it over here. Y'all gotta move around."

"We ain't honoring that, Draco. My mama live down the street. This our shit, too," Maniac spoke up.

Cookie looked back and forth from the car to the porch during the exchange. Something bad was about to happen. She could feel it. And she was stuck in the middle. Her only hope was to get to her car and get the hell out of there, but the Monte Carlo had her boxed in. And right when she decided to make her move, Jay went for his waist. He pulled the black 45 automatic and fired recklessly. The hand cannon roared like a beast, sending death towards the Monte Carlo at lightning speed.

Boom, boom, boom, boom, boom!

Maniac jumped to the ground, lying on his stomach.

Draco pulled a Glock 17 and returned fire as the Monte Carlo sped away.

Pop, pop, pop, pop, pop, pop, pop, pop, pop!

Jay ran from the porch, Swiss-cheesing the fleeing car, emptying the clip. "Bitch-ass nigga!" He got off the ground, laughing and dusting himself off. "You's a fool, my nigga!"

"H-help!"

The men spun at the distressed voice and found Cookie lying on the ground. She held a hand against her throat. Blood leaked through her fingers, turning the gold one-inch crucifix around her neck red.

J-Blunt

CHAPTER 1

The darkness moved.

That's what Dennis O'Flaherty thought as he blinked a couple of times, straining his eyes to see better. He moved the assault rifle from his shoulder, finger on the trigger, barrel leading the way as he went to investigate. There were fifteen large wooden crates near the wall at the back of the warehouse. He walked behind them, heart pounding in his chest like a kick drum. His nerves weren't what they used to be and he was terrified at the thought of having to shoot the gun. But the property he guarded was important and he had a job to do. He looked left, then right. No one was there. Nothing moved. But he could've sworn...

"I need to get high like a mutherfucker." He chuckled, slinging the assault rifle onto his shoulder.

Dennis was a little man, barely 5'5" tall and rail thin. Blotchy pale skin, thinning blonde hair, and a large forehead made him far from handsome. Being involved in high crimes was supposed to be a thing of the past. After burning out in the Army and doing a year in prison, the last thing he wanted to do was be involved in something that could get him in trouble. But then the drugs came. And heroin cost money.

The wooden crates were marked in big block letters that read PROPERTY OF THE U.S. GOVERNMENT. But Dennis didn't care about the crates or their contents. What he wanted most was a sniff of the powder in his pocket. He hadn't had a taste in more than five hours, since he began the watch shift. His body was fiending for the opioid. But he had to remain sober. Big brother's orders. So for now, he would have to settle for a cigarette.

He fished through his pocket for the pack of Marlboros and popped a nicotine stick between his lips. After striking the lighter, the blackness around him vanished as the small flame flickered. Dennis puffed clouds of smoke. And that's when he saw it. The darkness moved again. But it wasn't the darkness moving at all. Someone was moving in the dark!

Dennis dropped the lighter and went for the gun. Before he could handle the weapon, a sharpness pierced his throat. The cigarette fell from his lips, fire sparking from the cherry as it hit the ground. Dennis tried to scream while reaching for the object protruding from his neck. No words came out; only a gurgle. And when he tugged at the sharp object, blinding pain flashed behind his eyelids. His body convulsed. Consciousness escaped him as he teetered and fell.

Strong arms caught the body before it hit the floor. Dennis never felt the hands of his killer.

After hiding the dead man on the floor behind the crates, the darkness moved, using the shadows inside the warehouse to remain concealed. One down. Five to go.

***

"Where the fuck is Dennis?" Martin O'Flaherty cursed. Standing a couple inches over six feet with a lean build, the red-haired Irish native was pissed.

"Dumb ass is probably in the john passed out high." Eddie Hagen laughed.

The running joke amongst the security team was Dennis's incompetence. It was legendary. Not only was Dennis a burned-out alcoholic drug addict, but he was also, according to most of the squad, unfit for security. The junkie couldn't babysit a dead man, let alone help guard a shipment of precious cargo. The only reason he was put on the crew was because Martin O'Flaherty, their boss, was throwing his piece of shit little brother a bone.

"Go find him," Martin ordered, his voice booming with authority. "The boys will be here in twenty. We need to look alive."

"When I find him, can I shoot him?" Eddie laughed.

"You shoot my brother and I'll tie you up and make you watch while I fuck your mother and kill your father," Martin threatened.

The smile vanished from Eddie's face. When the boss was angry, he wasn't to be fucked with. Period. Eddie left the room, nodding towards the two men that guarded the door.

"You guys seen Dennis?"

Sammy glanced towards the lower level. "Yeah. 'Bout ten minutes ago he went downstairs to make a round. He's probably in the bathroom shooting that poison in his veins. You might find him in the stall passed out."

"Everybody knows he's a piece of shit except the boss." Eddie chuckled. "The buyers will be here in twenty minutes. Look alive," he said before heading down the iron stairwell.

The warehouse was relatively small and dimly-lit, two hundred square feet of mostly open space. Built in the nineties, it had been a paper mill and then a store house. Now it was vacant. Owned by Martin. He used it for deals, like the one he was making tonight. Inside those fifteen crates were arms stolen from the United States Government - five million dollars' worth.

"Hey Dennis! Where are you? Get out here!" Eddie called as he neared the bathroom. He stopped at the door to knock. "Dennis, you in there? Your bowels collapse?" he joked.

When no one answered, he tried the knob. The door opened and he took a step into the bathroom. A sudden pain at the base of his skull made his body freeze. He tried to reach a hand back to find the cause of pain, but his legs gave out and the cold floor met his face. When he realized his limbs didn't work, he began to panic. He tried to scream, but couldn't open his mouth. A blinding pain flashed in his brain and his body began seizing. Eddie could feel death robbing him of sight. And right before he died, he saw the darkness move, dragging his lifeless body out of sight.

"Cobra Command, this is Cobra. Over," the darkness whispered into a communications device embedded in his ear.

"Cobra Command reads you loud and clear."

"The target is on the second level. Two guarding the door. Another in the room with him. An iron staircase is the only way up. Stealth will be compromised if I attempt. How long will it take to knock out the power?"

"One moment." After a pause, Cobra Command spoke. "I'm checking the schematics. I can have power out in about a minute.

But the backup power is not accessible. When the lights go out, you have about ten seconds before the backups come on. Will that do?"

Cobra let out a dissatisfied grunt. "It will have to. Give me a chirp before lights out. Cobra out."

The trained assassin opened the bathroom door slowly, gripping a poisoned stiletto, ready to let it fly while listening for sounds of movement. When satisfied that no one would jump out, he moved, edging along the wall, hiding in the shadows. The iron staircase was in sight, thirty feet away. He flipped on the night vision shades and waited. The time ticked slowly, allowing him to think on the dangers of the mission. He was in another country. The only firearm he carried was a Walter PP7. Fifteen shot magazine. Two extra clips. And the poison knives. Twelve of them. His enemies were armed with enough weapons to start a war. Not to mention the crates of missiles. If he was compromised, it would be a worldwide political nightmare. And he would be killed. The healed scars on his body attested to the dangers that were part of the job.

When the chirp sounded in the earpiece, he snapped to attention. He gritted his teeth, gripping two knives, muscles twitching, anticipating the action. The darkness came in an instant.

The trained killer covered the space to the stairwell in six steps. His boots clanged against the steel stairs as he took them three at a time. He could hear the guards talking about the darkness. They came into focus at the top of the stairs. Behind the goggles, their features were back and white. They were armed with automatic rifles. Pointing them at the stairwell.

"Eddie, is that you?"

Cobra let the knives fly. One of them hit a guard in the eye. The second guard caught it in the throat. On the way to the ground, one of their guns fired.

"Shit!" Cobra cursed. The element of surprise was gone. The backup lights would be on any moment. He grabbed another poison knife as he reached the door. After yanking it open, he charged the room. Two men were standing, pointing handguns at the door.

"Borris, that you?" Martin questioned, wondering if the guy in the room with him had opened the door.

The stiletto whistled through the darkness, landing in Borris's throat. Martin began shooting blindly. The cobra dove forward into a tuck roll, removing the night vision glasses and getting out of the line of fire. He was on his feet in the blink of an eye, his motions fluid and catlike.

The lights came on and Martin saw the big man dressed in black fatigues and face paint standing an arm's length away. He turned the gun towards the stranger, but never got off a shot. The big man grabbed his wrist and twisted. Bones cracked and the gun fell.

"Aaahh shit!" Martin screamed, taking a swing with his free hand.

The trained killer easily blocked the punch and returned a hard elbow to the Irishman's throat. Martin collapsed to the ground, holding his bruised neck. He stared up at his assailant, the fear of God in his eyes.

"Please don't kill me!"

"Shut the fuck up! You stole from the United States and we came to collect."

***

"Look at the real life GI fucking Joe!" Marshall "The Slayer" Sanchez laughed, slapping the bar.

"C'mon, Slayer. Why don't you tell the whole fuckin' world we SEALS," Desmond said, embracing his friend and brother in arms.

"Beat it with the Bruce Wayne shit. Being a SEAL is like being a superhero. Bitches love superheroes. Bruce Wayne would get way more pussy if he let everybody know he was Batman. And so would we. We're in Paris, France. These bitches love us. I got that Latino swag from Mexico and you got that Zulu sauce from Africa. C'mon, bro. If bragging about being a SEAL gets us pussy, let's do it."

Desmond shook his head, taking a seat at the bar. Like Slayer said, he was a Navy SEAL, the best of the best, trained in weapons, stealth, torture, hand-to-hand combat, explosives, and survival. He had been with the Navy's Sea Air Land and Special Operations unit for five years. He had spent all of his adult life in the armed forces:

three years in the Army, three years in the Marines, and five years as a SEAL. At thirty years old, he was in the best shape of his life. Standing 6'3" and a solid 225 pounds, the extra-large black T-shirt fit snugly, showing off defined traps and sculpted arms. Hair cut low. Dark-brown complexion. Eyes deep set and black. A wide nose. Strong jawline. A healthy white smile. Desmond was a handsome man, but the discipline of a military life kept him humble.

"We also gotta worry about enemies and our CO finding out you're telling the world that America's most dangerous weapons are exposed. If Colonel Jones finds out, you taking the heat."

Slayer shrugged. "I ain't exposed. I got a gun in my back and an AR in the room. I already spotted two ways to get out of here if things go bad. But fuck that, homie, order a drink. Bartender!"

The bartender was a large older man with a face weathered by many of life's storms. "What're ye having, mate?"

"An American beer, or whatever my friends is having."

"Irish whiskey," Slayer said, holding up his glass.

The bartender smiled. "Be right back."

"How many you kill this time?" Slayer asked.

"Can't talk about missions. I took an oath," Desmond said, keeping a straight face. "And there are three ways out. Window near the back, by the bathroom. You missed it."

Slayer turned to look towards the bathroom. He didn't see the window, but saw light from the sun reflecting off the floor. The window was there. "I missed that one. But fuck that window. We took the same fuckin' oath, fool. And we're in the same fuckin' squad, smart guy."

"But you didn't go on the mission. What happened anyway? Why'd they keep you on the base?"

The bartender returned with the drink and set it in front of Desmond. Slayer paused until he left, letting out a breath before taking a sip from the glass of dark whiskey. "Fuckin' bitch in Brazil is saying I raped her, bro. I'm being investigated."

Desmond's eyes popped. "You mean the chick from the bar after the Celeste mission?"

Slayer nodded. "I don't gotta take no pussy, bro. I might get a little rough, but I ain't no rapist. When we get back to base, they will talk to the rest of the squad."

"What do you want me to say?"

"Tell the truth, bro. We had drinks and got some girls. But I don't wanna talk about that right now. Shit is depressing. I'll deal with that later. Right now I'm focused on tomorrow's mission. Get these Parisian fucks."

"We're never out of the fight." Desmond nodded.

"Damn right. I'm not laying down for nobody. I'm from South Central, California. I was born fighting. Tell me about Ireland. What happened? If you don't tell me, Lester will. How many did y'all get?"

"Les does have a big mouth." Desmond laughed. "I got five."

Slayer looked disappointed. "A team of SEALS only killed five? You tellin' me they only had five people guarding fifteen Tomahawk missiles?"

Desmond nodded. "Just five. But the team didn't go in. Just me."

Slayer downed the drink and slammed it on the bar to get the bartender's attention. "Barkeep, fill me up! Now we're talking. How'd you do it? Sniper shit?"

"Throwing knives."

Slayers eyes grew wide as child's that had been told Santa left their favorite presents under the tree. "Throwing knives?"

The bartender came and filled the glass halfway before walking away.

"Couldn't risk a shootout and alerting the police. Had to get in and out with stealth. They had missiles and we couldn't explain that away. Shit would've started an international crisis."

Slayer pushed him in the chest. "Damn, man. Shit! You a beast, bro!"

"I can do a lot of shit. We're trained to kill." Desmond chuckled. "Now where these girls you called me about? Don't tell me you fakin' again because you lonely."

"What! Fuck you, bro. I'm Latino heat. Papi chulo," Slayer bragged, looking towards the door. "Matter of fact, they just walked in. They're pros, so let's get a couple drinks and get 'em back to the hotel. I already got us rooms."

After a nod, Desmond spun to get a look. Two women walked in. The blonde wore a form-fitting green dress that showed off big breasts and a slim figure. The brunette had on a loose-fitting purple summer dress and was also slim.

Slayer stood and waved them over. "Mamacitas! How are you doing? Nice to meet you."

The women smiled like they were meeting superstars as they hugged the men.

"Hi guys!" The blonde smiled, her Parisian accent heavy.

"Have a seat. Have a seat. You ladies are lookin' real fine. This is my friend, Desmond. Bro, this is Lexi and Grace."

Desmond nodded and smiled. "Nice to meet you."

"Hi, Dezmin," the brunette attempted, looking him from head to toe like she wanted to mix him in a drink and swallow him.

"Hey, Grace. I like the dress. Purple is your color."

"Thank you." She grinned. "Are you army man? Zuper hiro, yes?"

Desmond cut his eyes at Slayer. The Mexican gave a smile and wink before turning to Lexi.

"I'm not a superhero, but I am in the military. Don't believe everything Marshall says. He's a bad liar."

"Ahh, I zee. You have big muzles. I touch, yes?"

Before he could consent, Grace was feeling his arms.

"Zo zexy, yez. I like."

"Hey, bartender! Bring us some drinks!" Slayer called.

After a couple of rounds, the foursome left the pub and hopped a cab to the hotel. Slayer had already booked them separate rooms.

"I like a black-a-man, yez. Zo black. Zexy. And you have big ztick." Grace smiled, grabbing his crotch as they entered the room.

"And I like you, too. I like your blue eyes. Your body. And your accent is so sexy." Desmond smiled, falling onto the bed.

Grace climbed on top of him, her face hovering inches above his. "I like black-a-man's lipz. Big an zoft. Can I kizz?"

Desmond lifted his head, sucking her thin bottom lip into his mouth. She kissed him back aggressively, moaning as their tongues wrestled.

"I take thiz drezz off and you take off pant."

She stood and took the dress off, revealing that she wasn't wearing panties or a bra. Her breasts were small and perky, the pink nipples hard. Her athletic body was toned and sculpted, her pussy clean-shaven.

"You like?" she asked, doing a little shimmy.

"No." Desmond licked his lips. "I love it."

Grace lay back on the bed, her fingers dancing between her thighs as she watched him undress. Desmond took his time, first removing his shirt and showing his chiseled chest and eight pack abs, then his shoes and pants. After removing his underwear, he paused, hypnotizing the European woman with his magic stick. As if in a trance, Grace got on her knees and crawled to him, never taking her eyes off the prize. She grabbed it in her small hands and fondled him before opening wide. He was as big as a cucumber and she couldn't get that much in her mouth, so she focused on sucking the head and using both hands to jack him off. Desmond shuddered, closing his eyes as she went to work. She licked up and down the side and sucked his balls before focusing on the head again. When he'd had enough, he pushed her onto the bed and grabbed a condom from his pants. While he put on the protection, Grace fingered herself roughly.

"Do it hard," she ordered, her blue eyes crazed and serious.

Desmond smiled as he climbed between her legs. Unable to wait any longer, Grace grabbed his dick and shoved it in her box.

"Oh zhit! Yez! Fuck me, Dezmin! Fuck me!"

Her pussy was snug, so Desmond started off slow, giving her half the meat. He watched it go in and out, stretching her pussy lips, her juices making his dick shine. When she had loosened, he went deeper.

"Oh, yez! I feel it. Oh zhit!"

He got into a rhythm and gave her long strokes, beating the pussy up. And Grace loved it. She thrashed around the bed and screamed his name, making ugly sex faces.

"Yez, Dezmin! Yez! I love your big black dick! Yez!"

He lifted one of her legs onto his shoulder and went even deeper. His pelvis slapped into her pussy so hard that it sounded like someone being beaten.

When he got tired of looking at her ugly faces, he flipped her over and hit it from the back. Grace took the D like a champ, wanting it hard and fast. Her ass was red from him hitting it so hard.

"Oh, yez, Dezmin! Yez, yez, yez! Feelz zo good! Cum in my faze."

He slowed down to make sure he heard her. "What you say?"

"No, don't ztop. Keep going. Cum in my faze."

Desmond chuckled as he picked up the pace again. Grace was a straight-up freak and he loved it. And he also couldn't wait to bust in her face, so he pounded her pussy hard and fast. A few moments, later he could feel the load building. He pulled out of her, snatching off the condom and jacking off. Grace spun around, opening her mouth and sticking out her tongue.

"Aw shit!" Desmond grunted.

Thick white semen shot out of him, splashing onto Grace's face, tongue, and hair. Then he used his dick to smear the cum on her face like he was spreading mayonnaise on a piece of bread.

"Oh, yez, Dezmin! That waz zo hot!" she moaned, using her hands to rub his juices all over her neck and breasts.

The hot sex continued for another hour, finishing in the shower. After washing their bodies, Grace was on her way and he lay in bed and went to sleep.

It wasn't long before his phone rang. He thought about not answering. It was late and he was tired. But he had a mission coming up, and it might be someone from his squad. After checking the screen, he saw it was his commanding officer.

"Colonel Jones, why so late?"

"Hey, Desmond. Sorry so late, but it's urgent. I have a number for you to call. They want you to call as soon as you can. Like now."

Desmond memorized the number. "A Milwaukee area code? Whose number is this?"

"I wish there was an easy way to tell you this. But there's not, so I won't. I'm no good at this shit. I wish I could tell you more, but I can't. Just make the call. And if you need anything, I mean anything at all, don't hesitate to give me a call. Okay?"

Desmond wanted to know more, wanted to ask another question. But he knew the colonel well enough to know that was all the information he would get.

"Okay, Colonel. Thanks. I'll make the call."

Desmond felt a lump form in his throat as he dialed the number with the Milwaukee area code. He hadn't lived in the Brew City in almost ten years. And a call in the middle of the night told the news was probably bad.

"Detective Perry. Who's this?"

When Desmond heard the man's voice, he immediately questioned why a detective in Milwaukee was looking for him.

"Hey! Who's on the line? Hello?" the detective said in an irritated voice.

"Oh, sorry about that. I didn't know I called a police officer. I'm Desmond Harrison. Why are you looking for me?"

"Oh. Harrison. I hear you're over in Europe. What time is it over there?"

"Quit the shit, Detective. It's late. Why are you looking for me?"

He chuckled. "I should've known that you can see through bullshit. Look, soldier, there's no easy way to say this. I'm sorry. Do you know Mary Harrison, a.k.a. Cookie?"

Desmond felt a pain enter his chest, like he was having a heart attack. "Yeah. That's my mother."

"I'm sorry to have to tell you this. She was killed four days ago. Had a hard time tracking down next of kin. All we found for relatives was you in the computer. If it's possible, can you make the trip back to the States to identify and claim her body?"

J-Blunt

CHAPTER 2

"Good morning, sir. Good morning, Detective. I'm M.E. Gary Sandberg. If you and the gentleman would follow me, I'll need you to confirm the identity of the deceased."

Desmond eyed the short balding white man in the lab coat before nodding. "Let's do it. I'm ready."

The morgue was cold and it smelled of antiseptic cleaners and dirt. The combination made Desmond uncomfortable. It reminded him of a graveyard. And thinking of graveyards reminded him that he was a killer. In the name of freedom and defending the country he loved, Desmond's kill count was nearing a hundred. Ninety-six confirmed kills, to be exact. Ninety-six people that would never walk, talk, laugh, or breathe again. Did they deserve to die? Most of them, yes. But being in a place that reminded him of death was making the blood on his hands seem a little too real. It unnerved him. And he was further disturbed when they stopped at the refrigeration unit that held the dead bodies. His heartrate increased and palms turned clammy as images of Cookie flooded his mind. There were no good memories; only pain. No love; only hate. But he still hoped it wasn't her on the slab.

"You ready?" Detective Perry asked, laying a hand on his shoulder. The homicide detective was an inch shorter than Desmond. Tanned skin, broad shoulders, a thick frame, and slight gut. At forty-three years old, he had most of his brown hair, but was graying around the temples. He wore a dark suit and blue tie, his demeanor screaming "I'm a cop".

"I'm as ready as I'll ever be," Desmond managed.

The medical examiner opened the cooler and pulled out the slab. The deceased was a slim, dark-skinned female. Her hair was matted, facial features sunk in, skin blotchy, lips white. A numbness crept into Desmond's body when he saw her. To his dismay, it was Cookie, the woman that gave him life, whom he didn't feel an ounce of love for. But he did feel something: guilt.

"Do you need a moment?" the detective asked.

The SEAL remained stone-faced. "No. I'm good. That's her. My mother."

"Will you claim the body? The autopsy has been done. She died from a single GSW to the neck," the M.E. confirmed.

"Yes. I'll contact a funeral home and make the arrangements."

"Okay. If you'll come with me, I'll need you to sign a few papers, and then you can be on your way."

***

"So, what happened? Do you have anyone in custody?" Desmond asked as he and the detective stood outside the coroner's office.

"No. No witnesses either. You know how it is. Snitches get stitches. I think she was caught in a shootout. Two sets of shell casings were found. 9 mil and a 45. Your mom got hit by the 9. Drugs were in her hand. Crack. My guess is she was making a buy and got caught in the crossfire. There's a turf war going on over there. Narcs believe a clique of dealers is trying to take over the area and is kicking out and murdering rivals."

Desmond looked the cop in the eyes. "So what happens with Cookie's case? Honestly."

Detective Perry read the "don't bullshit me" look in the soldier's eyes. "I'm not going to lie to you. You're a good man and have sacrificed a lot for the country. And I've never met an actual Navy SEAL, so just being in your presence is an honor. Your mom's case has no priority. She was a crack addict shot dead while buying drugs. There is no community uproar, no Black Lives Matter protests, and hardly any media coverage. No family members came to identity her body or claim her. We found your name in the computer for bailing her out ten years ago. And trying to contact you was an investigation in itself. Taxpayers and the brass don't care about your mom's murder. We're understaffed and overworked. They don't want us to spend resources on a drug user. I don't think her murder will be solved unless a snitch comes forward."

Desmond became quiet, thinking about what the homicide detective said. Cookie died trying to get high. No one mourned or missed her. Her case wouldn't even be investigated. No one cared.

"I appreciate your honesty, Detective."

"I'm sorry, man. I wish I could do more."

"I know how it is," Desmond said before shaking his hand and heading towards the rental car.

From the coroner's office, Desmond drove to Serenity Funeral Home to make arrangements for Cookie's funeral. An hour later, he was pulling into the parking lot of the Pfister Hotel. After taking an elevator ride to the room, he plopped down on the bed and pulled the gold crucifix from his pocket. He had gotten it from the coroner. It was Cookie's only possession. Thoughts of his life giver filled his mind.

As a child, he had wished her death many nights after he got his ass whooped. Cookie had been a terrible mother. She beat him without mercy or reason, neglected him in every possible way. He had to steal food because she sold the food stamps for dope. The only time he got new clothes was when he stole them or committed a crime to get the money to buy them. School ended in the sixth grade. Since Cookie couldn't buy school supplies or clothes, she didn't bother enrolling him. She didn't care about his education or future. All that mattered was getting high. The verbal and physical abuse was constant. She never told him she loved him, but made sure to remind him how much she hated him. He was a trick baby. An accident. Wasn't planned. She didn't want him, but was forced to keep him. When he started running the streets and didn't come home at night, she didn't go looking for him or call the police. As a teenager, he roamed the streets, getting into all kinds of trouble. Cookie was a terrible mother. And now she was dead.

After a fitful night of sleep, Desmond awoke the next morning filled with dread. The weary feeling had nothing to do with the death of his mother. She chose to ingest poison into her body and was killed because of it. The dread was because of the visit he had to make.

After a shower and change of clothes, he jumped in the rental car and hit the highway. An hour later, he pulled into the parking lot of Fox Lake Correctional Institution, a medium-security prison in Fox Lake, Wisconsin. Fifteen foot electrified fences with razor wire atop surrounded the prison. And if being shocked with one hundred thousand volts or having limbs severed with razor wire wasn't enough to prevent an attempted escape, the thirty foot towers with armed guards inside surrounding the prison were an added safety measure.

Desmond emptied his pockets of everything except the military ID and twenty-five dollars before getting out of the car. He entered the prison through the front doors. The visitor processing desk was to the right. A slim blonde-haired white woman with big green eyes sat behind a laptop computer.

"Good morning, sir. How can I help you?"

"I'm here to visit Larry Harrison."

"Okay. What's your name and relationship to the inmate?"

Desmond pulled out his ID. "Desmond Harrison. We're brothers."

She began typing on the laptop. "Okay. I see you're approved. If you fill out a form with your name, I can send you in. Give this form to the officer at the desk. Have a nice visit."

After getting an invisible stamp on the back of the hand, he was allowed inside the prison. The visiting center was located up a long flight of concrete steps. It was a hundred feet of open space littered with little tables that looked like they were made for toddlers rather than adults. There were high resolution cameras in every corner of the room and vending machines with high-priced processed food and snacks near the door. Desmond stopped at the officer's desk and handed the C.O. the paper he had filled out in the lobby.

"Thank you, sir. I'll make the call for your visitor. You and your visitor will be seated at table 15-B," the middle aged white man explained before picking up the phone.

Before going to find the seat, Desmond went to the vending machine to buy snacks and drinks. After finding table 15-B, he sat to wait.

Ten minutes later, his brother walked into the visiting room. Larry Harrison, a.k.a. Lucky, didn't look like the typical prisoner. He didn't look mean, put extra sauce in his walk, or view everyone he passed as a potential enemy or victim. Larry was bald, light-skinned, had light brown eyes, and a smile that could disarm Donald Trump's toughest Secret Service agent. He was tall, 6'4", and long-limbed, and he walked with the grace of a cheetah.

"Des! What's up, li'l bro!"

Desmond put on a fake smile as he stood to hug his big brother. "Lucky! What's good, man?"

After sharing an embrace, the men had seats.

"What's with the surprise visit, nigga? You know I'm coming home in two days. They let you off the base? They ain't got you tied up in no secret missions?" Lucky cracked.

Seeing the joy on his brother's face from being so close to free-dom made Desmond want to keep the death of Cookie to himself.

"Yeah. I just left Paris. I had to come to Milwaukee. Man, I don't know how to say this." He paused, looking away.

Lucky's demeanor got serious. "What's up, brah? Did some-thing happen? You good?"

When Desmond looked at his brother again, there were tears in his eyes. It was the most emotion he had shown since learning of his mother's demise. "Cookie dead."

Lucky's face went flat, devoid of any emotion as he stared at his brother. The words shocked him, and it took a few moments to process. Then slowly, the realization dawned. His eyes turned red and watery. His brows furrowed and his forehead creased. For a moment he was speechless and the brothers sat in silence. After try-ing to unsuccessfully blink away the tears, they began to spill.

"What happened?" Lucky questioned, his voice deep with grief and pain.

"Wrong place, wrong time. Got shot tryna buy some work."

Lucky got mad, raised his voice a little. "How the fuck you know she was buying dope, nigga? You just sayin' that shit to shit on her."

Desmond was hurt by the accusation. The pain quickly changed to anger. "She dead, brah. Why the fuck would I be tryna shit on her? I talked to the detective. She still had the dope in her hand."

Lucky's anger towards his brother was rescinded. "My bad. I know how you feel about what she did to us and I thought you was tryna shit on her."

Desmond acknowledged the apology with a nod.

"Tell me what else they said. Do they know who did it?"

"They don't know much. Ain't nobody talking. It happened on 41st and Clarke. Said it was two different guns. Think it was a shootout. I guess they beefing about who can hustle over there. That's what the cop said."

"I been hearing about them Clarke Street niggas. Can't believe she got killed a couple blocks from where we grew up. Did you ride through there and see if anybody we know heard something?"

Desmond shook his head. "Nah. I really didn't wanna get involved. The detective said they probably won't even solve it either."

Lucky's anger was rekindled, the tears that spilled down his face burning with rage. "How the fuck you gon' go fight for this racist-ass country but you won't even go look for who killed yo' mama, nigga? You serious?"

"C'mon, Lucky. You know she wasn't no mother, man. And this country did way more for me than she did. She didn't send me to college. She didn't help me get my life together. She didn't teach me how to survive. I learned that from you and the military. She gave us life, and that was it. She didn't even want me, nigga. I was a mistake. She told me that all the time. You don't know what that feel like 'cause you know who yo' daddy was. You wasn't no trick baby."

"She was hurting, Des. She was broken. That's what America do to the poor and black people. They fuck you up and give you drugs then shit on you. Reagan allowed drugs into the ghetto to fund the wars in South America. She was a victim. She was sick. She needed help."

"Look, I ain't tryna argue with you over this. Our mother is dead. Fighting won't bring her back."

28

Lucky nodded, wiping tears from his eyes. "You right, man. We can't let this divide us. Damn, Cookie."

"You want something from the vending machine?"

"Nah. But I'ma drink this soda. So what the rest of the family say? Did you talk to anybody?"

Desmond shook his head. "Nah. You know I don't fuck with them. They didn't fuck with us growing up. Knew we was fucked up, but they never offered help. They didn't even claim her body. She died a week ago. I had to come from another country to identify her."

Lucky suppressed another bout of rage. "That's fucked up. But we gotta send her out in style. I know how you feel about her and the family, but we need to let everybody say one last goodbye. It's the right thing to do."

"Yeah, I know," Desmond breathed. "I already talked to the funeral home. I'm thinking about having the funeral over the weekend. Give you a couple days to shake the prison out yo' system. Give the family some time to make or change plans."

"Yeah. I like the sound of that," Lucky agreed. "And I don't need long to get this prison shit out of my system. I been waitin' on this moment for fourteen years. I just wish she coulda been there, you know. See everything I did. Even though she was a smoker, I still wanted to make her proud. It meant something to me to have her approval. If she could've seen me be successful after doing all this time, it might've made something click in her head. I wanted to try to help her shake that shit. But now..." His words were choked away by a painful sob.

It fucked with Desmond to see his big brother in pain. He reached a hand out and put it on Lucky's shoulder. "I'm proud of you, man. For real. For surviving fourteen years of torture and still having a good head. I can't imagine what it feels like to do time. To be locked in a cell for half of your life. I would've gone crazy. But you found yourself. Discovered you could write. I'm proud of you for finding your talent and publishing all those books. And I know Cookie woulda been proud of you too."

Lucky wiped the tears from his face. "Thanks, man. For every-thing. You held me down through it all."

"You know it ain't nothing. We all we got. Just keep yo' head up. It's gon' be over in two days. You almost home, man. Just stay focused."

CHAPTER 3

Tupac's song "Dear Mama" blared on repeat from the five-inch tablet. Lucky lay on the top bunk with his eyes closed, headphones turned up as loud as they would go. A white hand towel was draped over his face, hiding and catching the tears that spilled from his eyes. He was mourning the loss of the mother he never had. He hadn't gotten a visit, letter, or money order from her the entire fourteen years he'd been gone. Nor did he expect it. He knew what she was: an unfit mother and addict. Nothing meant more to her than getting high. But he still loved her and had been looking forward to seeing her when he came home, to help her shake the addiction and get to know her.

Despite the odds stacked against them, her sons were accomplished. She had so much to be proud of. Desmond had graduated college with a Bachelor's degree in political science and Lucky had published ten books from prison. And she would never get to celebrate the successes of the men she had given birth to. He would never be able to tell her that he didn't blame her for the neglect or his coming to prison. It wasn't her fault. The responsibility belonged to America. Racism and capitalism made the ghetto and the people in it. Cookie was a victim. A hurting woman. And hurt people hurt people.

When the key was inserted into the cell door, Lucky didn't hear it over Tupac's lyrics.

"Yo, Luck!" Frank Nitty called, walking over to grab the dominoes from the drawer.

When his cellmate didn't answer, Frank Nitty tapped the bunk. "Lucky!"

Lucky removed the headphones from his ears and towel from his face, showing red-rimmed eyes. "Yeah?"

The sad countenance surprised Frank Nitty. "Damn, brah. What's up? You good?"

Lucky shook his head. "Nah, man. Moms died. Fucked me up, brah."

Frank Nitty's eyes popped in disbelief. "Damn, my nigga. I'm sorry to hear that. What happened?"

"Wrong place, wrong time. Got caught in the middle of a shootout."

Frank shook his head. "Damn, bro. That's fucked up. Two days before you get out. Damn. I was finna come tell you let's go whoop these niggas' ass in dominos, but never mind. Fuck them niggas. You need me to do anything for you? You want some pills or something to smoke?"

"Nah, I'm good. I ain't got high in years. That shit might make it worse. I'ma just lay back. Call my girl in a few minutes. I'm just tryna stay focused on going home."

Nitty nodded. "That's what's up. I'ma get outta here and give you some time to yo'self. Let me know if you need anything."

"What that phone line look like? Is it long?"

"I don't know. But it don't matter. I'ma grab one for you."

"Good looking, my nigga. I'm finna be out in a second."

After his celly left the room, Lucky grabbed his photo album from the shelf and flipped to the only picture he had of Cookie. It was 1989. Cookie had a healthy smile, thick and shiny hair that hung past her shoulders. She wore a creased denim Guess jacket, jeans, and Nike Air Max and a small gold crucifix around her neck. Her eyes reflected the happiness of life as a first-time young mother. Lucky was eighteen months old when the picture was taken. He hung from his mother's hip, smiling for the camera. Ken stood next to her, an arm wrapped around her shoulder. They looked like the perfect young black family. But what Lucky could not see were the demons surrounding his parents. Three months after the picture was taken, crack would begin its rule over his parents' lives.

After taking a few moments to gather his thoughts, Lucky jumped from the bunk and slid into the white Nike Cross Trainers. He grabbed the prison ID and room key from the shelf and hit the door. The hallway was long, fifteen cells on each side. At the end of the hall was the small dayroom, about forty-five square feet. The sergeant's bubble was near the front of the unit. A flat screen TV hung on the wall. Two tables sat in the middle. A group of niggas sat at one playing dominoes and talking shit. To the right were the phone banks. Frank Nitty held out a receiver.

"Here you go, my nigga."

"Good looking, my nigga." Lucky nodded, grabbing the phone and entering his inmate number and passcode. After following a series of instructions, he dialed his girlfriend's number.

Melissa was a thirty-six-year-old divorcée with two kids. She had written to him five years ago after reading one of his books. A relationship sparked and love conquered the distance between them.

"Hey, baby. Why didn't you call earlier?"

He exhaled and tried to find the words to say. "Desmond came to visit. When I got back to the unit, I fell asleep."

"Desmond is in Wisconsin? Why didn't he call me?"

"He came to tell me our mother got killed." Lucky closed his eyes after he said the words, tears refusing to stay away.

"Oh, baby. I'm so sorry to hear that. Oh my God! I wish I could come visit you right now. I'm coming tomorrow. Are you okay?"

"I don't know. I guess. You know how bad I wanted to see her. I wanted to show her that I'm okay. That I did something with my life. And try to help her get off that dope. Now I won't get that chance. That shit hurt," he emoted, wiping away tears.

Near the bathroom entrance, a small commotion arose. Rio was getting loud.

"Aye, brah! I had that phone next. I went to piss real quick."

Lucky didn't hear the remark. His eyes were closed, listening to Melissa.

"I know, baby. I can hear your pain. I'm hurting with you. I feel like I should've tried to do something. I should've tried to talk to her. What happened?"

"Desmond said she got caught in a crossfire tryna buy some dope. A bystander - "

"Aye, Lucky! I had that phone next," Rio interrupted.

Lucky opened his eyes and saw the big youngster standing close. At 6'2" and 230 pounds, he had the build of an NFL linebacker. They locked eyes, Lucky's reflecting a deep pain and anger.

"I'm on the phone, my nigga. You got it when I'm done."

Rio was undeterred by the angry expression. He had been bigger than most people his entire life. When he wanted something, he got it. "Let me get it right now and you get next. I don't need that much time."

"Aye, leave him alone, li'l nigga!" Frank Nitty called from the dayroom table.

Rio blew him off. "Man, I ain't tryna hear that shit. Ain't nobody phone call more important than the next. I had that bitch first. C'mon, Lucky. Lemme get that. I need to make a move before they call for rec."

Lucky's stare was stone, his voice firm. "Use it when you get back. I'm already on it. I'm not finna hang up my call."

Anger flashed in Rio's eyes. He raised his voice. "You ain't finna hoe me, nigga! Let me get that line."

"Lucky, are you okay?" Melissa asked, listening to the confrontation. "Is he saying something about the phone?"

Lucky didn't respond to his girl. Instead, he focused his attention on Rio. The youngster had his chest poked out, looking for action. Not many people challenged the street-bred goon. Lucky knew the type. Loud and reckless. Always looking for a challenge. Thriving from confrontations. Up until this point, that hadn't had a problem. Respect had been given from both sides. But now a line had been crossed and needed to be addressed. Lucky wasn't looking for a fight. He was going home in forty-eight hours. But he also wasn't about to take shit. Death before dishonor was more than a saying. He had been living it since he was born.

"Listen, li'l brah. I don't know what you think you finna get, but it won't be this phone until I'm done with my call. I ain't finna talk about this no more."

Lucky put the ball in his court. The stare down was serious, filled with animosity. The dayroom became still. Everyone was on edge, waiting to see who would throw the first punch or back down.

They didn't have to wait long. Rio rocked forward, leaning into a jab. Lucky shifted to the left, moving just enough to take some of the steam away from the blow as knuckles raked across his jaw. The phone receiver became a weapon. He threw it at Rio's face, following behind it with a right cross. Both phone and punch smacked the younger man in the face. Rio stumbled backwards, losing his balance and running into the microwave. Taught not to have mercy on his opponents, Lucky kept up the assault. He fired punches in bunches. Stiff blows landed to Rio's face. The young goon caught one punch too many and the lights went out. His body went limp and he fell into the microwave head first. After hitting his head on the microwave, he hit his head again on the table, opening up a gash. The fight was over. Rio lay on the ground bleeding from the nose and temple.

"Harrison, get against the wall! Stop fighting!" the sergeant screamed, running into the unit pointing his Taser.

***

Lucky lay on the concrete slab staring at the white paint on the ceiling. He couldn't sleep. It was five o'clock in the morning and he had been staring at the same spot on the ceiling all night. Fucked up way to spend your last day in the joint. He had been trapped in the cell for twelve hours. He had one more day to go until he would be a free man. It felt unreal. Like a dream. He spent most of the time thinking about his dead mother. It put a damper on what would normally be a joyous occasion. He had done fourteen calendars. He was supposed to be thinking about eating some real food. Getting some pussy. Melissa wasn't the best-looking woman in the world, but she was loyal. Sepia brown skin, a short curly afro, chubby cheeks and a pretty smile. She stood average height, was a little on the chubby side with big-ass J-cup titties and a wide, flat booty. What he liked most about her were her brown eyes. They reflected her truest emotions, everything she felt. They were empathetic and warm. He couldn't wait to look into them when he slid inside that pussy for the first time. Just thinking about busting that first nut got his dick hard. He reached for his piece, massaging it through the thin orange pants. It wouldn't be long.

Keys jingling made his ears perk. A few moments later they stopped outside his door. C.O. Johansen stuck his head in the small window.

"Harrison, you ready to go?"

"Where am I going?"

"You're being released."

Lucky looked surprised. "Right now?"

"Yeah. C'mon and cuff up. Your ride is waiting downstairs," he said before opening a trap in the middle of the door.

Surprise lit Lucky's eyes as he jumped up from the bed and stuck his hands out the trap. Some kind of mistake had been made, but he wasn't about to argue. "Let's go! I thought I wasn't leaving 'til tomorrow."

"I don't know. Guess they came early," the officer said as he put on the handcuffs. He radioed the control center to get the door opened and escorted Lucky downstairs to a holding cell.

"Gimme those state clothes and I'll get your release clothes," Johansen said before walking away.

He came back a few moments later with a shopping bag. Inside was an all-white True Religion fit. T-shirt, jeans, and shoes. Also a pair of Polo underwear and socks. Lucky smiled as he put on the brand new clothes. It was finally over.

As he was sliding into the shoes, Captain Murasaki and a white man he had never seen before stepped in front of the holding cell.

"You Larry Harrison?" The white shirt asked.

"Yeah. What's up?"

Instead of answering the question, he held up a white piece of paper, looking from it to Lucky. "What's you doc number and date of birth?"

"January eight, 1987. 456931."

"Alright. You're discharging from the Department of Corrections. From this moment forth, you are no longer a prisoner at Fox Lake Correctional Institution. Good luck."

Lucky smiled. "Yep. Thanks."

When the white shirt stepped aside, the unknown man stepped forward. "I'm Detective Sumner with the Fox Lake Police Department. You had a fight the other day with an inmate named Joseph Addison that required him to be sent to the hospital. As a result, charges are being filed against you for substantial battery. I'm going to have to arrest you."

An indescribable pain gripped Lucky's chest. "What? You serious? That muthafucka hit me first! I was defending myself."

The white shirt and detective laughed.

"You did a little more than defend yourself. I seen the footage. Kid almost died. Might even need brain surgery."

Lucky was devastated. He had been so close to freedom, and now it was being taken away. And there wasn't a damn thing he could do about it. He wanted to explain some more, try to get the detective to understand what freedom after fourteen years felt like. But as he looked at the cop's face, he knew that no amount of reasoning would have an effect. So he swallowed the fear and pain, putting on a soldier's mask.

"A'ight. Let's go, man. Get me out this cage. Where I'm going?"

"After I read you your Miranda rights, I'm going to take you to the Fox Lake County Jail to get booked. You can make a statement if you want. You have the right to remain silent. Anything you say..."

J-Blunt

CHAPTER 4

The black 2015 Camaro cruised slowly down the dark street. It was after 10 p.m. and 41st and Clarke was still alive with activity. Groups of men hung out on street corners, kicking it and hustling. Abandoned and rundown houses lined the block. Trash littered balding lawns, sidewalks, and curbsides.

Desmond pulled the car to a stop in front of the house where Cookie had taken her last breath. An indescribable feeling drove him to the house. For some unknown reason, he wanted to see the place where she took her last breath. The house was rundown and dilapidated. Thin green slabs of wood covered the windows and doorway. Most of the gray paint on the outside had chipped away.

After climbing from the car, Desmond walked up on the porch and sat down, trying to visualize his mother's final moments. He wondered if she felt any pain or if she went quickly. He began to feel the guilt he experienced at the coroner's office. He had abandoned his mother, used the army to start a new life. He had the money and resources to get her clean, but didn't even make an attempt. It wasn't his fault that she died, but he wondered if she might still be alive if he had at least made the attempt to help her clean up.

He had been sitting for a few minutes when two men walked up. One was tall and skinny with uncombed hair, the other short, bald, and fat. Both were in their early twenties.

"What'chu doin over here, nigga?" the tall one asked.

Desmond stood, not wanting to be caught off-guard as the young men approached. "This y'all house? It looks abandoned."

"All this shit ours." The fat man mugged him. "Who is you? What you doin' over here?"

Desmond thought about what Detective Perry said. A turf war was brewing in the hood. Outsiders were being purged. These were part of the welcoming party. And that meant they probably knew who killed Cookie.

"It's enough money out here for er'body," Desmond acted. "Let me get mines. I'll shop wit' y'all."

"No, it ain't. Ain't no money out here for you, nigga. This Clarke Street Goons shit. We the only ones gettin' money over here. Move the fuck around and don't come back 'round here."

Desmond sized up the young thugs. The bulges in the front of their shirts told him that both were armed. The only thing Desmond had in his pockets were car keys, an ID, credit card, and key card to the hotel room. But being unarmed didn't make him any less dangerous.

"A'ight. I'ma leave. But I just need one thing."

"We don't give no fuck what you want, nigga. Move the fuck around." The tall one mugged him.

Desmond let out a chuckle. The youngsters were so eager to do violence that they didn't want to hear anything, so Desmond gave them what they wanted. "And if I don't leave, fuck y'all gon' do?"

Snarls crossed the young gunners' faces and they went for their guns. Desmond moved with a speed neither man had ever seen. He chopped the skinny man in the throat, crushing his larynx. The slim thug released the grip on his pistol, grabbing his throat as he fell to the ground. Desmond grabbed the fat nigga's wrist in a vice-like grip, not allowing him to pull the gun from his waist. The big man tried to wrestle his arm away from Desmond and accidentally pulled the trigger.

Pop!

"Ahh shit!" he screamed, releasing the pistol and hopping on one foot.

The black 40 Glock fell to the ground. Desmond bent down and picked it up, glancing at the skinny nigga that thrashed around on the ground struggling to breathe. A black 9 millimeter Beretta lay near. Desmond picked that up too. The fat man tried to hop away. Desmond clipped his good leg. He fell hard.

"Ahh shit!"

"Quit screaming, bitch-ass nigga! I tried to be reasonable, but y'all don't want that. Now tell me who killed Cookie."

"I don't know no Cookie, nigga. Ah shit! My leg!"

Desmond pointed both guns in his face. "I'ma make you hurt even more if you don't tell me what I wanna know. Who shot Cookie?"

"Fuck you, nigga! I told you I don't know," he cursed, wincing in pain.

Desmond stepped on his wounded leg.

"Ahhhh! Okay! Okay!" the fat man pleaded.

"Who shot my mama?"

"It was an accident, my nigga. She was at the wrong place at the wrong time. She - "

Desmond stepped on his leg again.

"Ahhhh fuck! Ahhhh shit!"

"I know what happened, nigga. Gimme a name."

Deductive reasoning shone in the fat man's eyes. He was weighing his options. "Draco and Jay. Them niggas had a shootout. I don't know who hit her."

"Where they at?"

"I don't know. Jay mama used to live in 40th and Center. Draco always be in the hood."

Desmond took his foot off the fat man's leg. His friend had stopped thrashing around and wasn't breathing. In a moment he would be dead. The fat nigga deserved to die with him. He was a punk and bully. Desmond defended America against punks and bullies. He looked around for witnesses. No one was close enough to see what was happening. He moved the 40 to the fat man's face and pulled the trigger.

Pop!

Desmond left the scene with a lot on his mind. He thought about calling Detective Perry with the information. He had done more in ten minutes than the police had done in a week. Then he remembered the detective's words about Cookie's murder not being a priority. Nobody cared. A call to the police would probably be a waste of breath - not to mention he would probably have to explain how he got the information and the two dead bodies. So he kept the information to himself. And now that her killer's information had fallen into his lap, he wondered if he should try and bring justice.

That's what he did for a living: hunt down America's enemies and deliver justice. Did the woman that gave him life deserve the same devotion?

He was wrestling with the thought when he pulled up to the gas station. The rental car needed a fill-up. He used the debit card to make the payment at the pump and started the fill-up. A white Lexus truck pulled to the pump opposite him. A man drove and was arguing with the woman in the passenger seat. The windows were down and Desmond could hear every word.

"But that don't mean you hug the nigga. I don't give a fuck how long you knew him. You with me. I'm yo' nigga. Show me some respect."

"Please, Drew. You flirt with every girl that walks by. I don't know your phone's password, but you know mine. You the one with something to hide. Not me."

"Bitch, this ain't about me. This 'bout you hugging niggas and shit. Tryna be slick. I wasn't hugging no bitches. What you tryna flip it for? You fucking him?"

"Fuck you, Drew! I got yo' bitch. Just go pay for the gas and take me home. I ain't finna listen to yo' insecure bullshit. I can do bad by myself."

"You know what, bitch? Get the fuck out my car! Get the fuck out! I ain't takin' you nowhere. Walk home."

"I ain't walking nowhere. You dropping me off where you picked me up at."

Drew reached across her lap and opened the passenger door, trying to push her out. A wrestling match began. Desmond looked up when she began screaming, and that's when he saw her face. "What the fuck?" he questioned.

"Get your hands off me, Drew! Stop!"

"Get the fuck out! Go tell that nigga at the club to take you home. Get out, bitch!" Drew yelled, slapping her.

The woman slapped him back before getting out of the car and attempting to run. She couldn't get far with the heels on. Drew caught up to her quickly, clipping her feet. The woman took a major spill, landing on her stomach. He spun her over and climbed on top, cocking an arm back to deliver a mighty blow. The woman closed her eyes, bracing herself for the punch.

But it never came. Desmond had approached quickly and quietly, interlocking Drew's arm in his.

"Get the fuck off me, nigga! Let me go." Drew mugged him.

Desmond didn't let him go. He yanked Drew's arm back, throwing him on the ground. When he extended a hand to help the woman up, recognition flashed in her eyes. Then fear. Desmond could hear Drew's footsteps and see his shadow cast on the ground by the bright gas station lights. The spinning back fist landed perfectly on Drew's jaw, breaking the top and bottom mandibles. He fell to the ground like dead weight and didn't move.

***

"Desmond! Oh my God, man! I can't believe it's you. You look good, man. All grown up now." The woman gawked from the passenger seat of the rental car.

"Forget me, Lasonya. Look at you. Milk does a body good. Damn!" He laughed, checking her out for the millionth time.

Lasonya stood 5'7" with unblemished light brown skin. She wore a pink blouse and white jeans that flexed her curvy frame. Her hair was thick and flowing past her shoulders. She had a round face with delicate features, almond-shaped hazel-brown eyes, a button nose, full lips, and the smile of a movie star. Growing up, Lasonya was the finest girl in the hood. Eighteen years later, she had gotten finer.

"C'mon, Des. Stop looking at me like that. You making me blush."

He reluctantly took his eyes off her, focusing back on the road. "So, where am I driving to? Where do you live?"

"On 77th and Brentwood. I need to stop by my mom's house. She will be so happy to see you."

"I got you. I can't wait to see her. She still crazy?"

Lasonya laughed. "What? Stop playing. She got crazier. Most people calm down when they get older, but she the opposite."

After sharing another laugh, Desmond got nosy. "So who was that clown you was fighting? What's up with that?"

She let out a hot breath, anger spreading across her face. "That was Drew, my on again/off again boyfriend. I hope his ass never wakes up."

"He'll wake up. Might need surgery on that jaw though. How did you hook up with a dude like that? He sounded like a sucka. All jealous and shit. But I guess I can see why," he said, sneaking another peek at her body.

"I don't know what I was thinking about messing with him. I guess he was charming at the beginning. Then he changed. Got jealous and insecure. And full of shit. We were at the club when he started tripping. Got mad because I hugged Jamar. I haven't seen him in forever. Remember him?"

"Yeah, I remember Jamar's jug-head ass. How he doing?"

"Looks like he doing good. I'ma check him out on Facebook later. But forget him. What's up with you? Where you been? You're in good shape. Did you just get out?"

Desmond laughed. "That's how you stereotype me? Every nigga in good shape ain't been to the joint. I'm in the military."

Lasonya's face showed surprise. "Military? Seriously? So that's how you knocked Drew out like that. Damn. How long you been in the service?"

"Enlisted when I turned eighteen. I lived all over the world. Germany, China, Japan, Korea, South America."

"Wow! I'm amazed. I just remember you as this skinny little boy. Now you're all grown up, in the army, and traveling the world. What are you doing in Milwaukee?"

Desmond paused a moment. "Somebody killed Cookie."

Her eyes popped. "Oh my God, Desmond! For real? When?"

"'Bout a week ago. Got caught in a shootout. Innocent bystander. Having the funeral this weekend."

"Oh, man. I'm really sorry to hear that."

"It's all good. I don't know if you remember, but me and Cookie wasn't that close."

"Yeah, I remember. She was out there bad. But she still your mom. Me and my mama used to feel sorry for you and your brother. Where is Lucky? How is he?"

"He locked up, but get out tomorrow. Wrote some books. He's good."

She smiled. "I'm happy to hear that. Both of y'all turned out okay. Cookie woulda been proud."

"No, she wouldn't. All she cared about was that dope. We was only family because of blood. She hated me. Your mother did more for me than Cookie. I owe Marcy for all the times she let me spend the night."

Lasonya could see that nothing would change the way he felt about his mother, so she focused on her own mom. "She's going to be so happy to see you."

"You sure she still woke? It's kinda late."

"It's only ten o'clock. My mama a night owl."

Fifteen minutes later, Desmond parked the Camaro in front of a peach ranch style house on Brentwood. "So this where y'all moved to when y'all left 39th, huh?" he asked.

"Yeah. Mama had to get us out the ghetto. But it really ain't no better out here. C'mon in. And be quiet. I want to surprise her."

Desmond followed the switching of her hips up the walkway. After using the key to let them in, he remained in the living room while she went to look for Marcy. She wasn't hard to find. The TV in the bedroom could be heard in the living room. It sounded like women arguing.

"Mama! Where you at?"

"I'm in the room."

Lasonya walked in and found her mother lying in bed, eyes glued to the TV. Marcy was a small woman with a petite frame. Although she was fifty-three years old, she had the aura and presence of a younger woman. She still spoke street lingo, loved going to the club, and binge watching *Real Housewives* and *Love and Hip Hop*.

"Dang, woman. You gon' be deaf. Turn that down."

"Shhh! Porscha and Candy about to throw hands!" Marcy said excitedly, not looking away from the TV.

"I hate to bust your bubble, Mama, but the show is scripted. All this is fake."

That got Marcy's attention. She gave her daughter a sideways look. "Why you gotta throw shade at my - wait! Girl, what happened to you? Why yo' clothes all dirty? Is that a bruise on yo' face?"

Lasonya looked away in shame. "Yeah. Me and Drew had a fight."

Marcy shot out of bed, heading for the closet. "I told that bitch I was gon' kill him if he ever put his hands on you again!" She came out of the closet a moment later with a large black revolver. "Where that bitch at? He outside?"

"Wait, Mama! Chill. He not here. I left him at the gas station. He probably in the hospital now."

Marcy paused, a crazed look in her eyes. "Which one? I'ma shoot his ass while he in the hospital so he won't have to go far to get stitched up."

"Stop, Mom. Put the gun back. I'm good. I got help from some-body. You not gon' believe who I ran into."

The anger in Marcy's eyes turned to rage. "You bet' not say Quaysha's daddy!"

Lasonya frowned. "Hell nah! I hate his ass. Just look in the liv-ing room. And put the gun down before you make him nervous."

Marcy eyed her daughter before tucking the gun in the waist of her pajama pants, leaving the butt of the pistol exposed. "Let me see who you brought in my house. Knowing you, I might need this." She walked to the living room and had a stare down with Desmond.

"Hey, Marcy." He waved.

She didn't recognize him. "Who is you?"

"Mom, you really don't know who that is?" Lasonya asked. "He used to live across the street from us on 39th and Clarke."

Desmond continued to stand there and smile. Marcy eyed him suspiciously. And then it clicked in her head, recognition showing on her face and in her eyes.

"Desmond! Lil D, is that you, nigga?"

"Yeah, Marcy. It's me. 'Sup?"

"Oh shit! Nigga all grown up and shit. Come gimme a hug, nigga!"

Desmond swallowed Marcy in his arms. After the embrace, she stepped back to look him up at him. "Shit, boy. You got big and strong. I feel all yo' muscles. You must've just got out, huh? How long you do?"

Lasonya laughed. "I said the same thing, Mama. But he wasn't in jail. He in the army."

Marcy looked from her daughter, back to Desmond. "Aw shit, nigga! I'm proud of you. Good Lord, this is a good surprise."

"Yeah. I joined on my eighteenth birthday. Been in ever since. Saved my life."

"Oh, I know Cookie so proud. How is yo' mama? She still on that shit?"

"She dead," he said flatly.

Marcy softened up. "Oh, I'm sorry to hear that, baby. When she pass? What happened?"

"Happened about a week ago. Got shot. Tryna buy dope. Walked into a shootout."

Marcy clutched her chest. "Oh, baby! That is so sad. Did they find who did it?"

"Nah. They really don't care. Dope fiend got killed buying crack. Nobody care. And the police told me that. But I'm looking into it."

"You be careful out there, Desmond. You know these niggas crazy. Poppin' all them Percocets got 'em ready to shoot anybody. That's why I stay strapped," she said, patting the butt of her pistol.

"I see you. And I'm good. I got a particular set of skills."

Marcy smiled. "Right. My nigga in the army. Can you fuck up her boyfriend for me?"

Desmond and Lasonya laughed.

"What's funny?" Marcy asked.

"He already did that. You should've seen it, Mama. He did a spin around karate punch. Knocked Drew's ass clean out."

Marcy laughed, clapping her hands. "My nigga! When I get off work tomorrow, I'ma take you to eat. My treat."

"You don't gotta do that. My brother get outta prison tomorrow. I gotta pick him up."

"Oh, I forgot about Lucky. Glad he gettin' out. Y'all stop over and say hi. Don't be no stranger. And text me yo' mama funeral time. I'ma come pay my respects."

"I got you."

"Where is Quay-Quay?" Lasonya asked.

"In yo' old room asleep. Go on get her." When Lasonya left the room, Marcy stepped closer to Desmond. "How long you in town?"

"I don't know. Another week at least. Gotta tie up some loose ends."

Marcy smiled. "So, you gon' give my daughter a ride home? Her car is broke."

"Yeah. I got her. Who is Quay-Quay?"

"Her daughter. Lasonya got a knack for fuckin' wit' no-good niggas. But I'm happy she had my grandbaby. Maybe you came at just the right time to give her love life a good spark."

Desmond frowned.

"Boy, stop lookin' crazy. I knew y'all had that puppy love crush thang. If we didn't move, y'all might've started having sex. She told me you was the first boy she kissed. Don't tell her I said none of this."

Lasonya walked into the living room carrying a sleeping toddler in her arms. Marcy and Desmond wore guilty looks. "Was y'all talking about me?"

"What? Nah." Desmond laughed nervously.

Marcy waved her off. "Girl, we got better stuff to talk about than you."

***

Rick Ross's "Apple of My Eye" played softly from the car speakers as Desmond drove towards Lasonya's house.

"I don't even like Rick Ross, but I love this song," she said, nodding her head in the passenger seat.

"How could you not like Rick Ross? That shit you just said sounds blasphemous."

"I don't know. I'm not really a fan of rap. It's stupid. And they all be lying and disrespecting women."

Desmond agreed with her. "Yeah. All that is true. So, what you listen to? Country?" he cracked, checking his phone when it began vibrating.

"Is that your woman calling to check up on you?" Lasonya fished.

"I don't have a woman. This is Lucky's girl. Hold on. Let me answer. What up, Melissa?"

"Why didn't you tell me you were in town? Your brother just called and he's in jail."

"I know he's in jail. We gotta pick him up tomorrow. And I didn't call because I didn't want to bother you."

"Bother me?" she said, sounding irritated. "Whatever. We'll talk about that later. But your brother is really in jail. Not prison. Jail jail."

Desmond's face twisted. "What do you mean?"

"He's in the Fox Lake County Jail. He had a fight last night and put somebody in the hospital. They charged him with battery and arrested him. He's in jail waiting to see the judge in the morning for bail."

Desmond couldn't believe his ears. "What the fuck? He put somebody in the hospital? Fuck is wrong with him? He knew he was getting out tomorrow."

"I said the same thing. But he said the guy punched him first. They was arguing over the phone. He was talking to me and I heard it all. But I didn't know he put him in the hospital."

Desmond shook his head. "Okay. I gotta drop my friend off and then I'ma come over. Stay the night on yo' couch and we can go get him in the morning. Hopefully they let him get a bail and don't be on no bullshit."

"Alright. Call me when you're on the way."

Desmond sounded like an airbrake, letting out a long breath after hanging up the phone.

"That's so messed up," Lasonya commented. "Send him to jail the day before he gets out for a fight. That sounds like some bullshit."

"Don't it? But he know better. He did fourteen years. Shouldn't nothing be more important than coming home."

"Damn. I didn't know he did that long. Yeah, he probably should've walked away from that one. But Lucky did have a temper growing up. I remember he beat up Brandon and li'l Chris for talking shit about Cookie."

Desmond laughed at the memory. "Yeah. Bro was a fool."

"Do you mind coming to get me so I can ride with you to pick him up? I got the day off and I wanna see that nigga."

CHAPTER 5

Lucky sat on the concrete slab, back against the wall, eyes closed, trying to keep positive thoughts. He had spent the night in the holding cell. He slept in a sitting position, surrounded by four petty criminals also awaiting arraignment and bail hearings. He hated being in jail. It was even worse being moved from prison to jail the day before you were to be released for a fight you didn't even start. He had replayed the situation over in his mind all night, wondering if he had fucked up his release. But he couldn't let nobody hoe him. During his younger years, he beat niggas' asses for looking at him sideways. No way could he let a nigga get away with putting hands on him. So here he sat, in jail, wondering if he would be released.

Noise at the holding cell door got his attention. When it opened, a courtroom bailiff stepped inside.

"Okay, guys. You're about to appear before the judge. I'm going to lead you into the court. You'll all be sitting together in the second pew. The court reporter will call your names and you'll each come to the defendant's table to meet with your lawyer or court-appointed counsel and have your case heard. Let's go."

Nostalgia gripped Lucky when he stepped into the courtroom. Justice seemed to look the same no matter the county, city, or state. A white judge sitting high up on the bench looking down upon the accused. Court reporter and stenographer sitting close. District attorney sitting at a table on the left with piles of case folders in front of him. An overworked and underpaid public defender sitting at the opposite table. Visitors and family members sitting anxiously in the gallery to witness the proceedings.

For a moment, Lucky allowed himself to feel comforted by the presence of loved ones. Desmond and Melissa sat together, offering supportive smiles. He gave them a nod before having a seat in the second pew.

The first case on the docket was a fifth offense drunk driver. He was not given a bail and was escorted back to the holding cell. A sinking feeling went through Lucky's body and he glanced back at his supporters. Melissa smiled. Desmond nodded confidently. And a fine woman he had never seen before waved.

"Larry Harrison?" the court reporter called.

"That's me," Lucky said.

"Take a few moments to have a word with your counsel before we begin," the judge spoke.

Lucky went to the defense table and shook the clammy chubby hand of his mouthpiece.

"I'm Michael Sarawak. This is going to be quick. I read over the charge. You had a fight in prison. Being charged with assault. Hopefully we can get you a bail and get you out of here. Is there anything you want to let me know before we begin?"

"Yeah. I didn't start it. Dude punched me and I beat him up. The prison got it on tape. Dude hit his head. I didn't try to hurt him."

The lawyer nodded. "Okay. I'm just here to get you through the hearing. We probably won't ever see each other again after this. When you get a lawyer, you can tell them the story for them to build a defense. I just need to know if you can pay bail if granted."

"Hell yeah!"

"Your Honor, my client is ready to proceed," the lawyer called.

The judge peered down his nose at Lucky before picking up the paper on his desk. "While you and your lawyer were talking, I read the charge. Is this correct that you had a fight in prison?"

"Yes, Your Honor." Lucky nodded. "But I didn't start it."

"Okay. We'll get to that. How long were you in prison and what were you locked up for?"

Lucky felt uncomfortable answering the question. His answer would probably determine the outcome of the hearing. But he also knew he couldn't lie. That would make the situation worse. "Fourteen years for felony murder."

The judge's eyes squinted before he turned to the district attorney. "How bad were the injuries, Mark?"

The district attorney looked through a stack of papers. "Very significant. Several head injuries that required a lot of medical attention. The victim hit his head on the table after being punched several times by the defendant."

The judge turned back to Lucky. "One punch wasn't enough?"

"He hit me first," Lucky answered sheepishly.

He turned back to the district attorney. "And what does the State recommend?"

"State recommends he remain in custody, considering his criminal past. It's obvious spending fourteen years in prison did nothing to quell his penchant for violence. In the interests of protecting the community, he should remain behind bars."

Lucky mugged the district attorney, wishing he could get up and whoop his ass.

"Okay, Counsel would you like to say anything?" the judge asked the public defender.

"Yeah. He says the guy started it and we don't have the prison footage yet. Larry Harrison paid his debt to society for the crime for which he was convicted. No need to keep him locked up for a fight. Give him bail and let him go be with his family."

Lucky looked at his fake lawyer, expecting more. The fat white man shrugged his shoulders as if asking "what more can I do?"

"Um, Your Honor, can I speak?" Lucky asked.

The judge looked amused. "Are you sure you want to speak? You don't have to."

Lucky looked to his lawyer one last time. It was no wonder the prisons were overcrowded. The court-appointed representation was terrible, at best. "Yes, Your honor. I spent too much time in prison to let my freedom get put in the hands of a man who barely said a whole paragraph in my defense."

The judge smiled briefly. "Alright. Proceed."

"Your Honor, this fight happened a day before I was supposed to be released. I wasn't looking for trouble. The guy I fought was a bully. You can check his prison record. He hit me first. I just found out my mother died and was on the phone talking to my girl, who is in the gallery. He tried to take the phone. When I didn't give it to him, he punched me. I reacted. I went to prison when I was an eighteen-year-old boy. I'm leaving a thirty-two-year-old man. I educated myself. Got a degree in business administration. I've published ten books. I wasn't in there trying to become a better criminal. I spent my time becoming a better man. I'm just asking that you gimme the opportunity. I worked hard for this. I didn't mean to hurt him."

The judge peered down his nose at Lucky, taking off his glasses. "When people enter my courtroom, rarely do they speak for themselves. And when they do speak, they normally make excuses and beg the court for forgiveness. And I can't remember the last time I heard someone call out their counsel for their deficient performance. This case is different from a lot of those I've proceeded over. Considering the victim's injuries and your past criminal history, this could turn out badly for you, Mr. Harrison. But I believe you are a shining example of what the criminal justice system is supposed to do: rehabilitate. Minus the fight. I'll grant you bail. Five hundred dollar signature bond. Don't make me a liar. Go be with your family. The court will draw up the papers and you can sign them and be on your way. Report back for your next hearing two weeks from today."

Lucky smiled for the first time since entering the courtroom.

***

"My boy is a free man!" Desmond yelled, opening his arms for a hug.

Lucky smashed his body into his younger brother's chiseled frame as the men shared a long embrace in front of the Fox Lake Courthouse. The tears came without warning. Happy tears. Freedom tears.

"Man, Desmond. I can't believe this day finally came!" Lucky cried.

"We good, brah. It's over. You back, baby!"

After hugging a little longer, Lucky broke the embrace turning to hug and kiss his girl. "Hey, baby. We did it. I'm free."

Melissa stared lovingly up at her man, tears rolling down her face. "Thank God. I'm so happy. Welcome home, baby. Welcome home."

"Hey, Lucky! Welcome home."

Lucky looked over and saw the fine woman that had waved in court smiling at him. Now that he was up close, she looked familiar, but he still wasn't sure how he knew her.

"Thanks. Do I know you? You look familiar."

She looked offended that he didn't remember her. "I'm Lasonya, nigga. I stayed across the street on 39th."

Recognition flashed in Lucky's eyes and memories of Lasonya as a skinny preteen played in his memory. "Oh shit! Lasonya! What up, girl?" He smiled, opening his arms for a hug.

"You, man. I see you still knocking people out. Bad ass."

"I don't start nothing, baby. But I'm a man before anything."

"I can love that," Desmond agreed. "So what you wanna do first? Get something to eat? Go shopping?" He nodded towards Melissa. "Go home with yo' girl and have yo' own party?"

Lucky smiled, catching his drift and looking towards Melissa. "We got time. Right now I just wanna go see Mama. On the way, stop at Popeye's so I can check out that chicken sandwich. I heard people been going crazy over them mugs."

From the courthouse, they hopped in Melissa's Ford Escape and headed for Milwaukee. On the way, she stopped at Popeye's to order Lucky five chicken sandwiches. The newly-freed man destroyed the fast food, eating the first sandwich in four bites.

An hour later, Melissa parked the SUV in the lot of Serenity Funeral Home. The mood was immediately changed from festive to somber. When they walked inside the funeral home, the first thing Lucky noticed was the silence. It was a hollow, echoing quiet made by the lifeless bodies inside caskets spread out in the large room. A man sat at a big oak desk near the back of the room. He had dark skin, a shiny bald head, and black and distant eyes that had seen many things.

"Good morning. I'm Edmond. How may I help you?" he asked, extending a hand to Desmond.

"Good morning. We're here to see my mother, Mary Harrison."

Some kind of creepy delight flashed in the man's eyes. "Ah, yes. She's right this way. We just finished putting her in the casket this morning."

The group followed Edmond towards the back of the parlor and into another room. Three caskets lined the wall. He stopped at the second. It was made of polished redwood with shiny silver accents. The casket was opened. Tears immediately filled Lucky's eyes and a part of him died when he saw Cookie's lifeless body. Her eyes were closed like she was sleeping, like she would get up if he called her name. She looked prettier in death than she had in life. The last time Lucky seen her, she looked a mess: uncombed hair, wide eyes, and dirty clothes. But the funeral home had done a good job, dressed her with a lace front wig, light makeup, and a purple dress.

"We gon' make it, brah. We good," Desmond said, wrapping an arm around his brother's shoulder.

"I wanna know who did it. I wanna know who killed my mama," Lucky said, wiping away tears.

"We gotta let it go, brah. You just got out. You already caught a case. Just let it go. Live yo' life."

Lucky pushed Desmond's arm from his shoulder and spun to face him. "Our mama dead, nigga! She in a casket. Look at her. That don't piss you off? That don't make you wanna find who did it? The police told you they not gon' even look into it. And you want me to let it go. How you go out there and fight for America but you won't even fight for yo' own mama?"

Melissa grabbed Lucky's arm, trying to calm him. "Baby, calm down. We just don't want you to get in trouble. It's going to be alright."

Lucky gave her a dead stare. "My mama dead. It's not gon' be alright. Stop saying that shit."

Desmond turned to the women and funeral home director. "Can y'all give us a minute to be alone with our mother?"

"Take all the time you need," Edmond said before leading the ladies away.

When they were alone, Desmond turned to Lucky. "I'ma take care of it. I know who did it."

Lucky's eyes shone with the hope of revenge. "Who did it?"

"Some young punks from the neighborhood. Draco and Jay. I had to drop a couple bodies to get the info and got it hot. I'ma go back over there in a couple of days. Maybe after the funeral."

"I'm coming with you," Lucky promised.

"Nah. I said I got it."

Lucky's stare was serious, the same look he gave Desmond when they were kids. He was making a big brother call, a.k.a., an OG call. "I said I'm coming with you. She was my mama too."

Desmond returned a stare of his own and spoke with finality. "You know I'm trained to kill, right? I don't need no help. I got it."

"I'm the big brother, Des. You not about to start telling me what to do. And if push come to shove, I'ma go by myself. Either way, I'm going."

Desmond let out a frustrated breath, realizing he wasn't going to be able to talk Lucky out of sitting on the sideline. "Alright. But we doing it my way. You gotta do what I say."

Lucky smirked. "Yeah. I'll think about it."

Desmond shook his head again, then remembered the necklace in his pocket. "I got this from the coroner."

Lucky took the eighteen-inch gold chain with the small crucifix, examining it like it was a priceless artifact. "She was wearing this in the only picture I got of her."

"It's the only thing she left behind. Keep it."

Lucky put the chain around his neck, instantly feeling connected to his mother. "Thanks, man. Let's get the fuck outta here. I'm tired of crying. This supposed to be a celebration."

After leaving the funeral home, the brothers went to visit family members they hadn't seen in ages. Most were surprised to hear about Cookie's death and Lucky's release. After taking a few moments to catch up, everyone promised to attend the funeral to pay their final respects. When they finished making their rounds, the brothers went their separate ways - Desmond with Lasonya, Lucky with Melissa.

***

"Damn. You got a nice house," Lucky commented after Melissa pulled the truck into the driveway.

"No. We have a nice house," Melissa corrected, leaning over to kiss him.

The house was a blue and yellow townhouse on the upper east side. Three levels, three bedrooms, and a furnished basement for twelve hundred dollars a month. They were getting out of the truck when the front door burst open. A long-limbed ten-year-old boy and a curly-haired seven-year-old girl bounced down the stairs.

"Hey, Lucky!"

"Welcome home!" the kids sang, mobbing the newly-freed man.

"'Sup, Brandon! Hey, Brandy!"

"Where y'all was at? What took y'all so long to come home?" Brandy pouted, hanging onto Lucky's hip as they walked up the stairs.

"We had to visit some people."

"You wanna come in the basement and play my game? I'll fade you in Mortal Kombat," Brandon challenged.

"No, he won't be playing games tonight," Melissa spoke up. "Y'all about to leave with Grandma. Where she at?"

"I'm right here," an older woman with wide hips and a slight limp said as she walked into the living room. Brenda, Melissa's mother, was a big-bodied fifty-five-year-old woman that loved taking care of family. "Hey, Lucky. Welcome home." She smiled, opening her arms for a hug.

"Hey, Brenda," Lucky said, drowning himself in the soft arms of the older woman.

"Glad to see you in street clothes. I'ma take the kids with me for the night. Y'all have fun." She winked.

After hugs and kisses from the matriarch and children, Lucky and Melissa were finally alone. She was locking the front door and Lucky stood near the couch, eyeing her wide booty with lust. They had lots of phone sex and she'd sent him sexy pictures over the years. Now that the moment of truth was upon them, he was ready to feast.

"Finally, we alone," Melissa sang, spinning around.

Lucky went to her, wrapping arms around her love handles and tonguing her down. The kiss was noisy, erotic, and wet, the kind shared by adult film stars on porno sets. He gripped the flesh of her waist, hips, and ass while grinding his hard tool against her stomach.

"Let's go upstairs to the room," she managed between kisses.

"We ain't gon' make it," he mumbled, kissing her again and pawing at her big-ass titties through the T-shirt.

They made it to the couch, where Lucky pushed her down and stood over her. "Take that shirt off and let me see them mu'fuckas. I been waiting on this!" he said, licking his lips.

Melissa wrestled the T-shirt from her upper body, exposing the black Wonderbra. Lucky had seen the stretch marks on her stomach in the pictures and didn't allow them to concern him one bit. What he hadn't been able to see were those J-cups. When she took off the bra, her titties spilled out like a chocolate flesh avalanche. Gravity had taken its toll so they hung to her stomach. Lucky bent down and began motorboating the sweater puppies and sucking the nipples. Melissa moaned, rubbing his bald head. After a few minutes he stood to undress.

"That's what I'm talking about." Melissa smiled, her eyes wide with lust. "Let me see it. I been waiting on this!"

Lucky took his time taking off the True Religion fit. When he was naked, he stood before her, basking in the glory of his fit and trim nakedness. He stood 6'4" and 190 pounds. He had the build of a professional basketball player. Lean muscles and six pack abs. Melissa couldn't take her eyes off his hard meat. She stared at it like it was the Holy Grail before grabbing it and shoving it in her mouth. She didn't know how to deep throat, so she focused her mouth on the first couple of inches and used her hand to jack him off.

"Aw shit!" Lucky groaned as fourteen years of forced abstinence rushed out of him in less than thirty seconds.

Melissa had never had so much cum in her mouth, nor was she a swallower. Instead, she let it drip from her mouth onto her big-ass titties. Not yet done, Lucky pushed her back onto the couch and gripped her sperm-coated titties in his hands, smashing them together. Then he shoved his dick between the cum-slicked breasts and humped away. Melissa grabbed a pillow to prop her head so she could suck his dick when it slipped out the top of her breasts.

Lucky's lack of sex made him a minute man and he exploded onto her face. Then he stared down at his handiwork and smiled. Melissa was coated in his jism from her face to her stomach.

"You got me all dirty." She laughed, loving the lewd acts. It had been years since she had dirty sex, and she liked it. "Now let's go to the bathroom so you can clean me."

Sex in the bathroom remained dirty. Melissa stripped naked and bent over the tub to run bath water. Her wide ass was lumpy and full of stretch marks, but Lucky didn't care. He slipped behind her, spreading her cheeks apart and diving deep.

Melissa sucked in a deep breath of air. "Huh! Oh, gawd!"

Lucky didn't even let her vaginal walls adjust to him. Her insides felt way too good. He gripped her fleshy hips and pounded her pussy from behind like a man possessed. Every time his pelvis hit against her ass, it sounded like someone being slapped. Melissa held onto the tub, crying out to God as he drilled away. The third nut took slightly longer to come. He stood behind her and fucked her ass for a full ten minutes straight, giving her a knee-weakening orgasm before erupting. Both of them were sweaty and had to take a moment to catch their breath.

While they recuperated, she poured a sweet-smelling potion into the water before they climbed in the tub. He sat down and she climbed on top. They kissed some more as she slipped his member back inside her sugary walls. She rode him slowly, making love to her man inside the warm water of the bubble bath. When it got good, she picked up the pace, losing control when he started playing with her titties. Water splashed loudly, spilling from the tub all over the floor as she rocked violently in the bath. Neither cared about the damage the water might do. They were too lost in the moment. And when they came, both were able to mark the moment in their minds as the best sex they ever had.

CHAPTER 6

"I feel sorry for your brother's girlfriend." Lasonya laughed.

Desmond took his eyes off the road to shoot her a questioning glance. "What is you talking about? Melissa good."

Her eyes grew wide. "He was locked up for fourteen years. What do you think I'm talking about?" She laughed again.

Her laugh had an effect on him. It was girly and soft, a sweet-sounding giggle that made him laugh with her. "Yeah. Oooh wee! I might have to call them later to make sure she still alive."

"She gon' mess around and have to have a hysterectomy when he done with her." After another bout of laughter, Lasonya got nosy. "So, who do you share your bed with?"

Desmond gave her a side eye, wondering how much to tell about his sex life. "I don't really do the dating thing. My job won't let me."

She picked up on his attempt to be vague. "But you didn't answer my question. Just because you don't date that much doesn't mean you don't sleep with somebody. Must be kinda serious if you don't want to tell me. Have you known her for a while?"

Talking about his sex life to his childhood crush made his shoulders and neck get suddenly tight. He lifted a hand to massage away the ache. "It ain't nothin' like that. I have somebody on base that I see every now and then. Nothing serious."

She let out a smacking sound and pursed her lips. "You don't have to sugar coat nothing with me, Desmond. Why are you being so vague? Is there more than one?"

He didn't look at her but could feel her watching him. He realized she wouldn't let the issue go until she got the answers she wanted. "There have been others, but Amber is the only regular. I'm constantly on the move and don't have the time to get serious with anybody. She understands that because she lives the same life. What's up with this interrogation? You worse than the military police."

She smiled bashfully, like a child caught dipping a finger in a bowl of cake mix. "I just wanted to know how you've been. It's been almost twenty years since we talked. So, you don't have kids? Have you ever been in a serious relationship?"

"No. I've been focused on my career. I don't want to bring kids in this world if I can't be there to raise them."

She nodded in agreement. "I like that you know what you want. I wish all men thought like that and could be that honest with themselves. Most niggas say what they need to say to get you in bed and then bounce."

He detected a bitter memory coming from her lips. "So, that's your story, huh? No-good nigga after no-good nigga?"

Lasonya shook her head. "If you only knew."

"What about Quaysha's daddy? He still around?"

She cut her eyes, fires of hatred burning in her irises. "Worst decision I ever made. And one that I don't even want to talk about. Just thinking about him puts me in a bad mood."

An uncomfortable silence came and sat between them, changing the mood from light to heavy as a pregnant elephant. Desmond was enjoying her company too much too let a bad memory ruin it. "I hope yo' mama won't be mad that Lucky didn't come."

Lasonya snapped out of the temporary funk and came back to the moment. "She might be. But she will understand once she finds out he went home with his girl. Shoot, she might tell you to call and check on Melissa to make sure she not damaged," she joked.

Twenty minutes later, Desmond parked the rental car in front of Marcy's house. Lasonya led the way inside. A symphony of sweet-smelling foods punched them in the nose when they walked in the house. It smelled spicy, and sweet, and tangy all at the same time. Desmond hadn't had a home-cooked meal in a long time so for him, the house smelled like a food paradise.

They found Marcy in the kitchen standing over the stove, putting the finishing touches on a rump roast. Quaysha was standing on a chair at the table holding a wooden spoon, stirring brown liquid in a small pot.

"Hey, babies!" Marcy sang, sauntering over to hug the new arrivals. "Where is Lucky?"

Lasonya turned to Desmond, her eyes wide with humor as she held in laughter. "Tell her."

It took all of Desmond's military training to keep a straight face. "He went home with his girl."

Lasonya busted out laughing. "I told him to call and make sure she okay. Lucky did fourteen years. He might break that girl in half!"

Marcy's mouth dropped open and eyes popped like Melissa's life was really in danger. "Ooh! Somebody betta call 9-1-1! That nigga 'bout to catch a case!" she cracked.

Everyone in the kitchen laughed.

"Hey, Mommy! I'm cooking. Want some?" Quaysha asked, holding out the wooden spoon and spilling the liquid on the table, chair, and floor.

"You wasting it everywhere, Quay-Quay. What you making?" Lasonya asked, walking over to inspect the bowl.

"It's a surprise. Granny said we can eat it later."

Lasonya frowned at her mother.

"It ain't nothing but chocolate sauce in water," Marcy whispered. Then she turned to Desmond. "I hope you ready to eat, nigga. I put my foot in this shit!"

The meal turned out to be a succulent rump roast that melted in your mouth every time you took a bite, macaroni with three different cheeses, biscuits made from scratch, and candy carrots. The conversation flowed smoothly around the table, most of it a Q and A aimed at Desmond.

Two hours later, they left with their bellies stuffed and Quaysha sleeping in the backseat. When he pulled up to Lasonya's house, Desmond thought about how much he liked being in her presence. Around her, he felt free to be himself. He could laugh and joke, let his guard down and be vulnerable, feel free from judgement. It was much the same way he felt around her as a kid. Even though seventeen years had passed since he'd seen her, she still felt familiar. And as he watched her grab Quay-Quay from the back seat, something inside made him want to let her know how he felt.

"Want me to get her for you?"

"Yeah. Thanks. Wanna come in?" she asked, reading his thoughts.

"Yeah. Sure. Nice house," he complimented, trying not to sound too eager as he got out and took the sleeping toddler in his arms.

"Thanks. It'll officially be mine in fifteen years. I want to be able to leave Quaysha something."

He nodded, staring at the pink and gray home. "That's good thinking. Equity. This could be the beginning of generational wealth."

She smiled back at him while unlocking the door. "That's the plan. Marcy taught me that. You want to bring her in the room and lay her in bed?"

Desmond carried the sleeping beauty down the hall to a pink princess room. After laying the kid in bed, Lasonya undressed her and tucked her in before the grownups retired to the living room.

"You want something to drink?"

"Yeah. What you got?"

"Water, juice, or liquor. I'm having a drink."

"Kinda early for that, ain't it?"

She got sassy and put a hand on her wide hip. "I'm grown and it's after five o'clock. I'm having a drink. What you want?"

"Since you put it like that, I'll have what you having."

She smiled before spinning and walking to the kitchen. Desmond watched her ample booty bounce in the white cotton pants. She was having an effect on him. He liked everything about her: the way she walked, talked, smiled, laughed, and smelled. In his eyes, she could do no wrong.

She came back from the kitchen a few moments later, carrying two glasses half-filled with clear liquid.

"Here you go."

Desmond took the drink and tried to ignore the electricity that went through his body when her leg rubbed against him as she sat down. "What is this?" he asked, sniffing the glass.

"Ciroc. My favorite." She smiled before taking a sip.

Desmond took a slow drink, the sweet-tasting liquor burning a little as it went smoothly down his throat. "How long you been with Drew?"

Her hazel-brown eyes danced across his face before she responded. "Couple years off and on. Is that what you and my mom was whispering about last night when I was getting Quay-Quay?"

Desmond laughed as he remembered Marcy's words. "She told me not to tell you. She carry a gun, so I gotta keep my word."

"Well, she ain't here. And I know how to keep secrets."

He laughed harder. "That's bullshit. You told her we kissed."

It was Lasonya's turn to crack up. Her breasts jiggled while her body rocked with laughter. "In my defense, I tell my mother everything. I don't have brothers and sisters. I'm surprised she said something. What else did she say?"

"That she knew we was crushing on each other. And that if y'all hadn't moved, we probably woulda had sex."

Lasonya turned red, blushing. "She said all that?"

Desmond nodded, taking a sip of the Ciroc.

"I'ma kill her ass."

"It's all good. Everything happens for a reason. Marcy believes that I might've showed up just in time to give your love life a 'good spark'. Her words, not mine."

Lasonya was quiet. She had felt an immediate connection to Desmond as soon as she got in the car with him after he knocked out Drew. It was deeper than the joy of seeing a long-lost friend. She figured it might've stemmed from the puppy love she felt for him as an adolescent, but whatever it was, she wanted to be around him all the time. Wanted him on every level. And when she looked in his dark eyes, she could see that he felt the same.

"Do you believe in coincidences?"

Desmond shook his head. "Nah. What's supposed to happen will happen."

"I believe the same thing. I know this might sound funny, but I feel this crazy connection with you. Am I tripping?" she asked, engaging him in an intense and erotically-charged staring contest.

Desmond held her eye contact, trying to find the right words. None came to mind. His only thoughts were for him to stop thinking and go with it. So he did, and leaned in for a kiss.

Lasonya met him halfway, meeting his hungry mouth with burning kisses. Their glasses found the table, freeing their hands to touch, squeeze, and rub body parts. The clothes started flying next and they were naked in seconds.

Desmond was mesmerized by Lasonya's perfect body. As far as he was concerned, she never needed to put on clothes again. Laws should be created allowing her to walk around naked so the world could see what perfection looked like. Her skin looked soft as buttermilk, defined shoulders and collarbones like she worked out. Her breasts were big firm globes with large dark areolas and hard nipples. Her stomach was flat, waist snatched like she wore a corset, hips wide like she birthed royal babies. The V between her thick thighs was bald and meaty. Even her calves were sexy, and her toes didn't have a corn or hangnail.

After taking in each other's nakedness, she pushed Desmond onto the couch, staring seductively into his eyes while straddling his lap. Desmond was hypnotized by her beauty and stare. He wanted her more than he had ever wanted any other woman. Putting on a condom never crossed his mind. Or hers. And there was no need for foreplay. He was harder than steel. Lasonya's treasure box was so wet that juices dripped down the inside of her thigh. She grabbed his prize and sat down on it, loving the way it filled her.

"Oh, Desmond!" she sang, biting his earlobe as she eased down slowly.

"Ssss! Oh, shit!" Desmond groaned. Her pussy felt better than any he'd ever been inside. It was hot as a preheated oven, wet as a waterfall, and snug as an insulated glove.

She moved her hips slowly, grinding in a circular motion and lifting her head to the ceiling to moan in pleasure. Desmond's lips found her breasts and started sucking.

"Oh, yeah! That feels so good, baby," she encouraged, loving the feel of his mouth on her nipples. It drove her crazy, and she began to ride him faster and harder.

Desmond had one hand on her hip and another gripping a handful of a fleshy ass cheek. He could feel himself about to bust. He tried to think of anything and everything to keep his mind off the goodness of Lasonya's pussy. Sports. Working out. At the shooting range. Nothing worked. Her sex was too good and he had wanted her for too long. He erupted prematurely, toes curling as his body went stiff.

"Aw shit!" he groaned.

Lasonya didn't slow her pace one bit. Desmond remained hard and she was in the zone. Feeling his spasming dick inside her turned her on even more. She dug her nails into his shoulder and rode harder.

"Oh, Desmond! Yeah, baby! Oh, my God, you feel so good!" she cried as the orgasm began building from somewhere deep inside. A few moments later it peaked, releasing waves of pleasure through her body.

"Oh shit! Oh shit! Oh shit! Oooohhh!" she cried, shivering and collapsing on top of him.

He kissed the side of her face and whispered in her ear. "You a freak, you know that?"

"Shut up," she managed through deep breaths, biting him on the neck.

A jolt of electricity shot through his body. "Oh! Bite me again. That shit felt good."

She did so. Without warning, Desmond gripped her ass cheeks and stood up. Lasonya had to wrap her arms around his neck and legs around his hips and thighs to keep from falling. His strength and vigor turned her on even more. His shoulders, back, and bicep muscles flexed as he began lifting her up and down, bucking his hips as he fucked her while standing. They quickly got into a rhythm. Lasonya was suspended in sexual bliss. The way he manhandled her was exciting and new, taking her to new carnal heights.

"Oh, Desmond! Oh, Desmond! Yeah, baby. Oh, my God, this feels so good!"

The words and the sounds of her moans were a beautiful melody, swimming through his ears, getting lodged in the pleasure part of his brain. He continued to stand and fuck her, his legs getting weak and beginning to burn. But he couldn't stop. His second nut was coming on fast and he had to get there. So he powered through the pleasure and pain, bucking his hips ferociously and slamming into her pussy as hard as he could. When he busted the second time, he knew that it would be hard to leave Milwaukee for his next mission.

***

The first thing Desmond noticed was the smell. Fried eggs and bacon. The scents tickled his nose and reminded him that he was still on leave. What surprised him was that he didn't hear or feel Lasonya get out of bed. He was a light sleeper. The slightest sound would force his eyes open and he would be ready to fight or flee. Being with Lasonya had relaxed him so much that he slipped. And that could be dangerous. He couldn't allow it to happen again.

Vibrations from his pants pulled him from thoughts of training. He grabbed the phone from the pocket. The screen read Alpha One. Duke was the Team Leader of SEAL Team Alpha. Officially Alpha One. Desmond was Alpha Four.

"Hey."

"Hey, Alpha Four. You sound asleep. You okay?"

Desmond cleared his throat. "Yeah. Had a late night. But I'm okay. How did it go in Paris?"

"Tango got the bandit. Crisis averted. Got a good team. We aren't completely handicapped without you," he cracked.

"I know. I didn't mean it like that. I just wanted to make sure everybody was good."

"I know what you meant, Desmond. I'm just giving you a hard time. We're fine. But how are you? When is the funeral?"

Desmond thought about Cookie for a fleeting moment. "I'm good. Funeral is this weekend. I'll be back with the team in three days. Four tops."

"You don't have to rush back, Alpha Four. Take time to grieve with the family and get it all out. You're one of the best I've ever recruited, but I don't want you to come back before you're ready.

The mind and emotions are tricky. You have to make sure you're good. No doctors can put a time limit on the proper amount of time to grieve. Clear your head."

"I'm good, Duke. She was my mother, but she wasn't a mother, you know? She gave me life, but didn't raise me. I'm giving her a proper and respectable burial because she birthed me. And as soon as she's buried, I'm flying back to base. I'm good."

"Okay. Call me if you need anything."

"Will do. Bye."

"Good morning, sleepy head." Lasonya smiled, sauntering into the room wearing his T-shirt. "I was about to come wake you. You hungry?" she asked, leaning over and kissing Desmond on the jaw.

Hearing her cheery voice, seeing her smile, and his T-shirt barely covering her blue panties turned him on. He grabbed her around the waist, pulling her on top of him and kissing her. "I'm always hungry."

Lust and excitement flashed in her brown eyes. "Wait. Quaysha is awake. Breakfast is ready. Come and eat. What do you want to drink? Apple juice or orange juice?"

He released her from his grip. "Orange juice."

"Get up. I put a towel and toothbrush on the sink."

When Lasonya left the room, he yawned and stretched, limbs popping like Rice Krispies cereal when adding milk. After finding his jeans, he went to freshen up. On the way out of the bathroom, he ran into Quaysha.

"Hi, Desmond!" She smiled, showing a missing front tooth.

"Hi."

"Are you my mommy's friend?"

"Yes. Is it true you're only four? You seem older."

"Yes. I turn five next month. Mommy said I can be a princess."

"You already are a princess. Where is Mommy?"

"In the kitchen. Want me to show you?"

"Yes. Please."

Desmond followed the bouncing little girl through the house and into the kitchen. Lasonya was standing over the stove making his plate.

"Mommy, I found Desmond!"

"Thank you, baby. Sit down, Desmond. I talked to Jamar on Facebook while you were asleep. He wants to talk to you. I couldn't find you on Facebook. What's your name?" she asked, setting the plate of food in front of him. Fried eggs, bacon, hash browns, and toast with jelly.

"I'm not on Facebook. Or any other social media," he said before taking a fork full of over-easy eggs into his mouth.

Lasonya couldn't believe her ears. "What? Everybody is on social media."

"Not me. You can cook. You did yo' thang with these eggs."

"Thank you. Why don't you have a Facebook page?"

"My job," he mumbled between bites.

"The army won't let you be on Facebook or Instagram?"

"It's a little more complicated than that. I'm not in the army. I'm a Navy SEAL. I have to keep a low profile."

Intrigue flashed in her eyes as she sat down across from him. "Are you a spy? What is a Navy SEAL?"

"Kind of like a spy, but not really. We do secret missions. Do you remember when President Obama said he killed Bin Laden?"

She nodded.

"I work with those guys."

Her eyes got big as the moon. "What? Seriously? Shit! I never woulda thought. Damn, Des."

"Oh! Mommy said a bad word!" Quaysha bugged.

"I'm sorry, baby. Hey, why don't you get ready to take a bath? Go find some clothes so you can go with Granny."

"I wanna wear my princess dress!" Quaysha screamed as she ran from the kitchen.

"Call Jamar. You can use my phone. I told him I would tell you to call when you woke up. I gotta go give her a bath," Lasonya said before heading for the bathroom.

Desmond grabbed her phone from the table and searched for Jamar's number and called.

"What up, love?"

"This not Lasonya. This Jamar?"

There was a slight pause. "Desmond, this you, nigga?"

"Yeah. This Jamar?"

"First of all, beat it with that Jamar shit. I'm J-Money. But what's good, nigga? Fuck you been at?"

"All over the world," Desmond said as the doorbell rang. "I went to the military."

"Desmond, can you get the door!" Lasonya called.

"I got it!"

"Lasonya was telling me that earlier. She said Cookie died too. That's fucked up. How long you in town?"

"I'm leaving after Mama's funeral. Two days. Three at the most. Hold on, Jamar. Somebody at the door," he said as he looked out the peephole. A tall light-skinned man stood on the porch. He looked familiar, but Desmond wasn't sure why. "Who is it?"

"It's Tony. Lasonya here?" the man on the porch called.

Desmond opened the door, surprised when feelings of jealousy filled his chest. The same emotions played over Tony's face as the men stood face to face.

"Who should I say you is?"

"I'm Quaysha's daddy," he answered, studying Desmond intently. Then recognition flashed in his eyes. "Don't I know you, man? Yo, you Desmond?"

J-Blunt

CHAPTER 7

Lucky lay in bed with his eyes closed, listening to the sound of freedom. It was quiet. Peaceful. Relaxing. No keys jingling on the hips of correctional officers. No doors being opened or slammed shut. No loud talking or arguing about things that didn't matter. No sounds of cards and dominoes slapping the table or people calling out chess moves over the tiers. The sound of freedom was still silence, a blessed polar opposite to the sounds of incarceration. And he was thankful to be free. He had been awake for five minutes, appreciating his first morning of freedom and the feel of a real mattress. The California King was the softest thing he'd ever slept on. It felt like sleeping on a cloud.

When he finally opened his eyes, he took a moment to gaze at his surroundings so he could remember what the first morning of freedom looked like. The master bedroom was decorated simply. Royal blue walls. Black curtains. Blue carpet. An oak dresser with a lighted mirror. Visiting room pictures of Lucky, Melissa, and the kids were on the mirror and in frames on top of the dresser. Flat screen on the wall. This was home.

After forcing himself to climb out of bed, he went to freshen up. To shower in a real tub instead of a shower stall or community shower felt freeing. After washing his body and drying off, he dressed in a pair of boxers and went to find Melissa. She was sitting on the couch in the living room wearing a T-shirt and panties, focusing on her laptop.

"Hey, baby." He smiled, bending to kiss her. "What you doing?"

"G'morning, free man. I'm doing what I normally do on my lunch breaks. Posting and sharing some stuff on your Facebook and Instagram. You were sleeping so good and I didn't want to wake you."

"Best sleep I ever had. I been sleeping on cardboard mattresses for fourteen years. That California King is the truth. I don't even remember my dream," he expressed, sitting down next to her on the couch. "Let me see what you doing."

"I'm posting about your first day of freedom. What do you want to say to your people?"

He thought for a moment. "Freedom is priceless. Don't give it away."

Melissa typed the word as he spoke. "Is that all?"

He shrugged. "Yeah. What more can I say?"

"Whatever you want. If you want me to leave it like that, I will. Maybe take a picture of you holding your books and put it on Instagram. I have a box of them in the closet."

It was a good idea. "Good shit, baby. Stay right there." He said before running upstairs and looking in the closet. There was a handmade wicker basket near the back. Inside were brand new copies of all ten of his books. He grabbed the box and went downstairs. Lucky spread the books out on the table and stood behind it. Melissa took the picture on her phone and put it on Instagram with the caption "From a Prisoner to a Prince".

"That's good shit right there, baby. You remembered what I told the judge, huh?"

"Baby, I listened to and remembered everything. I was scared they wasn't gon' let you go. I'm glad you spoke up for yourself, because that public pretender was worthless."

"Yeah. I couldn't leave my freedom up to him. Especially after all the time I did. I needed to get home to you."

"I know that's right!" she agreed. "So, are you ready for today? We have to go see your P.O. at 8:30 and you have a call with the book agent at 10:00. And we have to go to the DMV to get you an ID."

"Yeah. I'm ready when you is. I need to get my license so I won't be pulling you away from work to drive me around."

"I already took care if that, too." She smiled proudly. "You start Driver's Ed next week. Monday."

He was impressed by her efficiency. "Damn, baby. I don't know what I would do without you. Thank you," he said, leaning over and kissing her lips. He tried to peck her once, but Melissa wasn't having it.

"Nah, baby. Bring them lips back over here. We ain't got no guards watching us."

The make out got hot and heavy, eventually turning into sex on the sofa and another round in the shower. After they were Zestfully clean, the lovers got dressed and went to take care of business.

The Probation and Parole Building was only a ten minute drive from their house. The big white office building turned Wisconsin Department of Corrections extended supervision headquarters seemed to have a thousand windows. It took three hundred people to operate the building when it was fully staffed, most of them underpaid and overworked. Melissa pulled the SUV into the parking lot at 8:20 a.m., wanting to be early so Lucky could make a good first impression.

They left the truck and walked hand in hand towards the building. Directions hanging on the wall led them to an elevator. Three floors later the door opened. A walk down a short hall brought them to a door that read Department of Corrections Adult Division Of Probation and Parole. Behind the door was a small waiting room. Four wooden park style benches made a U in the middle of the room. On the opposite side of the room was a door, and next to it, a bulletproof check-in window. An older black woman with graying hair sat behind the glass looking at a computer screen. Lucky walked up and spoke.

"Hi. Is this where I check in?"

She looked at him like he had asked a stupid question. "That's what the sign says, don't it?"

Lucky was momentarily taken aback by her sarcasm.

She didn't seem to care if he took her comment the wrong way and continued speaking. "Sign your name on the clipboard. Who you here to see?"

"Gary Graham," he answered flatly, grabbing the clip board and using the pen that hung from it to sign his name.

"He'll be out to get you in a minute. For future reference, you can't bring guests into the building with you. They have to wait outside."

Lucky walked away understanding why the office had a bulletproof window.

"She was rude," Melissa said, mugging the woman behind the glass.

"Now I see why they got bulletproof glass. Old bitch need to be shot," he mumbled.

A few minutes later there was a buzz at the door beside the bulletproof window. When it opened, a bald black man in his fifties stepped into the waiting room. He looked at Lucky. "Larry Harrison?"

Lucky stood. "Yeah. That's me."

He extended a hand. "I'm your parole officer, Gary Graham. Welcome back to the free world."

Lucky nodded as the men shook hands. "Thanks."

"Alright. Follow me. Gotta holla at you for a minute. Have you sign some papers," he said before leading the way down a long hall with small offices on both sides. After a right and left turn, they stopped at an office door that looked exactly like the other twenty they'd passed.

"After you, son," Gary said, opening the door and letting Lucky go in first. "Have a seat. Let's get this started."

The office was small. The only thing that could fit inside were the desk, the computer atop it, two chairs, and a file cabinet. Lucky sat at the chair in front of the desk while Gary sat behind.

"I read your file, man, and I see you did a long time," Gary opened, staring at Lucky with watchful sharp dark brown eyes.

"Yeah, man. Fourteen years. Feels good to be free."

Gary gave a hmph. "I bet it does. Considering you killed a man, a fourteen year bid don't sound that bad. So, what are yo' plans?"

"Can't bring nobody back from the dead, and I know people who got more time than me for doing less. I know I was blessed," Lucky expounded. "And my plans are to keep writing. I saved up a little money while I was in and I want to use it to start my own business. I was thinking a publishing company."

Gary nodded. "I like it. I see that you wrote some books while you were in. That's good. Takes a lot of talent to do that. How far have you gotten with your plans to start this publishing company?"

"Wrote a business plan. Now I gotta get out here and put it down. I'm thinking about going to register a trademark in the next couple days. Probably after my mother's funeral."

Gary nodded again. "Yeah. Heard about that. Is that why you beat the guy up the day before you got out?"

Lucky couldn't tell how the older man felt about the fight. Nothing showed on his face. "Nah. That was over the phone. Young dude tried to take the phone while I was on it. When I didn't give it to him, he punched me. And I'm sure you know the rest."

"Put his ass in the hospital!" Gary laughed. "I didn't trip on that because it happened while you were still in prison and technically you wasn't on my case yet. So, what came of that? You were arrested, right?"

"Yeah. I go back to court in two weeks. Charged with felony battery. I'ma look for a lawyer later today."

"Okay. Keep me posted on what happens. Sounds like you have a good head on your shoulders. I talked to your girlfriend and you have a residence. Have you bought a car yet? If so, I need to see the papers."

"Nah. No car yet. But I start Driver's Ed next week. Buy one as soon as I get my license."

"Okay. Again, just keep me posted. I'm not gon' be on yo' ass all the time. I don't roll like that. You a grown man and I ain't cho daddy. I'll give you a lot of rope. You gon' either use it to get ahead or hang yo'self. Yo' choice. If you make me do my job, I'ma do it. I don't like sending black men to prison because it's enough of us in there already. But again, if you force my hand, I'ma do my job. I'll help you in any way I can, just let me know. Since you just got out, we gon' meet every other week for ninety days. After that, it's once a month. You have to deal with me for the next ten years, so let's try to make it a good ten."

Lucky nodded. "I like the sound of that."

"Okay. I'ma have you sign these rules and give you a copy. Make sure you look them over and remember them. These are the conditions of your release. You was supposed to sign them before you got out, but you went and got Mayweather on that young nigga," he cracked before sliding a paper with rules printed on them and a pen across the desk.

After reading the rules, Lucky signed.

"Alright. Got any questions?" Gary asked.

Lucky shook his head. "Nah, I'm good. I'm just ready to live, man."

Gary smiled. "I got a good feeling about you. You gon' be alright. Let me walk you to the door."

After walking down the long hall, the men stopped in the waiting room to shake hands before Lucky and Melissa were on their way.

"How was he?" Melissa asked when they walked into the hall.

"He seemed cool. Told me he gon' give me a lot of rope and not to hang myself."

When they stopped at the elevator, Melissa stood on her tippy toes and kissed his lips. "I ain't gon' let you do nothing with that rope but tie me up."

A flash of danger shone in Lucky's eyes as he pulled her close and kissed her. "Betta stop playin wit' me before we get it poppin' on this elevator."

She met his look with a challenge. "Who said I was playing?"

The elevator dinged and the couple's make-out session was interrupted by a youngster wearing way too much jewelry and smelling like weed.

"What's poppin', mane?" He nodded before swaggering down the hall.

Lucky shook his head. "That nigga 'bout to go to jail. Let's get the fuck outta here."

When they left the P.O.'s office, Lucky tried to call Desmond, but didn't get an answer. "Where this nigga at?"

Melissa gave him a side eye. "Where you think? Where we dropped him off with that pretty girl. What's her name? Lasonya?"

Lucky smiled. "Right. Yeah. Go over there. Gimme that book agent's number so I can call her."

Fifteen minutes later, Melissa pulled up to the curb of Lasonya's house and parked behind a white 750 Mercedes Benz. Two people were in the car. A tall light-skinned man was walking up on the porch. Something about the man caught Lucky's eye.

"That's a nice car," Melissa mumbled, taking the key from the ignition.

Lucky didn't respond. He was climbing from the truck, eyeing the back of the man's head. He wore all-white fitted designer clothes and had curly short hair. When the front door opened, Desmond appeared shirtless and the men had a few words. Lucky and Melissa approaching from behind made the man spin around. He and Lucky exchanged long stares and Lucky was able to see his eyes. They were blue. He would never forget the blue-eyed light-skinned nigga.

"Lucky? That's you, brah?" the man asked.

"Tony?" Lucky questioned.

The man smiled. "Yeah! What's good, my nigga?" he yelled, opening his arms for an embrace.

Lucky glanced at Desmond. His little brother didn't look happy. "What you doing over here, man?" Lucky asked after the embrace.

Tony gave a sly grin, adjusting the gold Patek on his wrist. "I just came over here to see my daughter and baby mama. I didn't know li'l Des was over here," he said, nodding to the door.

"I ain't li'l Des no more," Desmond said in a serious tone.

Tony looked back at Desmond like he felt disrespected by the tone. "What's good wit'chu, brah?"

Lucky didn't want to see his childhood friend get his shit split by a Navy SEAL, so he intervened. "He good, Tone. Niggas just kinda fucked up 'cause Moms passed a li'l while back."

Tony gave Desmond a lingering stare before turning back to Lucky. "I heard about that, brah. And I'm sorry to hear that. If it's anything I can do, let me know."

The two men in the Benz climbed from the car wearing mean looks. Neither spoke, just watched the porch.

"Fa sho'. So you got a baby by Lasonya?" Lucky asked.

Tony smiled, cutting his eyes at Desmond. "Yeah. Been a minute since I seen Quaysha, but I was hoping to change that."

"Who at the door, Desmond?" Lasonya asked, appearing behind him. When she saw Tony, her face showed a mix of emotions. Shock. Surprise. Exasperation. And then anger. "What the hell you want?"

Tony lifted his hands, palms up, a peaceful gesture. "Ay, chill, baby. I just wanna see my daughter."

Lasonya's face went from anger to rage. She stepped out onto the porch, not seeming to care that she was only wearing a T-shirt. "After three fuckin' years? You wait all this time and then just show up like everything supposed to be okay?"

Tony lost the cool demeanor and got serious. "Listen. This why I stayed away, 'cause yo' ass be talkin' shit. Now I'm tryna do the right thing, but you gettin' in my way. My daughter needs her daddy."

"No she don't! She don't need shit from you. Only thing you was is a sperm donor. I'm her mama and her daddy. We good. I got it. Go on, finish doing you, 'cause as you can see, I'm doing me," she said, leaning into Desmond.

Tony's top lip quivered in anger as he mugged her. He looked like he wanted to hit her. "Fuck you then, bitch. I came over here to talk to yo' stupid ass, but I see you still on that bullshit. Bet I won't make this mistake again," he said before walking away.

"Lose my address, nigga. We good. I got a real man now."

Tony looked back over his shoulder and smirked as he walked to the driver side of the Benz.

A maroon Cadillac truck on 28s pulled up alongside the Benz. The passenger window rolled down and the man inside the truck exchanged a couple words with Tony. After one last look towards the porch, Tony and his people climbed in the European car and sped away. The luxury truck parked at the curb and a tall light-skinned man with long dreadlocks hopped out. He had a husky build, pudgy around the midsection, and wore an iced-out chain.

"What's good, family!" he yelled, running towards the porch.

"Who dat?" Lucky asked.

"Jamar's crazy ass," Lasonya mumbled, still mad at seeing Tony.

"Yo, Lucky! What's good, nigga? Act like you don't know me!" he yelled, wrapping him in a bear hug that lasted too long for comfort.

"What's good, Jamar? Let me go, nigga."

Jamar broke the embrace and mugged Lucky. "Listen, I'm not gon' keep tellin' you and yo' brotha that my name's J-Money. J-Money, nigga! Beat it with that Jamar shit."

The brothers laughed.

"A'ight, J-Money," Desmond said sarcastically. "What's good though, brah? It's been a minute."

"Understatement. Show me some love, my nigga," J-Money said, opening his arms for a hug. Then he turned to Lasonya. "What up, sis? Why y'all ain't got no clothes on?"

"Hey, J-Money," she said, a little bit of anger in her voice and demeanor. "I was giving Quay-Quay a bath."

"And who is this thick, fine mu'fucka?" he asked, looking at Melissa.

"Slow down, li'l nigga." Lucky spoke up. "This my girl, Melissa."

He laughed at Lucky. "Okay, big brah. I was just complimenting yo' missus. What's good, Melissa?"

She blushed. "I'm fine."

"What that nigga Wacco was doin' over here?"

"Who?" Lucky and Desmond asked at the same time.

"Tony. What he wanted?"

Desmond turned to Lasonya, a hint of anger in his eyes. "They got a baby."

J-Money looked surprised. "Straight up? Damn! How you start fuckin wit' that nigga?"

Lasonya shook her head. "Being stupid. I don't even wanna talk about him no more. I hate that bitch-ass nigga. Y'all wanna come in? I need to put some clothes on."

J-Blunt

CHAPTER 8

"Desmond, I need to put on some pants. Can I talk to you in the room?" Lasonya asked, leading the way into the house.

Desmond gave her the look of a man that had been betrayed. "Nah. I'ma catch up with my nigga, Jamar. Go 'head."

She looked hurt. "C'mon, Desmond? It's really like that?"

"Yeah, it's like that," the soldier said, sticking to his guns and turning to his childhood friend. "What's good with you, Jamar?"

"I told you my name ain't Jamar, nigga! Call me by my government name one more time and we boxin'. On er'thang I love."

Lasonya rolled her eyes and stomped away.

"My bad, brah. That J-Money shit just take some gettin' used to."

"We good. For now." he joked. "So, what the fuck happened to Cookie, my nigga? How she get knocked off?" J-Money asked as everyone had seats around the living room.

"Got caught in a shootout tryna buy some work," Lucky said sadly.

"Damn, that's fucked up, my nigga," J-Money lamented. "Where that shit happen at? They know who did it?"

"On 41st and Clarke. Some niggas named Jay and Draco," Desmond said.

A look of surprise showed on J-Money's face. "Damn. That's a couple blocks from where we grew up. And Draco, shit, I think that li'l nigga is Wacco's nephew."

Lucky and Desmond shot each other glances.

"You got Wacco's info?" Desmond asked.

"Nah. We ain't in the same lanes, but we acknowledge each other when we see each other 'round the city. But he ain't hard to find. He still be on Clarke Street. And matter fact, Draco is Wacco's nephew," J-Money confirmed. "Li'l nigga is Carmen's son. Y'all remember Carmen, right?"

Lucky's eyes grew wide at the memory. "Tony's sister. Her son was a baby when I got locked up."

Desmond nodded. "Yeah, I remember her. That's crazy how little this city is. You know where to find this li'l nigga?"

"Shit, they all still over on Clarke. You know most niggas don't go far from the block they grow up on. Wacco got all that shit on lock. He the one that started that CSG shit."

"What's that?" Desmond asked.

"Clarke Street Goons. They be over there block bangin'. Don't want niggas that ain't CSG to get money over there. Cookie might've got caught up in that bullshit."

Desmond and Lucky shared another look.

"You know some of them niggas over there?" Lucky asked.

"Yeah. A few of them niggas."

"Take me over there and show me Draco."

"Wait, baby," Melissa spoke up, lines of worry playing across her face. "I don't want you to get in trouble. You just got out."

Lucky gave her a look that ceased all doubts about his next move. "This don't got nothing to do with you, baby." Then he turned to Desmond. "You coming?"

Desmond was already walking to Lasonya's room. "Let me throw my shit on."

Lasonya walked in the room with Quaysha in her arms wrapped in a towel as Desmond was getting dressed. "You gon' leave before we talk about this, for real?"

Desmond took a deep breath, rubbing both hands across his face. "What more is it to say? You got a baby by Tony. I mean..." His words trailed off.

"I didn't mean to get pregnant by him. I only messed around with him for a couple of months. I know y'all was all cool back in the day, but we lost contact for almost twenty years. I didn't know what happened to you."

"I asked you who her daddy was. You coulda told me instead of letting me find out like that. And Tony wasn't my guy. That was Lucky's friend. I hated that nigga."

"I'm sorry, Desmond. I know I shoulda told you, but I didn't know how. I was a little ashamed and I didn't want you to look at me differently."

He looked her from head to toe with disgust. "Too late for that." He mugged her before leaving the room. "Y'all ready?" he asked Lucky and J-Money.

"Let's hit it," J-Money said, standing and walking outside.

"Wait, baby. Don't leave. Please," Melissa begged, on the verge of tears as she grabbed Lucky's arm.

"I'ma be right back," he said, trying to walk away.

Melissa held on tight. "No, Lucky. Don't. I don't want you to get in trouble."

He snatched away. "Let me go, Melissa! Let me go!"

She grabbed him again and got in his face. "No! I'm not about to let you go out there and do something stupid. You just got out yesterday," she refused, fighting for his love.

"I said let me go!" Lucky yelled, pushing her so hard that she fell on the floor.

Melissa was surprised by Lucky's overreaction. She sat on the floor staring up at him like he had battered her. When Lucky realized his overreaction, he softened and helped her up.

"I'm sorry, baby. I'ma be back. I'm not gon' get in trouble," he said before leaving the house.

She ran towards the door, the tears spilling down her face as big as raindrops in a thunderstorm. "No, Lucky. I don't want you to go."

Desmond stopped her. His brother had made up his mind, and no one would be able to stop him. "I got him, Melissa. I'm not gon' let him do nothing stupid. We coming back. Stay here."

She continued to cry crocodile tears, the possibility of her worst nightmare playing across her face. "Bring him back, Desmond. Promise me you gon' bring him back."

A strange feeling entered Desmond's body as he stared into her eyes. For some reason, he felt like he couldn't keep the promise. But he made it anyway. "I'ma bring him back. I promise."

After leaving the house, Desmond walked out to the truck idling at the curb. Lucky sat in the passenger seat. The brothers locked eyes as Desmond approached, the look on his older brother's face telling Desmond to keep his comments about Melissa and the trouble they could get in to himself. So he climbed in the back seat and kept his peace.

J-Money could sense Lucky's foul mood and attempted to lighten it with humor. "I can't believe you went to the army, Des," J-Money said as he pulled the luxury SUV away from the curb. "You all buff and shit like one of them steroid using-ass niggas. *Universal Soldier*-ass nigga," he cracked.

"Fuck you, nigga. This all natural. I can help you tone that shit up if you want. Run a couple miles. Lift a couple weights."

"Pssst! Nigga, please. Only thing I'm lifting is stacks of money and bad bitches. Speaking of bad bitches, on what, you fuckin' Lasonya?"

Desmond laughed. "Why you gotta say it like that?"

"Aw, don't tell me you soft on her!"

"Nigga been soft on Lasonya since we was kids," Lucky chuckled.

"C'mon, man. Y'all niggas clownin'. I'ma always have a soft spot for her. We go way back."

"So when you go back to the army base or overseas, you want me to look out for her?" J-Money smiled, watching Desmond in the rearview mirror.

The look on Desmond's face told him that he didn't find the joke funny.

"Damn, nigga. Chill. I'm just fuckin wit'chu. But when you leaving, seriously? You know we gotta ball out one time. Plus, Lucky just got out. We gotta turn up one time."

"I don't know. After we bury Moms. The funeral this weekend."

"Say no more, my dude. I'm making us VIP reservations at Telly's for Freaky Friday. I damn near own that bitch and we gon' fuck it up! Y'all in?"

"What is Telly's?" Lucky asked.

"Strip club. Bad bitches all up through that bitch." J-Money nodded.

"We in." Desmond spoke up for both of them.

Ten minutes later, the Escalade turned onto 37th and Clarke, parking in front of a white townhouse. It was a few minutes past noon and the block was alive with the rhythm of hood life.

July in the hood was a special time. Kids ran around screaming while they played, not a care in the world but having fun. Porches were filled with people enjoying the short summer sun. Some had their grills on, barbecuing in full effect. Some sat around smoking or drinking, not believing the made-up rule of drinking after five o'clock. Others sat around like vultures, watching the block like they were looking for a meal. The birds of prey caught Desmond's eye. He felt a little uneasy being in the neighborhood when the sun was up considering what had taken place the last time he was around these parts.

"What we doing, J-Money?" Lucky asked.

The Cadillac driver pulled out a phone. "My nigga Six live here. He CSG. I'ma text him to come outside. See what he knows. Let me do the talking."

A few moments later, the front door of the townhouse opened and a slim brown-skinned man walked out. He wore a Milwaukee Brewer's jersey, acid-washed jeans, and white Air Force Ones, his hair braided to the back in six cornrows. The bulge in the front of his pants told that he was armed. When he got to the truck, he paused at the passenger door and looked inside, his eyes lingering on Desmond.

"What up, nigga?" J-Money nodded.

"You got it. What it do?" the newcomer smiled, showing a row of gold teeth.

"Get in and take a ride wit' me. Lemme holla at you."

He looked towards the backseat, eyeing Desmond again. "Who that?"

"That's my nigga from way back. He good."

"He look familiar. What you wanna holla at me about?" he asked, refusing to get in the truck.

"I'm tryna catch up wit' Draco. I need a new plug and wanted you to get up wit' him for me. I'll look out if you can make that happen."

Hearing that money might be involved seemed to change Six's demeanor. "He been laying low lately, but I might be able to catch 'em," he said, pulling out a phone. He eyed Desmond again while dialing a number.

"Who I look like?" Desmond asked, noticing Six adjust the bulge in the waist of his pants.

"Like the nigga that was on 41st a couple days ago. Changed my nigga Big Man."

The statement was an accusation, and Desmond knew that Six wasn't calling Draco to hook J-Money up with a drug connect. It was a call to let him know they found him. Somehow he had been revealed. He was unarmed, and they were sitting ducks in the truck.

"Pull off," Desmond whispered, hoping Six didn't hear him.

When Six locked eyes with him, Desmond knew he had heard.

"Pull off, Jamar! Pull off!" Desmond screamed, diving on the floor.

J-Money heard the panic in Desmond's voice and slammed the truck in gear. The powerful engine revved loudly as the tires on the truck squealed.

Pop pop pop pop pop pop pop pop pop pop pop!

Glass broke and metal slugs thudded into the frame of the truck as it sped away.

"Ah shit!" J-Money screamed, losing control of the truck.

Lucky reacted quickly, grabbing the steering wheel and keeping the truck from crashing. "You good, nigga?"

"Nah. I'm hit in the back." He groaned as the truck blew through a stop sign, almost hitting a car.

Lucky guided the truck through the intersection. "Take yo' foot off the gas. Hit the brake. I got it."

The truck came to a jolting stop.

"Ahh!" J-Money screamed, his body jerking violently in the seat.

"Drive, Lucky. I got him." Desmond said, remaining calm and springing into action. He had been trained to do emergency lifesaving skills on the battlefield. He pulled J-Money over the driver's seat and into the backseat and ripped open the back of his shirt. He was bleeding from a hole in his shoulder blade the size of pea.

"You gon be a'ight, brah. I need this shirt to slow down the bleeding," Desmond said before ripping most of the shirt from his body and pressing it onto the bleeding hole. "Lucky, you gotta get out so I can take him to the hospital. I don't want you involved in this. Drive back to Lasonya's house. I got it from here."

"Yep." Lucky nodded, watching the streets and mirrors.

"What the fuck was that about?" J-Money groaned.

"I think I killed his nigga the other day. That's how I found out Draco and Jay had the shootout that killed my mama. I thought I got away clean, but somebody must've seen me."

"Ah shit!" J-Money groaned. "This shit burns, brah. Get me to the hospital!"

***

Desmond tapped the gas pedal when the light turned green, the Camaro engine purring as it drove through the intersection. Although he was focused on driving, all of his actions were mechanical. He didn't think about hitting the blinker when he turned or slowing down for the next red light. His mind was stuck on J-Money. Because of him, his boy had been shot and was laid up in the hospital. Someone had seen him during or after the murders. But how? He did it at night and checked his surroundings. Now CSG wanted him dead, and they didn't care who got in the way. J-Money's friend had become his enemy. Then there Lasonya. Her baby daddy was Tony, a.k.a. Wacco. The leader of CSG. The uncle of the nigga that killed Cookie. A showdown seemed inevitable.

"Penny for your thoughts," Lasonya sang from the passenger seat.

Desmond let out a long breath. "I'm thinkin' about Jamar. That situation is messed up, and it's my fault."

She looked at him quizzically. "What are you talking about?"

Desmond shook his head, wishing he hadn't said anything. "Never mind. I'ma figure it out."

Lasonya leaned in close, searching his face, her voice raising an octave. "Wait, Des. Don't shut me out. You don't have to keep secrets. We're friends. Tell me what happened."

He glanced at her and smirked. "Keeping secrets, huh? Like you not telling me you got a baby by Tony?"

"C'mon, Desmond. I apologized. I'm sorry. How long is it going to take to get past this? What do you want me to do?"

Desmond took a moment to think on a response. Nothing she could say or do would take away the sting of betrayal he felt. And to make matters worse, Wacco was connected to the murder of his mother. While he was considering what to say, his phone rang. It was Detective Perry.

"Hold on. Let me get this. What's going on, Detective?"

"Desmond! Hey, man. You still in the city? I need to talk to you."

"Yeah. I'm here. What's going on? You find who killed my mom?"

"Not on the phone. Face to face. Where you at? I can come to you if you need."

"I'm driving. Headed up Mill Road."

"I'm close. You wanna pull over on Good Hope Road? I can be there in five minutes."

"All right. I'm in a black Camaro."

"What was that about?" Lasonya asked.

Desmond's face was hard and unreadable. Something in his gut didn't feel right. "I don't know. He supposed to be investigating Cookie's murder. I guess he knows something."

A few minutes later the blue unmarked sedan pulled into the parking lot. Desmond climbed from the Camaro as the detective parked. He tried to read the cop's face when he got out of the car, but couldn't. Detective Perry had a good poker face.

"How's it going, Desmond?" he asked, extending a hand.

"I'm making it. You?"

Something dark flashed in Perry's eyes before he pushed it away. "Same. Did you have the funeral yet?"

Desmond didn't like beating around the bush. "No. And I appreciate the concern, but I would rather get to the point of this meeting. Why did you want to talk? You know who killed Cookie?"

The cop let out a chuckle. "You got me again. You can see through the bullshit, huh, soldier?"

Desmond's face remained serious.

"Okay. I'll stop bullshitting. CSG wants you dead."

None of Desmond's training could hide the surprise that showed on his face when the detective dropped the bomb. "What? How do you know?"

The darkness was back in the detective's eyes. "You know those two clowns you thought you whacked in front of the house where Cookie died? One of them lived. You did a number on his throat and he probably won't be talking for a while, but he survived."

Desmond channeled his bearings and took all emotion from his face like a soldier standing at attention. "I don't know what you're talking about. And why are you telling me this?"

The detective chortled. "I didn't come to arrest you, man. We don't have enough evidence. Kareem isn't talking to us. That's the guy whose throat you crushed. Plus, I believe you did me a favor by ridding the earth of Big Man. It was only a matter of time before he ended up back in prison. You saved the taxpayers thirty thousand dollars a year. I came because I will make sure no one on my side will find out about Big Man's death if you do something for me. The whole wash my back and I'll wash yours type of thing. You can go places I can't. Do things that no one on the force can. I need your help."

Desmond stared in the detective's face for a moment. He was fucked and had nowhere to run. The tall skinny nigga had lived and could testify and get him cooked. Now the detective was offering him protection. But it was probably too good to be true. But what choice did he have? He needed the detective's help. "What do you need?"

The darkness came back in the detectives eyes. "You ever heard of a guy named Polo?"

J-Blunt

CHAPTER 9

"Hi, Larry. Were you able to look over the contract?" Renae Shaffer asked.

Renae was a petite Indian woman with bronze-colored skin, high cheekbones, brown eyes, and jet black hair. She was also a literary agent with Power in the Pen Literary Agency. She wanted to represent Lucky to help take his career to the next level. They were Facetiming to discuss the details.

"Yeah. I like the way everything sounds. I already signed it and emailed it back. I just wanted to discuss whether you'll be working with the stuff I already wrote too. I wrote ten urban books. Are those a part of the plan as well?"

"Yes and yes. I'm representing you and all your works. I've read some of the books, and I can say that you have a real talent. Now you just need to cross over into the mainstream and crack the *New York Time's* Bestsellers list. I believe the autobiography will do just that. I'm also going to set up some book signings with the urban books. You probably need to check with your parole agent to see if you can travel."

"I'll do that. He seems pretty cool. And I'm finishing up the edits for the autobiography. Lisa really went hard with the first round of edits, but I like it. I think it will make the story stronger."

"Yeah, Lisa is good and thorough. But like you said, it will make the story stronger. Do you have any questions or concerns with the contract?"

"Nah. I'm good. I cool with everything you're doing."

"Okay, if you think of anything, don't hesitate to call. Take care of yourself and welcome home."

"Alright. Thanks. Talk to you later."

After ending the call, Lucky let out a satisfied breath. He had dreamed of moments like these while he was in prison. Now it was all coming true. His book sales were about to increase, he had a real agent that was working to take his career to the next level, and he was a free man. The only thing missing was Cookie being able to see his success. Damn.

"How did it go?" Melissa asked, walking into the family room.

"Good." Lucky nodded. "She's working on setting up some book signings for the urban books. I'ma have to call Gary to see if I can leave the state."

"That's good." She nodded, sitting on the couch across from him and messing with her phone.

Lucky stared at her for a few moments. Her reaction to his success wasn't what he expected. She normally celebrated the smallest achievements. When he became a certified tutor while in prison, she acted like he graduated from college. When Renae contacted about wanting to represent him, she hooped and hollered like they won a prize on a game show. But now that things were finally in motion, all he got was "That's good." He could tell by her demeanor that she was mad.

"You got something on yo' mind?"

She shrugged, not even looking up from the phone. "No. I'm fine."

Lucky got up and walked over to sit next to her. "So, this what we doing? For real?"

She shrugged again, still not looking up. "I'm not doing anything. I said I'm fine."

Lucky let out a frustrated breath and ran a hand across his lips. Then he snatched the phone from her hands. "Gimme this phone! What's yo' problem, man?"

"Gimme my phone back!" she yelled, trying to take the phone.

Lucky moved it to his other hand and held it away. "No. We not finna be sittin' in this house mad and not talking about it. If you got something on yo' mind, say something. It's obvious that you mad. How we supposed to fix it if you acting all passive aggressive? Tell me what's wrong."

Tears welled up in her eyes. "I'm still mad that you went out yesterday and almost got in trouble. I don't understand how you can say you love me and want to be with me, but you almost went back to jail. And you could've got shot or died. Then what was I supposed to do? I stuck by you for five years. I love you, but I don't want to be visiting you in prison again. You said you changed and I believed you until yesterday."

"What you want me to do, Melissa? Huh? I said I'm sorry. And I didn't get shot. And I'm not in jail. I'm sitting on the couch with you at home right now. I'm here. We good. Why can't you let it go?"

"Because it's not about you being here. It's about you loving me and caring about me enough not to put yourself in situations that could hurt us. I tried to stop you, and you threw me on the floor like I was trash. You could've died or went back to prison. What don't you understand about that? That is serious to me and I'm not going to get over it immediately. I was hurt. You chose revenge over me. What else are you going to pick over me? How important am I really?"

"C'mon, Melissa. You reading into this way too much and over reacting. You know you important to me. I love you with everything inside me. C'mon, now."

Her eyes went from sorrow to anger. "I'm not reading into this. You just don't want to understand. You picked something over me. I was crying and you didn't care. You were too focused on finding who killed Cookie. Almost got yourself killed. So now what? Do you want revenge for J-Money getting shot, too?"

Lucky let out a stressed breath. "Look, I said I was sorry. I'm not about to keep apologizing for this shit."

Her eyes got angrier. "And I'm not about to leave it alone just because you want me to. You have a family now. It's not just about you, and you have to get used to that. You can't go out there doing whatever you want. You have responsibilities and you need to get your priorities in order. If you love me like you say you do, put me and my feelings first."

Lucky hung his head and took a couple deep breaths. The whining had him pissed. And he couldn't talk to her because she was too busy being mad. And apparently she wanted to stay that way.

"I need some air. Where the keys?"

"You don't have a license yet. You can't be driving. Where do you want to go? I'll take you."

"Nah. Stay here with the kids. I ain't going that far. I just wanna take a drive to clear my head."

Melissa didn't give in. "No. You can't - "

"WHERE THE FUCKIN' KEYS?" Lucky exploded.

Melissa reared back, terrified by the look in his eyes. She had never seen him so angry. "In the kitchen. On the counter," she mumbled.

Lucky threw her phone on the couch and went to get the keys. After grabbing them, he walked past a crying Melissa and right out the front door. He hopped in the Ford Escape and drove aimlessly through the city, letting his thoughts roam. He'd been out three days and was already second guessing coming home to Melissa. If he was honest with himself, she was a basic woman. As basic as basic could get. She was chubby with a fat face. She had stretch marks all over her body, and two kids that weren't his. In a world of Instagram models, ass shots, and everybody making songs for bad stripper bitches, she didn't fit the mold for the ideal woman of a successful man. She was a far cry from the eye candy that niggas bragged about. But because he loved her, he didn't care that she wasn't a beauty queen. Her love, loyalty, and devotion to him while he was down and out made her more beautiful than Beyoncé. But that was before the arguing. He didn't want to live in an environment that stressed him out. But he had made promises. Melissa loved him. Her kids loved him. And even though he was mad right now, he loved them, too. They were his family.

"Bullshit," he mumbled.

When he looked at the street signs, he noticed he'd ventured to the north side of the city. Everything looked so different from when he went in. Everything looked newer, even in the hood. Nostalgia gripped him when he turned onto 47th and Center. He remembered running through the area with his nigga Sam. He drove a few blocks and stopped at the bodega right off Sherman Boulevard. There was a silver Audi A-8 parked out front. Lucky whistled at the phat ride as he got out of the truck and walked in the store.

A short dark-skinned man stood at the counter laughing with the store clerk. He wore designer clothes, Cartier frames, an iced-out watch, and ice in his earlobes and on his pinky finger. They exchanged looks before the man went back to talking to the clerk. Something about the man looked familiar. Standing against the wall was a younger man that wore a permanent mean face. Lucky walked through the aisles and grabbed a bag of flaming hot Doritos, a fruit punch soda, and Snickers ice cream bar before going to the counter.

"This all you need, boss?" the clerk asked.

"Yeah." Lucky nodded, exchanging another look with the short dark-skinned man.

Recognition flashed in the eyes behind the designer frames. "Ay, I know you, man. Lucky?"

Lucky cocked his head to the side and smiled. "Yeah. Sam? Sammy-D, that's you, nigga?"

The ice wearer couldn't contain his joy and excitement. He fist pumped and grabbed the crotch of his pants. "Oh, shit! My nigga Lucky!" he screamed before wrapping Lucky in an aggressive embrace.

"What's good, Sam? Damn, I was just thinking 'bout you when I drove up."

Sam snatched off the glasses and took a step back to look Lucky from head to toe. "My nigga, I can't believe it's you, brah. Damn! What the fuck!" he said before giving him another hug. "When you get out, my nigga?"

"Couple days ago. I'm fresh." Lucky smiled. "But look at you. Look like you got on a million dollars' worth of jewelry."

He laughed. "This shit don't mean nothing, my nigga. That shit you did was the realest shit in the world. Ay, check it out, y'all," he said getting the attention of the clerk and young nigga against the wall. "This the realest nigga in the world right here. We go way back to Ninja Turtle draws and when gas was ninety-nine cent. This my nigga Lucky, fam. The realest nigga in the world. Matter fact, take this watch, my nigga. This a Patek. Worth forty. This you," he said, taking off the watch and handing it to Lucky.

"I'm good, brah. I don't need this watch. I'm straight, Sam," Lucky said humbly.

He frowned. "What? That's forty racks. That's you. I ain't taking that back. And my name Polo, my nigga. That Sammy-D shit over. Where you living at, man? You got some pussy? You need a whip?"

Lucky was speechless for a moment as he stared at the watch. The diamonds in the face twinkled and he could see rainbows in every piece of ice. "Uh, yeah. I stay wit' my girl on the East Side. Shit, I was about to head back that way."

Polo's eyes brightened. "Fuck that, my nigga. Change of plans. I need you to come with me. I need to do something for you. What you need? Let me know."

Lucky laughed. "I'm good, brah. You just gave me a forty thousand dollar watch."

"Fuck that watch. That ain't shit. I wouldn't have none of this if it wasn't for you. You just did what, ten or fifteen years?"

"Fourteen," Lucky corrected.

The store clerk and young nigga looked blown away by the number. Polo's eyes reflected regret and guilt. "That was because of me, my nigga. And you didn't snitch. You kept that shit all the way gangsta. That kinda shit is rare nowadays. Niggas puttin' bodies on they mamas out here. Real niggas is like dinosaurs. Extinct. My nigga, you like a fossil. Some *Jurassic Park* shit. What you did for me gotta be rewarded. Let's go hit this mall up and fuck up some commas. Breed, I'ma get with you later. Scooter, let's ride."

When Polo walked towards the door, the young nigga followed along like a trained pitbull.

"What I owe?" Lucky asked the clerk.

He smiled at Lucky like proud patriots did when soldiers came back from war, like being in the ex-con's presence was an honor. "That's on the house. Real nigga salute."

Lucky nodded before grabbing his stuff and going outside. Polo was walking to the driver's side of the Audi. "Give Scooter yo' keys. He gon' follow us in yo' truck to drop it off. You 'bout to ride wit' me."

Lucky handed the younger man the keys. He was getting in the luxury whip when a teenage girl walked up from the side of the store.

She wore next to nothing for clothing. A tiny tube top barely covered large breasts and the skirt she wore looked more like a small napkin than a piece of clothing. She had dark skin, full lips, long thick black hair, and dark eyes that told of the hardships life put her through. She looked at Lucky from head to toe, her eyes resting on his crotch for a split second before looking him in the eyes with an "I wanna fuck" look.

"Hey, Polo," she said, still staring at Lucky.

"What you doing out here, Laronda?" Polo asked as if scolding a child.

She cut her eyes at the baller. "Tryna catch a check, nigga. Who yo' friend?" she asked, looking Lucky up and down again.

"You want yo' dick sucked?" Polo asked. "Shorty got that mean top."

Lucky had to give it some thought. The young girl looked fun and her body was banging. "Nah. I'm good. Li'l too young for me."

"A'ight. Get in. I know some dimes that's legal and will suck yo' dick 'til the sun come up. Laronda, take yo' li'l bad ass home. And tell yo' mamma to stop playing and gimme the keys to the house before I come over there and fuck shit up."

The young girl rolled her eyes. "I ain't thinkin' 'bout Sharday. Bitch gettin' on my nerves," she mumbled before walking in the store.

Lucky got in the passenger seat of the Audi, his eyes following the young girl's round backside. "Her mama named Sharday?"

"Yeah. She ain't on shit. Back in the day she - " Polo stopped mid-speech, surprise lighting his eyes. "Dawg, you did used to fuck Sharday back in the day! I forgot about that, my nigga."

Lucky's face also showed surprise. The girl looked about fourteen or fifteen. Was it possible that Laronda was his kid? "That's my old Sharday's daughter?"

Polo nodded as he pressed the start button. "Yeah. Her mama fucked up, too. Got hooked on that ron. She out there bad. Let shorty do whatever she wanna do. You probably wouldn't even recognize her no more."

Lucky felt a tugging at his heart. He knew what it was like to grow up with an addicted mother and felt sorry for the little girl. "Damn. That's so fucked up. How old is Laronda?"

"Like fifteen or sixteen. Some shit like that. But she ain't yours, though. Nigga name Ricky her pops." Polo laughed. "You thought she was yours for a minute, huh?"

Relief flooded Lucky's body. "I did for a minute. I ain't gon' lie. Damn, I woulda been fucked up."

Polo laughed some more. "I wouldn't let yo' seed be out there like that, my nigga. But they live right down the street on 49th. You wanna see Sharday?"

Lucky smiled at the memory of his ex. She was fine, chocolate, and thicker than a Snickers bar. "Yeah. Why not? Fuck it."

A couple minutes later, Polo parked in front of a black and white two level house. They walked upon the porch and Polo rang the doorbell. Nervous energy flooded Lucky's body from the anticipation of seeing his ex. Fourteen years ago, she was beautiful. She had the same body that her teenage daughter flaunted. Long and thick natural hair. She had a job in a local boutique that kept her in the newest clothes. She had dreams to become a fashion designer. Now Polo said she was fucked up and he might not recognize her.

"Who is it?" a husky female voice called from behind the door.

"Polo. Open the door."

A lock clicked and the door flung open. Lucky immediately recognized Sharday. She didn't look anything how he remembered. Her thick natural hair was now thinning permed hair that barely went past the nape of her neck. Her face was blotchy with lots of blackheads and pimple scars across her cheeks. She had dark bags beneath her eyes like she never slept. And the thick Coke bottle shape was now skinny. She wore a faded T-shirt, a pair of loose-fitting jogging pants, and was barefoot.

"Damn, nigga. Why you didn't call first?" she asked with plenty of attitude, not even looking at Lucky.

"'Cause this my house. I own it. What's good? You got my money?"

100

A sad look flashed in her eyes. "C'mon, Polo. You gon' kick me and my baby out on the street, for real? I thought you fucked with me. We grew up together. I knew you before you was ballin'. That's how you gon' do?"

"C'mon, Shar. You ain't gave me no rent money in three months. Any other landlord woulda been put yo' ass out. I can't keep taking losses. Gimme my money or get out. Don't keep forcing my hand."

"Okay, okay. I need a little more time. Gimme two weeks and I'ma have last month's rent."

"You got one week. That's it. If you don't have my shit, I'm coming to put you out. That's my word. One week."

She smiled, happy to have the extension. "Okay. I got you. Good looking out, nigga."

"What up, Sharday?" Lucky nodded.

She looked him from head to toe as if seeing him for the first time. "Who is you?"

"Yo' old boyfriend. My nigga, Lucky," Polo answered.

Recognition flashed in her eyes along with elation. "Aw shit! My nigga, Lucky!" she yelled, stepping onto the porch and wrapping him in a hug.

"What's good, baby girl? What's good?" Lucky laughed, noticing she smelled like stale cigarettes.

She took a step back and looked him from head to toe. "Just out here tryna make it, baby. See, yo' friend tryna put me and my baby out on the streets. Damn, you look good." She smiled, running a hand through her short hair and becoming self-conscious. "I wished y'all woulda told me y'all was coming over so I wouldn't be looking a hot mess."

"You good," Lucky lied.

"When you get out? How you doing?"

"I'm good. Got out a couple days ago. Just rolled through and ran into Polo and seen yo' daughter. Wanted to see how you was doing."

She continued to play with her hair, the negative self-image making her wish she could curl into a ball and roll away from the door. "I'm just living, man. Trying to keep my head above water."

"Yeah, well, if you don't got my rent money, you gon' have to find another place to live," Polo cut in. "Let's get outta here, Lucky. Hit this store and get you fresh," he said before walking off the porch.

Lucky and Sharday shared an awkward moment, neither knowing what to say.

"Okay, Sharday. It was good seeing you, baby," he said, backing away.

She nodded, knowing he told a lie. "Yeah. You, too. Stay free and welcome home."

CHAPTER 10

Lucky's head was spinning.

Kicking it with Polo meant partying like a boss: VIP in the strip club, endless bottles of top shelf liquor, and throwing money like it was confetti at some of the baddest strippers in the Midwest. The combination of liquor and kicking it like a rich nigga had Lucky's head spinning. He had read about it in books and seen it in music videos and pop culture media outlets like TMZ. But to actually throw thirty thousand dollars in the strip club and drink thousand dollar bottles of champagne was a life-changing experience. Not to mention the new clothes. Lucky was dressed from head to toe in a five thousand dollar Louis Vuitton fit. The iced-out Patek gave him the aura of the rich and famous. He was currently talking to a dancer that had mistaken him for a professional ballplayer.

"I thought I seen you on TV before. In a basketball game," Black Barbie said, sitting in the lounge chair and draping an arm around his shoulder.

"Shit, I wish." He chuckled. "I can play, but not good enough to be on TV."

"That's the realest nigga in the city," Polo said, pointing the bottle of Ace of Spades at Lucky like he was holding it up in his honor. "Get to know him, Barbie. They don't make niggas like that no more. Just came home from a long bid. Didn't snitch. Show my nigga some love."

Respect and admiration shone on the stripper's face and she looked at Lucky through a new set of eyes. Before, he was a potential trick. Now she viewed him as a real nigga, and real niggas were shown real love. "What's yo' name, baby? How long you do?"

"Lucky. Fourteen long-ass years in that bullshit. Just got out on Tuesday."

"My real name is Rachel. I know I just met you, but I got a lot of respect for you. I love real niggas. My daddy got life because somebody snitched on him. My pops was a real nigga, but he was fucking with some fakes. I hate snitches."

The liquor haze was temporarily waved and Lucky saw Rachel clearly, past her soft brown skin, curvy body, and sex appeal. Her eyes told the story that not many people knew. She was more than a woman who took her clothes off and danced for money. She was a real person and had a story.

"I know a lot of niggas like that. Good niggas that might not get to come home. Nowadays, they call niggas like us stupid. Integrity and character don't matter no more. All it's about is getting money," Lucky explained, taking a drink from the bottle of liquor.

"Not with me, baby. I don't respect niggas just because they come in here and spend money. I appreciate it and I try to make them feel good because this my job. But I don't take a lot of them serious. They pay bills and that's it. But I like you and I want to get to know you personally."

Lucky looked her up and down, taking it all in. Rachel was bad. Auburn and black shoulder-length hair. Soft and seductive brown eyes that reflected strength born from adversity. A small beauty mole near her nose. Full lips. Thoughtful tattoos covering a body toned to perfection.

"I got something going on at home. Baby gave me five years of her life while I was in. Anybody that will fuck wit' a nigga when he ain't got shit don't deserve to be done wrong."

If it was possible to see respect grow in someone's eyes, Rachel's reflected it. Then she smiled. "That's why I love real niggas. Y'all always keep it real. Well, you know where I work at. If you ever wanna kick it, you know how to find me. Now watch the show on stage. Lady Boss is good, but wait 'til it's my turn."

An hour later, Lucky was slumped in the VIP booth, the champagne bottle in his hand feeling like a forty pound dumbbell. The liquor had caught up to him and he was faded. The club was still alive with dancing and partying but he was too throwed to get involved, so he sat and watched.

The phone vibrating in his lap grabbed his attention. He moved in slow motion, eventually picking up the phone and checking the screen. It was a text from Melissa that read: "Call me. we need to talk."

It took a couple minutes to find her number. "Hey," he slurred.

"Lucky, turn the music down. Where are you?"

"I can't turn it down. I told you I was out with my nigga. We at the club."

"What's wrong with you? Are you drunk?"

"Yeah. I'm fucked up."

"What club are you at? How are you getting home? You can't drive."

"I'ma have Polo drop me off."

"Don't you think you had enough? You sound like you can't even stand up."

He laughed. "I probably can't. I'ma have Polo drop me off in a couple minutes."

"What about my truck? I gotta get to work in the morning."

"I'ma tell him. I got you. I'm finna be on my way in a few minutes."

***

The only bad part of the evening came at a little after 10 p.m. when Lucky told Polo he had to leave. He was currently sitting in the passenger seat of the Audi A-8. Scooter trailed them in Melissa's Ford Escape.

"Dawg, I ain't neva kicked it like that before, my nigga," Lucky slurred. "I used to hear niggas talk that shit and see it on TV. Shit looked fun as fuck. And now I know for sure that it is fun as fuck. That was some boss nigga shit."

Polo took his eyes off the road to smile at his inebriated friend. "Rich nigga shit, brah. That's how we do. So what you doing to make money? How you eating out here?"

"I made a li'l money on some books I wrote. I was thinking about buying into a restaurant chain."

That got Polo's attention. "Straight up? That's what's up, my nigga. When you finalize them plans, let me know. I can put up some bread and we can get a bigger piece of pie. I'm always with investing. Gotta take lucrative steps to win out here."

Lucky nodded. "I like the way that sound."

"What you doing this weekend? I'm flying to Florida with my nigga, Shotta, for his concert. He the opening act for Corvette Corey. You wanna come?"

"Nah. Cookie's funeral this Sunday. Gotta bury Moms."

Polo looked surprised. "Cookie died and you just now telling me about it? When this happen?"

"'Bout two weeks ago? Wacco's nephew was shooting at some niggas. Cookie got caught up in it."

"You talkin' 'bout Tony?"

"Yeah. Jamar told me it was Carmen's son. He got shot yesterday when we went looking for them niggas. A CSG nigga named Six shot at us. Desmond fucked up some of they niggas and he tried to get back."

"Oh! That was y'all? I heard about that. Damn. What you wanna do, my nigga? I got shooters. Say the word and I'll send 'em."

Lucky let out a long breath. "I don't know what to do, my nigga. At first, I wanted them niggas dead. Shit, I wanted to do it myself. But Jamar in the hospital, me and my girl fighting about it 'cause she want me to leave it alone, and I think they got a green light on Desmond. I didn't know shit was gon' hit me this hard when I got out."

"That's how it is out here, my nigga. Life is a bitch. The streets is a hoe. You gotta figure out a way fuck 'em or pimp 'em. Stay ahead of these niggas. Get yo' perspective straight. You was fighting a different battle in them cages. Now you gotta learn how to fight out here in this concrete jungle. Niggas playin' for keeps. But I got you. I'ma look into that situation with Wacco and his nephew. Me and Wacco ain't seen eye to eye in a long time."

***

Cookie's funeral was the fakest event Lucky had ever attended.

The gravesite was crowded with about thirty grief-stricken mourners. Family and friends that didn't give a damn about Cookie in life cried like she was the most cherished and loved person they had ever known. None of them had tried to help her get off drugs. No one offered to take him and Desmond in when Cookie neglected them. And no one offered them a meal when Cookie spent her money to buy dope instead of food. Now they all tried to outdo one another for the best acting job, like they were auditioning for a role in a Tyler Perry movie.

Lucky stood in the front row wiping tears from his eyes as the casket was lowered into the ground. Melissa squeezed his hand and shed tears with her hurting man. Desmond stood near. His face was as hard as stone, showing no emotion. Lasonya stood next to him, drying tears.

"From ashes to ashes and from dust to dust," the preacher said somberly. "Cookie is with her maker now. May God rest her soul."

Family and friends each took turns hugging Lucky and Desmond, whispering words of encouragement before walking away from the grave. One of the final people to walk over for their final respects was Polo.

"She in a better place now," he said, wrapping an arm around Desmond's shoulder.

The soldier's face remained unchanged. "Yep."

Polo noticed the icy reception and turned to hug Lucky. "I'ma get them niggas. That's my word. I owe you. And I make sure to pay all my debts."

Lucky nodded. "Thanks, brah."

"Y'all be cool, my nigga. Call me later about those business plans," Polo said before nodding to Scooter and walking away.

"I'ma take the kids to the car," Melissa said before walking away with Brandon and Brandy.

Lasonya kissed Desmond on the cheek. "Take your time," she whispered before walking away

A few moments later, it was only Desmond and Lucky standing at the headstone, watching the graveyard workers fill in the dirt.

"That was the fakest shit I ever seen," Lucky said, his voice filled with discontent.

"I'm just glad it's over," Desmond breathed. "I don't wanna see none of them again."

The brothers stood in silences for a few moments before Desmond spoke again. "Why you invite Sammy-D?"

Lucky shrugged. "Why not? We invited everybody else that showed fake love. At least his was real."

Desmond turned to look at Lucky like he supported Trump. "That nigga the reason you went to prison. The reason I ended up in the group home."

Lucky hung his head, gathering his thoughts. "You don't think I thought about that every day I was locked up? I lost the most, nigga. But he a good nigga. Showed me a lot of love since he found out I was out. And he taking care of the niggas that did this to our mama. That's as real as it get."

"No it ain't," Desmond snarled. "Real woulda been him admitting he shot Gutta fourteen years ago. He shoulda been in a cell. Not you."

"What about what you did, Desmond? If you woulda stayed yo' ass in the car like we said, wouldn't nobody have got shot. You created the distraction that let Gutta get the pistol. You got blame in this too. I did that time because I wasn't no bitch-ass nigga that was gon' tell on his day one or li'l brotha. We was thuggin' in the streets, Des. That's the kinda shit that happens when you rob people. We had a real gun. We took that nigga's money and his life. We all got some blame in this."

Desmond shook his head. "You blind, brah. That nigga ain't no good. He had money all this time, but never reached out. And he a snake. I know snakes when I see them."

Lucky was tired of arguing. "Man, is you done? Damn. We just buried Mama. I ain't tryna argue with you."

Desmond turned back to the headstone, becoming quiet for a breath or two. Then he dropped a bomb. "The police know what I did on Clarke."

Lucky turned to look at Desmond, making sure he heard him correctly. "What?"

Desmond nodded. "I gotta call from Detective Perry the other day. One of them niggas survived. He knows I did it."

108

Lucky's eyes reflected the pain of a man who was just told he had a few months to live. "Nah, Des! What the fuck, brah?"

"I know. But he offered me a way out. Said he would make sure all the evidence against me never get seen."

Lucky knew when a deal was too good to be true. "And what he want? What's the caveat?"

Desmond took his time answering. "Wants me to help him get Polo."

Lucky got mad. "And you told him no, right?"

Desmond shook his head, unable to say the words.

Disgust shown on Lucky's face. "Brah, you finna snitch?"

"What choice do I got? They got me and offering me a way out. What, I'm supposed to be like you and spend half my life in prison for sticking to a code that don't nobody respect no more?"

"Hell yeah!" Lucky said defiantly. "You take yo' lumps when you get caught. That's the example I set. That's what Harrison's do. We got real nigga DNA."

"So I'm supposed to give up my military career and everything that I worked hard for to protect a nigga that didn't keep it real with you? He let you do a decade and a half with no money orders or visits. I did that. I was there."

Lucky's face was serious, the hardness in his eyes testifying his strong beliefs in keeping it real. "And I'ma be there for you if you get convicted. Being a snitch ain't an option," Lucky said with finality.

J-Blunt

CHAPTER 11

"No, Desmond. I don't want you to go!" Lasonya whined, wrapping her arms around his waist and holding on.

"I know. I don't wanna leave but I gotta go."

She looked up into his face, eyes reflecting true emotions. "No, Desmond! I still have so much to say. We can't leave it like this. When are you coming back?"

"I'm not sure."

She frowned, not liking the answer.

"Seriously. I'm not sure. I live mission to mission and stay on the base. I never really had a reason to leave, except to visit Lucky. That was every couple months. My life has been the military. I'm not even sure what we're doing. What are we doing?"

She removed her arms from around his waist and took a step back, creating a little distance between them, a thoughtful look upon her face. "I'm not really sure what to call it. This week has gone by so fast and I've just been riding the wave, I guess. But I know I like what we're doing and don't want it to stop. I wish you didn't have to go so we could figure this out. I care about you a lot and have always loved you since we were kids. How do you feel about me?"

Desmond paused to think of a response. He liked Lasonya. A lot. All of the puppy love they shared as children along with the couple of days he'd spent at her house had allowed him to develop real feelings. But he wasn't sure about a relationship. His commitment to the military wouldn't allow it. The last thing he wanted to do was lead her on or hurt her.

"I care about you. A lot. I have ever since we were kids. You've always had my heart. But I just don't know if we can be serious. My plan was to focus on my career. Save the world from the bad people type shit. I never imagined falling in love or having a family. The military and Lucky is all I've ever had. And you have a life here. I know you don't want to move to Virginia and live on an army base with Quaysha. You won't have friends or family around. It'll just be you and your daughter. I'd always be on missions. Our lives are in different places at the moment. I don't think we could build any-thing meaningful right now."

Lasonya thought on his words. Although he was right, she felt like a deflated balloon on the inside. "Yeah. I think you're right. I can't follow you to an army base with my daughter. My mama would go crazy if I took her only grandchild away. I wish we had more time."

"So do I," he admitted.

Silence stood between them for a moment. Lasonya broke it. "Can we talk about Tony?" she asked, giving a disgusted look. "I hate saying his name, but I feel like we should clear the air. I know you feel some type of way about me not telling you Quaysha is his daughter."

He shrugged, attempting to show aloofness. "Nothing you can really say. It is what it is."

She gave him a look. "Is that how you really feel, or are you acting like a man?"

He rolled his shoulders uncomfortably. "I just wish you woulda told me before the nigga showed up on your doorstep. That shit felt like a blindside. But I get it. You didn't tell me because you didn't want me to look at you differently."

"Do you? You saying it's all good now, but is it really?"

He chuckled and closed the distance between them, wrapping her in his arms. "We good. I was in my feelings a li'l bit, but I'm over it," he said before leaning down and kissing her lips.

She smiled. "That feels good. Will you come and see me when you get some leave?"

"Yeah. I'ma do that. Might be about a month. But I'm coming. Am I staying in a hotel or with you?"

Irritation flashed in her brown eyes. "I can't believe you just asked me that. I was going to let you stay with me. Just for saying that, book a hotel."

***

The Naval Air Station in Virginia Beach, Virginia housed the best of the best in the United States military. Heavy security surrounded the base. There was a checkpoint at the front gate and Military Police patrolled the grounds.

After being allowed inside the perimeter, Desmond headed towards the barracks. He was walking across the marching pad when he ran into the team leader.

"Desmond, how are you, brother? Welcome back." Vernon "Duke" Wilson grinned, greeting him with a handshake and hug. Duke was a forty-year-old white man from Philadelphia. He stood six foot tall with a muscular build. His face was clean shaved, he had piercing blue eyes, a crooked nose from many breaks, and low-cut salt and pepper hair. He had been a SEAL for twelve years and a team leader for eight.

"Hey, Duke. I'm just glad that shit is over with. Ready to get back to work."

"Are you sure that you're ready?" he asked, looking for a sign that Desmond wasn't all the way together.

"I'm good, brother. One hundred percent. Mom is at peace now. And so am I. Where is the team?"

"In the barracks. We have a debriefing at sixteen hundred. Get yourself together and be ready. This is an important op. I'ma go find the colonel to let him know the team is back together."

After parting ways with Duke, Desmond headed for the barracks SEAL team Alpha was housed in. It had the feel of a college dorm room rather than an army barracks. He stepped inside and saw his team spread out across the room. Kim Lee, a.k.a. "Jackie Chan", was having a knife throwing contest with Artie "Big Country" James. The target was a life-sized picture of Bin Laden glued to the wall. Large throwing knives were stuck in the poster's face, neck, and chest. Across the room, Carter Spears was sitting on the couch locked in a heated debate with Marshall "Slayer" Sanchez about whether or not President Trump was a racist.

"Daddy's home!" Desmond sang as he stepped into the room.

"You ain't even old enough to have kids," Slayer joked, getting up to hug his brother from another mother. "How are you? Everything go good back home?"

Desmond thought about Lucky being free, his relationship with Lasonya, the deal from Detective Perry, and Cookie's funeral. "As good as could be. We're never out of the fight."

"We're never out of the fight!" the team echoed.

"How's the brother?" Kim asked, aiming a knife at the terrorist poster and letting it fly. It landed in the chest.

"Good. Getting adjusted. Fourteen years in a box changes a man. But he's good," Desmond said, walking over and grabbing a knife from Big Country. "Let me show you Girl Scouts how it's done." The knife throw was as effortless as a gymnast doing a tumble. His wrist flicked and the knife cut through the air, landing in Bin Laden's eye. "Look at the flick of the wrist!" he bragged.

"Challenge me to a rifle fight from two hundred yards," Big Country growled, admitting defeat. No one could beat Desmond at throwing knives.

"Say when, sugar." He laughed, flopping down on the couch. "How's the investigation going?" he asked Slayer.

"I don't know. Bullshit. Bitch is lying. They questioned everybody. Now we're just waiting for the findings."

"You'll be okay, brother. They're letting you go out with the team, so that's a good sign. Everybody knows you didn't do anything wrong. I'll tell them that when they question me."

At 1600 hours, 4:00 p.m. Eastern Time, SEAL Team Alpha gathered in the debriefing room. A map of India covered the entire wall. Lieutenant Colonel Jones stood at the front of the room with General Legge.

"SEAL Team Alpha, welcome. Desmond, welcome back to the team. This mission will officially be off the books. Can't leave a trace. We need you to capture a tier one asset. We've got Intel that Grenandish Muhammad is hiding at an apartment building in Hyderabad, India. As you all know, he is very smart and very dangerous. He was responsible for multiple terrorist attacks in Asia and

Europe. He also kidnapped an American journalist in Pakistan," Colonel Jones explained.

The general cut in. "Your mission is to get him back to the States alive. We'll leave the details to you. This is a very important mission. He is very cunning. Our friends at the FBI said he's converted agents to join his team. This is why he has eluded the government for so long. But you men are our best and brightest. We need this capture. Be careful. Good luck."

***

Desmond walked into The Last Stop and paused to look around. The Last Stop was a bar near the naval base, frequented by soldiers and military personal that needed to wind down. It only took a moment to find who he was looking for.

First Mate Amber Maldonado sat on the barstool, sipping a drink. She had soft tan skin, bright brown eyes, an oval face with nice teeth and thin lips, and brown hair braided into a ponytail. The Latin woman was beautiful without makeup, but never used her looks to get ahead. She worked hard and played harder, which is why Desmond liked her. She sat on a barstool dressed in a navy T-shirt, jeans covering her athletic body, Nike cross trainers on her feet. He walked up silently, placing his elbows and forearms on the bar.

"That kinda day, huh?"

She glanced over. "What did I tell you about sneaking up on me, man?" she lectured. "Commanders are pains in my ass."

He took a look behind her. "It's a nice ass."

"Shut up! And leave my ass alone." She smiled, pushing him playfully. "How did everything go back home?"

Desmond let out a stressed breath. "Highs and lows. Barkeep, can I get a Henny on the rocks?"

The bartender nodded.

Amber's face softened and she turned to face him. "What happened? Did you fall out with the family? Is your brother okay?"

"Yeah. He's fine. And the family didn't cause problems. I kinda got in a little bit of trouble. I went looking for who killed my mother and killed a guy."

Concern and worry shone in her eyes. "Oh my God! What's going to happen? Are you in trouble?"

He paused as the bartender sat the drink in front of him. "A little bit," he said before taking a sip. "The dude was a street punk and a drug dealer. Him and a friend thought I was in the neighborhood selling drugs and tried to jam me up. I turned the tables and killed one. Wounded the other. Thought I killed both. Now the gang has a hit on me and at least one police officer knows I did it. The same one who is investigating my mother's murder, that no one really cares about solving. He told me that."

She grabbed his hand. "Shit, Desmond. This sounds like a *Rambo* movie. What did the cop say?"

"A detective. Wants me to help him get charges on a guy I grew up with. Guess they've wanted him for a long time but can't get him. He's actually the reason my brother went to prison and I ended up in the army. But my brother doesn't want me to help the police. The whole don't snitch thing. He wants me to be like him and accept whatever happens. Lucky didn't have to go to prison if he would've told the police who shot the guy. But he didn't snitch. Wants me to follow his example."

"But what about your career? Are you supposed to give that up?"

Desmond took another drink. "Yep."

"I know you're not going to be that stupid? You didn't spend twelve years fighting for our country just to give it up like that."

Desmond let out a stressed breath. "I don't know what I'm going to do."

"What did Duke say? Did you talk to him yet?"

"No. I didn't tell anyone but you."

"You can't live by a code that doesn't apply to you. You're not in the street. You're not a drug dealer. You're a Navy SEAL. You uphold justice around the world. Don't try to live up to your brother's standards. Don't go to prison if you don't have to. You track down America's bad guys and bring them to justice. Do the same thing in your hometown. Work with the police. Don't be like your brother. He might be a good guy, but you're better than him. And smarter. Be smart."

"I know."

She waited for him to say more. "Is that all you got?"

He drained the liquor from the glass and waved the bartender over for a refill. "Yep."

Amber rolled her eyes. "Don't be stupid."

"I won't. What commander is hurting your ass?"

She gave him a look. "Watch it or I'll hurt your ass. But it's Anderson. I hate him. Wish he would choke on a shit sandwich."

"Hell of a visual." He laughed.

She visualized the scene in her mind. "It is. So, when is your next mission?"

"Tomorrow. We leave at zero six hundred."

Her eyes popped and jaw dropped. "But you just got here. Damn."

"The world needs saving. That's my job."

"Whatever, Superman." She smirked. "My body needs saving. You down for a couple rounds?"

Desmond polished off the second glass of Hennessey in one gulp. "I'ma make you cum faster than a speeding bullet."

The Hotel 6 was a few blocks from the bar. Amber and Desmond were frequent visitors and known by the front desk employees.

After paying for a night, they touched and kissed all the way to the room. When the door closed behind them, the petting got heavier and the clothes came off. Two years of sleeping together had allowed them to explore one another's bodies and find their spots. Desmond's was just below his earlobe. Amber kissed and licked him there like she was trying to get to the center of a Tootsie Pop.

"Mmmhhh!" Desmond moaned in approval, gripping her toned backside and grinding his hard dick into her stomach.

"You like that, papi?" she whispered.

"You know I do."

"Mmmm. Tell me what else you like?" she asked, looking him in the eyes and biting her bottom lip.

"I like when you put your mouth on me."

She grabbed hold of his dick and stroked it. "Where do you want me to put it?" she teased.

He looked down, loving the sight of his big black snake in her little sand-colored hand. "I want you to put it where yo' hand at."

Her eyes dimmed to sexy slits. "Say it. You want me to suck it?"

"Suck my dick."

Compliance shone in her eyes and she bent over, taking him in her warm mouth. Desmond shuddered, thrusting his hips forward and letting out a groan. His eyes closed on their own and his head leaned back. Amber worked her mouth on him like she got paid for sex. She gave good head and loved to please. She took three quarters of him down her throat, bobbing her head rapidly.

"Damn, baby! Shit!" Desmond groaned, reaching an arm behind her and sticking a finger in her ass.

Amber let out a little moan, loving the sound of his pleasure and the finger moving in and out of her ass. It got her pussy wetter. She moved her mouth and began licking and kissing up and down the length of his dick before going to his balls. She sucked them in her mouth, flicking her tongue on them while jacking him off. Desmond clenched his ass cheeks and curled his toes. And just when he thought he was about to bust a nut in her hair, she put his dick back in her mouth and began sucking again.

"Aw shit!" he cursed, shooting his load.

Amber continued sucking while he squirted in her mouth, swallowing every drop.

"Mmmm. Damn," he grunted after he was drained.

She stood, lust burning a fire in her brown eyes as she walked backwards to the bed, her index finger telling him to come to her. "Now come and pet the pussycat."

When she lay back on the bed, he kneeled over her and began kissing and licking his way up her leg. When he got to her inner thigh, a few inches from her pink and bald pussy, he paused to pay the area some attention. It was one of her spots. He wiggled his tongue against the soft flesh.

"Oooh, Desmond! Oh my God!" she moaned, running her hand across the top of his head.

A few moments later, he moved to her pussy. It was dripping wet. He kissed the lips, sending a shiver through her body. Then he attacked her mother pearl with his tongue, flicking it across the little ball of flesh as fast as he could.

"Oh, papi! Yes, Desmond! Oh yes!" she moaned, holding onto his head like she was birthing him.

He continued to lick her and stuck the finger back into her ass. Amber bucked, barked, and ground her pelvis onto his face.

"Suck it, baby! Oh, suck it right now! Do it!" she demanded.

Her wish was his command. He wrapped his lips around her clit and began sucking like he was trying to remove sugar from his fingertip. Then he ran his tongue across her clitoris while he sucked it. Amber went mad.

"Ssss! Oh God! Oh God! I'm cumming! Oh God!"

Her body locked and Desmond could feel her juices wetting his mustache, lips, and chin. When she let go of his head, he stood on the floor and dragged her to the edge of the bed. After lifting one leg and spreading the other, he dove deep into her wetness.

"Oh, papi!" Amber moaned, her head rolling around on her shoulders, loving the way he filled her.

Desmond played no games. Sex with Amber was an event, and he planned on taking it all the way there. He started with deep, short strokes, loving the tight wetness. A few moments later he was hitting her with a fast stroke, his clean-shaved pelvis slamming into her wet pussy and making a slapping sound.

"Oh, yes, Des! Oh, yes! Oh shit, yes!"

He continued drilling her, showing no mercy while watching his dick pump in and out of her. Her labia looked like they were being stretched. His meat was shining with a coating of her juices. Amber moaned and sang his name, making beautiful, ugly, and painful sex faces. When he felt his nut coming on, he pulled out and masturbated, shooting onto her stomach.

***

119

Hyderabad is bustling city in south central India with a population of over two and a half million people. Located within the Indian metropolis was the terrorist Grenandish Muhammad. He had been tracked to an apartment building in a rough neighborhood. It was after 10 p.m. and the sun had disappeared two hours ago.

SEAL Team Alpha rode in a brown 90's model Volkswagen minivan that looked ready for the scrapyard. Dark tinted windows kept the soldiers hidden from prying eyes as the van motored through the dark city. The van's driver was a local asset named Ahmed Singh. When he pulled the van into the alley behind the apartment building, Duke took a look around. There were two lights illuminating the alley.

"Do a final ammo and com check."

All of the SEALS checked their silenced fully automatic weapons and secondary silenced pistols. When they were good, they checked their com links.

"All right. Now somebody kill those lights."

Big Country opened the sliding side door and took aim. Two silenced pops killed the lights.

"Let's go!" Duke called before hopping out.

The SEALs flipped down night vision goggles on their helmets as they piled out of the van. The kill team moved with precision, their weapons ready, scanning the alley for signs of life. They made it to the back of the building without incident and located a fire escape. Desmond and Slayer covered both ends of the alley while the team climbed the ladder.

"Get up there," Slayer whispered.

"I'm after you," Desmond responded.

"Get your ass up there. I got the six," Slayer snapped.

Desmond didn't argue. He jumped up on the fire escape and followed the team up. During the climb, he looked down, expecting Slayer to bring up the rear. When he didn't see his Mexican brother, a bit of panic gripped his chest. With the help of the night vision glasses, he could see the entire alley. Slayer was nowhere to be found. A terrible sinking feeling entered his chest.

"Alpha One, Alpha Three is MIA. I repeat, Alpha Three is MIA."

All the members of the SEAL team paused to look down the fire escape, confirming that Slayer was really missing.

"Shit," the team leader cursed. "Proceed to the top of the building and we'll do a recon."

When the team climbed to the roof of the ten story building, Kim and Lester began assembling a zip line. Duke and Big Country were looking through the scopes of their rifles to the building across the street, where two terrorists stood guarding the roof of the building. Desmond looked over the edge of the building, scanning the alley for Slayer. "Duke, Slayer is still missing."

Fwap. Fwap. The rifles sounded as the enemy sentinels on the building across the street went down.

Duke turned to Desmond. "Where the fuck is he? What happened?"

"Slayer didn't come up. I looked in the alley and he's gone."

Confusion spread across the team leader's face. He hit the com and tried to make radio contact. "Alpha Three, this is alpha One. Where you at?"

They waited. Didn't get an answer.

"Alpha Three, this is Alpha One. Where you at?" Duke tried again.

Still no answer.

"Shit," Duke cursed. "Alpha Three must've been compromised. They may know we're here. We gotta go in hot."

Desmond didn't agree. If they had captured Slayer, the last thing they needed to do was enter a building full of hostiles. It could be a trap. "Sir, we have to fall back. Call it off."

Duke looked at Desmond like he had spoken out of line, superiority lighting his eyes. "No. There is a tier one asset less than a hundred yards away. We move. Let's go. Kim, you boys got those lines ready?"

The Asian nodded. "We're ready."

"All right. Go," Duke ordered, walking towards the edge of the building.

Desmond grabbed his arm. "Duke, call it off. Slayer is missing. Radio to the CO that he's missing."

Battle lust danced in the team leader's eyes. "This is my team. Get your ass in the game. Watch our six. We'll locate Slayer after the mission."

The order was final. The mission was on and there was no calling it off.

"I got it," Desmond mumbled, grabbing his rifle. He watched their backs until the team crossed over to the building across the street on zip lines.

When their backside was clear, he grabbed the zip line and made ready to cross. Then he got a funny feeling, like he was being watched, and glanced behind. The door on the roof was opening slowly. Alarms went off in his head and he went for the rifle. Before he could aim, Big Country's silenced rifle sounded.

Fwap, fwap, fwap, fwap!

The door opened and the body of a man in dark clothes fell onto the roof. But he wasn't alone. More men poured from the door onto the roof. The SEALs' rifles lit up the night. Desmond got low and joined the fire fight. Enemies continued to die, but more rushed the roof.

"Alpha One, move!" Duke called in the com. "We got enemies coming out of our building too. Get out of there!"

Desmond could hear the panic in his team leader's voice, but had no time to consider it. He was on the rooftop alone with enemies trying to kill him. He ran towards the fire escape, holding the trigger on the rifle and spraying bullets towards the enemy. Then his gun clicked. It was empty. He dropped it and ran as fast as he could to the edge of the building.

He had just made it to the fire escape when something caught his eye. The rooftop door opened and a man ran onto the roof with a rocket launcher. Desmond jumped onto the fire escape and slid down the ladder, all the while watching the roof for the rocket launcher. He hoped to get as close to the bottom as he could before jumping. When his feet clanked onto the scaffolding, he ran to the ladder on the opposite side. He grabbed the ladder rung when the rocket launched from the gun.

There was a pop and whistle. Then an explosion. The building shook and Desmond was blown off the fire escape. He fell thirty feet and landed on the roof of the rusted van the team had arrived in. Debris from the building fell around him, a large piece of the structure falling on top of the van and crushing Desmond.

J-Blunt

CHAPTER 12

Chicago, Illinois, a.k.a. the Windy City, was well-known for cold winters with bone-chilling wind gusts. Twelve foot snow drifts were as common as birds flying south when the temperature dropped. And the summer was the exact opposite. Brutal heat waves scorched the Midwest city during the summer solstice. In July and August, the weather could be oppressive.

Chi-Town was currently in the middle of a heat wave and the weather was sweltering. Heat indexes above one 100°. Humidity above ninety percent. Going without moving air or an air conditioner was as deadly as the gun fights that took over three hundred lives every year. Staying hydrated was as important as taking a breath.

Lucky was thankful to escape the sweltering heat. He sat in a chair inside the air-conditioned bookstore, Books By Us. On the table before him were five stacks of his bestselling books. Sitting at the table with him was the book store owner and his literary agent, Renae Shaffer. The store was filled with fans of the up-and-coming urban writer, and there was a line of people that went outside waiting to get a picture and autographed copy of his book. The scene blew Lucky's mind. He couldn't believe that hundreds of people had shown up for the book signing. It made him feel like a star.

"Which book do you want?" he asked the woman next in line. She was tall and pretty. Purple hair. Green eyes. A nose ring. A healthy white smile. She wore a white half halter top that barely hid big breasts and showed a flat stomach and tight jeans that flexed a crazy curved body.

"You know I want *A Gangster's Code!*" She smiled, her eye contact serious.

He grabbed the book and flipped open the cover, thankful for the momentary relief from looking in her eyes. She was fine and the googly eyes she gave told what he already knew. She wanted more than an autograph. "Who do you want me to make this out to?"

"To me. Natasha. I'm a big fan of the series. You did yo' thang. You are one of my favorite writers. I don't even read urban books. but you changed my mind."

He looked into the tempting green eyes again. "Thank you. I really appreciate the support. I'm dropping another project real soon. It's a biography. Be on the lookout."

"Can I get the first copy? It would be nice if I could get it in person."

He held her eyes longer than necessary, trying to see if she was saying more than he heard. Then someone cleared their throat loudly.

"Uh uhhh!"

Lucky looked over and saw Melissa standing off to the side, arms crossed over her big breasts, shooting eye daggers in his direction. He got his focus back quickly.

"Uh, yeah. I'll be throwing another book signing in the Chi. You can come get a copy then."

She smiled like she got the number one answer on Family Feud. "Okay. I'll be checking for you on Facebook and Instagram. Check for me too. I'm natashawiththegreeneyes."

"For sure." He nodded, handing her the book. When their hands touched, he allowed it to linger.

"Nice watch. Can I get a pic?"

He glanced at the iced-out gift from Polo as he stood. "Thanks. Yeah. Sure."

Natasha snuggled up next to him like she was trying to wear his skin. Lucky tried to act like the smell of her perfume and soft curves didn't affect him. But it did. She felt amazing, and he knew one night with her would take him to the moon. He wished he hadn't brought Melissa along for the ride. Natasha was super bad, ready, and willing.

After snapping a picture on her phone, she squeezed his bicep and gave more seductive eye contact.

"I see you been working out. Talented and sexy. You are a woman's dream."

126

Lucky could feel Melissa's eyes upon him, so he kept his composure. "Thank you. I appreciate your support."

"Always, love." She smiled before strutting away.

When the book signing was over, Lucky stood outside and had a couple words with his agent while Melissa waited in the truck.

"Next week, you'll have another book signing in Detroit, Michigan. I'm working to set one up in New York in a few weeks. I'm trying to get you maximum exposure to create a buzz for the biography. You have an amazing story and people will want to hear it. Congratulations on everything."

Lucky couldn't wipe the smile from his face if he wanted. "Thank you. I like everything that you doing for me." He nodded. "I'ma work it out with my P.O. so I can travel. You coming with me again?"

"No. I'm gonna sit the next one out. I came with you today so you could see how the process goes. It's pretty easy, and I think you can handle it from here."

"Yeah. I can. Thanks for everything."

"No problem. Now go smooth things out with Melissa." She nodded towards the truck and cringed a little. "I think that purple-haired girl might've gotten you in trouble."

Natashawiththegreeneyes flashed in his head. "Yeah. That was something, wasn't it?" He chuckled. "I'll talk to you later."

After parting ways with Renae, he walked to the truck feeling like he could fly. Everything he told himself he would do while he was sitting in the cell was manifesting. He felt on top of the world. Significant. Like his life mattered. He had a purpose. He climbed in the passenger seat wearing the good feeling like a loud-ass cologne.

"That was crazy, wasn't it, baby? My first book signing. I knew I wanted to get out and do it big, but to actually do it feels crazy. I told you I was going to do it.

Instead of applauding and celebrating his accomplishment, Melissa let out an angry hiss.

"Hmph," she grunted, cutting her eyes at him before driving away from the bookstore.

Lucky rubbed a hand across his face and let out a frustrated noise. "We finna do this, for real?" he asked, his mood changing from sunny and happy to dark and gloomy. It was a time to celebrate, and he couldn't believe she wanted to ruin the moment with an argument.

"That's all you. You did this. How you gon' flirt with a bitch while I'm standing right there? You don't think I should feel some type of way about that?"

Her words were sharp and bitter with accusations. Jealousy and insecurity mixed with the verbal attack to make it poisonous.

"I wasn't flirting with her. She was a fan. I signed the book and took a picture like I did with everybody else."

"Don't play with me like I'm stupid, Lucky. You looking at her body and were staring in her eyes. Y'all exchanged social media information right in my face. She was grabbing your arms. I know what I seen. If I wasn't there, you probably would've went back to her house."

Lucky's eyes grew wide with surprise. Melissa had done a one-hundred-eighty degree turnaround since he'd come home and their relationship was becoming toxic. "What? Man, you sound crazy. I told her to look for my new book. She follow me online. Thousands of people follow me. I'm a writer. I got fans. What the fuck is going on? What is happening to us? To you?"

Anger blazed in her squinted eyes. "So, now you calling me crazy because you was in the wrong? You was the one flirting with the pretty bitch. If I'm crazy, it's because of you."

Lucky lowered his head and remained silent for a couple moments. He didn't want to argue. He wanted to celebrate. When he looked to Melissa, his eyes were soft and pleading. "C'mon, baby. I'm don't want to argue with you. That's all we been doing lately. I didn't leave with her. I'm in the truck driving home with you. Whatever you thought you seen, it shouldn't matter because I'm with you. I love you."

Lucky hoped the words would calm Melissa down, that she would see he wanted to be with her - only her. But Melissa was blinded by jealousy and anger.

"You saying that now, but I don't believe you. You said that when you got out, you wasn't gon' do these types of things and make me feel this way. But now that you out, you changing up. You almost got shot and went back to jail. You put your hands on me. You staying out all night with strange friends at strip clubs and coming home smelling like women and wearing expensive watches. And now you flirting with pretty twenty-year-old girls right in my face. You told me one thing, but you doing another. I'm starting to feel like I don't know you. Like you ran jail game on me to keep me with you while you was locked up."

Lucky flinched like she took a swing at him, leaning back against the passenger door, his face twisting in confusion. "Where the fuck is all this coming from? I ran game on you while I was locked up? What?" he scoffed. "If anything, I took care of yo' ass while I was in there. I was giving you money. I never asked you for shit. I paid the phone bill. I bought birthday and Christmas gifts for you and the kids. I didn't lie to you about shit. And you need to learn how to let shit go. I pushed you on the floor on accident. And I'm not back in jail. Or shot. I don't know where all this shit is coming from, but you need to take it easy and fall back from all this arguing and bullshit. You sounding real insecure, like you don't believe in me. In us. Like you questioning our relationship. I'm not the once who changed. It's you."

"What if I am insecure? I felt better about us when you was locked up. I knew I had all of you. I knew I was important to you. Now that you out, I don't feel that way anymore."

Lucky was so mad that he couldn't think straight. He knew the argument was based on insecurity, but he didn't have the words to address the situation. He wanted to celebrate, but the arguing was getting to him. It was all they seemed to do.

"Well, what do you want me to do? How you want me to fix this?"

"I don't know. I just know how I feel."

The answer was the stupidest thing he'd ever heard. It made him think she was crazy. He asked her how he could solve her problem, and even she didn't know. And it pissed him off. "Well, how the fuck am I supposed to know what to do if you don't fuckin' tell me? I'm asking you what the fuck you want me to do, and you don't even know. Why the fuck is we even arguing about this bullshit?"

Melissa's voice became high-pitched and tears rolled down her face. "Why are you screaming and cussing at me like I did something wrong? You the one that's doing all this and making me feel like this."

Lucky slammed a hand against the dashboard in frustration. "What the fuck are you crying for? I'm not doing shit. All of this shit is in yo' head and it's pissing me off. I asked you what's wrong and how I could fix it, but if you don't even know, how the fuck you expect me to know? We supposed to be celebrating. I just had my first book signing."

"I don't wanna talk about it no more," she whined. "I'm done."

"So am I." Lucky mugged her, becoming silent and focusing his attention on the sights outside the truck.

***

After dropping Melissa off at home, Lucky took a drive to clear his mind. He sat at the stoplight, playing pieces of the argument in his head. It didn't make sense. As much as he tried to understand her, he couldn't. Her logic was flawed and she created situations in her head that weren't real. He had only been out two weeks and felt they were drifting further apart. All they did was argue. And the love he had for her was starting to fade.

He remembered part of a conversation he had with his old cellmate, Frank Nitty. Nitty told him to get a house on his own for a while so he could adjust to being free after fourteen years. At the time, Lucky thought his celly was crazy for insisting such a thing. He was going home to a loving family. What could be better than the love of family after spending half his life in a box? But now that he was free, Lucky was starting to think his celly was right.

When the light turned green, he tapped the gas pedal and drove through the intersection. He was in a familiar part of town. North Side, heading down Sherman Boulevard. After a series of turns, he parked in front of a black and white townhouse. He sat for a moment, questioning if he should be there. He was playing a dangerous game. But he needed someone to talk to. He needed to get his mind off Melissa and her drama. So he climbed from the SUV, walked up on the porch, and rang the doorbell.

"Who is it?" a female called.

"Lucky. Sharday here?"

Locks clicked and the door swung open. Standing before him was his ex-girlfriend. She looked better than the last time he saw her. Her hair was twisted in box braids. She wore a white Gucci T-shirt, black jeans, and a pair of Nike's.

"Hey, Lucky. What's going on?" she asked, surprise lighting her eyes.

"What up? I was nearby and thought I'd stop over and see how you was doing."

She gave him a searching look. "Oh. Okay. I wish you woulda called. You wanna come in?"

"Yeah. Sure. Sorry for showing up unannounced, but I didn't have yo' number," he said, stepping into the house.

The living room was furnished with well-used blue suede couches, black and white linoleum tile, and on the table was a clear thirteen-inch flat screen TV like the one he had while in prison.

"It's okay. Sit down. How you been?"

He sat on the love seat. Sharday sat next to him.

"Good. Tryna get back adjusted to being out here, you know? A lot changed in fourteen years. When I left, MySpace was still a thing. Now it's all about Facebook and Instagram. All the females wearing wigs and stretch pants. Remember when we was growing up and only our aunties and grandmamas wore that shit?"

Sharday laughed, showing yellow, stained teeth. "You crazy for that, but I remember. Mmmm hmm. Lotta things changed. Bitches got them lace fronts poppin'. You want something to drink? I got some vodka."

"Yeah. Sure." He nodded.

She got up and went to the kitchen. While she was gone, a key was inserted into the front door. Laronda walked into the house carrying a small paper bag. She wore a tight-fitting green dress that showed the dangerously tempting curves of her young chocolate body. When she saw Lucky on the couch, curiosity flashed in her eyes.

"What you doing over here?"

"I know yo' mother. What's up?"

She looked him from head to toe as she approached. "You tell me, baby. Need to leave that dopefiend pussy alone and get you some of this wet-wet."

Before Lucky could respond, Sharday came walking out of the kitchen carrying a blue bottle of liquor and two glasses.

"Get'cho fast ass outta his face, bitch!"

Laronda smacked her lips and rolled her eyes. "Ain't nobody thinking about him, shoot. Here go yo' cigarettes," she said, throwing the bag on the table. "I'm finna be out all night. You need anything else before I go?"

"Nah. I'm fine. Bye, bitch."

The adult teenager rolled her eyes before heading towards the door. "Girl, bye!"

"That's my daughter, Laronda. Li'l heffer be gettin' on my fuckin nerves," Sharday complained, dismissing her daughter and turning her attention to Lucky. "I don't got no ice. You good?"

"Yeah. That's fine. Pour me up. How old is she? She acts grown."

"Fifteen going on thirty. All she wanna do is smoke weed, get drunk, and fuck. Don't wanna go to school or get a job. I told her ass I'm not taking care of no babies if her fast ass gets pregnant," she said, pouring the drinks and handing him a glass.

"Who is her daddy? Do he be around?"

"Ricky's punk ass wasn't shit but a sperm donor. Bitch-ass nigga. But forget about me. Tell me what you been up to since you been out. Where you staying? You got a girl?"

He took a sip of the warm drink, it burned on the way down his throat. "Yeah. Met her 'bout five years ago. I thought we was good, but I only been out two weeks and I'm starting to question everything. All she wanna do is argue and fight. I'm not with that. Especially after doing all that time. I wanna enjoy my freedom."

"And fuck!" Sharday laughed. "After all that time with no pussy, you should be laying at home being served like a king. Pussy ten times a day."

"On the real! You feel me!" Lucky laughed. "But it's not like that. She questioning everything. Being insecure. And crazy. Got to tripping at my book signing in Chicago earlier because a fan was getting flirty. I was tryna be cool and sign the book, you know. She was a supporter and I didn't wanna be rude. But my girl got jealous and mad."

"She did that because you fine and talented. Everybody can't handle a nigga with a spotlight. Make some bitches insecure. She don't think she can keep your attention."

Lucky thought on the words. They seemed real.

"I didn't know you wrote books. How is that going?"

"Alright. I'm doing good. I was able to take care of myself while I was in prison as well as her and the kids. Now I'm out here tryna do it bigger. Gotta go to Detroit next week for another book signing. I dreamed of this while I was locked up and it feels amazing to be living it."

Sharday licked her lips, looking at him like he was a gold mine. "I always knew you was gon' do something special. You had that quality about you back in the day. I love a nigga that know what he wants and makes it happen. That's boss nigga shit. You didn't let nothing stop you. Not even prison. Congratulations on everything. That's what's up."

Lucky nodded and smiled. Getting congratulated for his accomplishments pushed his self-esteem high. "I appreciate that. Thanks," he mumbled before taking another sip of the warm vodka.

Sharday slid close, their bodies touching, placing a hand on his thigh. Her eye was contact serious, reflecting deep emotion. Regret. Desire. Lust. "I want you to know that I never forgot about you, baby. You was my first love. I always remembered the times we was together. I wished you didn't get caught up with Polo like that. Ain't no telling where we would be now."

Lucky could feel his body grow warm. Small beads of sweat popped onto his forehead and his armpits got moist. He took another drink to cool down and ended up draining the glass. "I thought about us too while I was locked up. You actually inspired a character in my first book. Chardonnay."

"Oh, really!" She looked flattered. "You gon' have to let me get a copy of that. You want me to fill that again?" she asked, taking the glass before he could make up his mind. "Turn up with your ex one time. You don't gotta worry about nothing when you with me, baby. I know how to treat a real nigga. Here you go."

Lucky shouldn't have taken the drink. He could feel the liquor taking effect. Sharday was starting to look better by the moment. Her skin on his skin felt right. Her lies were starting to sound like the truth and he was past the point of rational thinking. But before he knew it, the drink was back in his hands and Sharday was wrapped in his arms, whispering sweet nothings in his ear.

"If you want, I can take care of you," she said seductively, sliding a hand across the crotch of his jeans. The quickly-growing bulge let her know he liked what she was doing. "I learned how to please real good. I'm not a little girl no more. We grown now. Anytime you feel stressed, you can come to me and I will make you feel good. You want me to take care of this?" she asked, leaning forward and kissing his chin.

Somewhere in the back of Lucky's head a voice screamed for him to stop. Polo's words about her being hooked on drugs played through his mind as well. Melissa's face flashed, too. Her empathetic eyes damp with tears of betrayal. Then he remembered the arguments and the stress. He was out of prison, but didn't feel free. Sharday made him feel free. Feel good.

He brought the glass to his lips and killed the liquor with one big gulp. Then he found Sharday's mouth. She tasted like vodka. Her tongue was warm and slippery. Their kiss was wild. She moaned, going for the zipper on his jeans and unleashing his meat. He groaned when her hands began stroking him. She broke the kiss and bent low to place a kiss on the head of his dick. A chill went through Lucky's body. Sharday smiled and took him into her mouth. Although she'd lost some of her good looks, she had never forgotten how to please a man and turn him on.

"Aw shit!" Lucky groaned.

Sharday sucked him hard and fast, moaning in pleasure, like she loved sucking his dick. Then she knelt on the couch to get leverage, grabbing his hand and putting it on the back of her head, forcing him to push her head down. She gagged and went all the way down until her lips were touching his pelvis. Every inch of him was down her throat. Lucky closed his eyes and lay his head back against the headrest. He never imagined getting his dick sucked could feel so good. It was better than the best pussy he'd ever had, easily the best head he'd ever had, so good that when he busted, it felt like someone was rubbing his brain.

After draining him, Sharday came up smiling, horny lust lighting her eyes. "Yo' dick taste so sweet, baby. Dayum! Wait right here. I got some condoms in my room. Take off these clothes."

When she left, Lucky stood and took off his shirt. He had just unbuttoned his pants when his phone vibrated in the pocket of his jeans. All of a sudden, the erotic mood was gone. Life choices and responsibility flashed in his head as he pulled the phone out. It was a text from Melissa that read: "come home. I miss you."

Guilt immediately gripped him, killing the buzz and erection. Melissa deserved better. She was a good woman. Had stuck by his side and helped him through the hardest time in his life.

"Why you still got them clothes on?" Sharday asked, coming from the bedroom naked and carrying two condoms.

Lucky looked over her nude body. She was slim and surprisingly curvy. Chocolate skin. C-cup breasts that were a little saggy. Pussy bald. It was all very tempting. He used to know her body so well. He wanted to know the ways she had learned to please. But Melissa...

"My girl just sent me a text. I gotta go. My bad."

Disappointment flashed in her eyes. "Damn. I'm sorry to hear that. I was about to fuck you so good. You sure you don't wanna stay?"

Lucky reached for his shirt. "I gotta go. But thanks for everything. For real. Yo' head game is... Oh my God!"

She drank up the compliment. "I wasn't playing when I said you can come over whenever you want. Any time you stressed, come over and I'ma make you feel better."

***

Lucky was gripped by guilt and consumed with thoughts of infidelity. He'd been out two weeks and had already cheated on Melissa. While locked up, he imagined things going a lot differently. During the late nights he lay awake listening to music or collecting his thoughts, he pictured coming home to the perfect life with Melissa. He loved her more than he'd loved any woman not named Cookie. She proved her worth by coming to him while he was in prison and staying by his side, helping him fight the good fight for five long years.

A part of him felt indebted to the woman that sacrificed years of her love life to wait for a man she believed would be the last man she loved, and he so wanted to be that man. Made promises. Then he was released and the real world happened. Problems happened. Trust issues grew and intimacy shrank. Now he was leaving the house of his ex-girlfriend with the feel of her lips still pressed against his flesh.

"Damn." He exhaled, stopping the truck at a red light.

The vibrating of his phone got his attention. It was a text from Polo that read: "Hit me asap"

Lucky dialed the number, putting the call on speaker.

"What up, brah?"

"Where you at?" Polo asked, excitement in his voice.

"On my way home. What's good?"

"You by yo'self?"

"Yeah, man. Why you sound like that? You good?"

Polo chuckled. "I got some good news, but I can't talk about it on the phone. Come holla at me. I'm at a spot on 26th and Brown."

"I gotta get to the crib, brah. Melissa just texted me and I told her I was on my way."

"Listen, my nigga. Melissa can wait. This is important. It's about Cookie. Come holla."

His mother's name got Lucky's attention. "Gimme the address."

Ten minutes later, Lucky parked the Ford truck in front of a green and gray house in the middle of the block. It was almost 10 p.m. and the streets were dark. He checked his surroundings as he exited the SUV. Nothing and no one moved. He walked upon the porch and rang the doorbell. It opened a moment later. Polo's eyes shone with excitement. His smile was sinister.

"'Bout time you got here. Come in, nigga," he rushed, stepping aside so Lucky could walk in. Polo took a look around outside before closing the door.

"What's going on?" Lucky asked, looking around the house. A dull lamp glowed in the corner of the living room. There were no furniture or appliances. The windows were covered with black sheets. Scooter stood between the doorways, peeking out of a bedroom.

"Come and look." Polo smiled, his eyes gleaming in the dull light of the lamp.

Lucky followed him to a bedroom empty of furniture. The windows covered with a black sheet. There was a blue tarp on the floor. A half-naked brown-skinned man with rainbow-colored dreadlocks lay on the tarp in his boxers. He lay on his stomach, hands and feet in the air, hog-tied. Tape covered his mouth. His face was swollen and bloody. The sight brought terror to Lucky as thoughts of a prison cell flashed in his head.

"What the fuck is this?" Lucky panicked, ready to get the fuck out of the house. He had already gone to prison for fucking with Polo. No way he was about to let that happen again.

Polo pulled a big black 44 Bulldog from his waist. "This the nigga that killed yo' mama. Draco."

The fear that Lucky felt slowly changed to anger, then rage. This was the nigga that killed Cookie.

"And they got a green light on Desmond," Polo added. "Somebody seen him off them bitch-ass Clarke street niggas. If we start knocking they ass off, won't be nobody left to move on that green light on yo' brotha."

The information about Desmond only added fuel to the fire for revenge that burned inside Lucky's chest. He took the pistol from Polo and walked over to stand in front of Draco. The fear of death shone in the swollen eye of his mother's murderer. Lucky stared him in his eyes for a long eerie moment, the sight of his mother in the casket playing in his mind. He had made so many plans for her while locked up. He was going to help her get clean and she would finally be the mother he wanted all his life. But Draco had taken that. And now they were trying to kill his brother.

"How much you think it hurt to die?" Lucky asked the beaten and bound man.

Draco whimpered something unintelligible through the tape on his mouth. But the look in his eye was unmistakable. He wanted mercy. Another chance. A different fate.

"I don't think it hurt as much as it should," Lucky finished before pointing the gun at the top of his head and pulling the trigger. His wrist flinched from the powerful kick of the handgun. Fire flew from the barrel and the slug exploded into Draco's cranium, creating a crater. Sulfur and smoke filled Lucky's lungs as another color was added to Draco's multi-colored hair.

Polo stood nearby, smiling like a proud father that had just watched his son ride a bike for the first time. Scooter stood nearby, the desire to spill blood lighting the young shooter's eyes.

"Let me get that," Polo said, taking the gun. "I'ma get this cleaned up. Won't be no evidence or witnesses, my nigga. We ain't gon' repeat what happened back in the day."

Lucky didn't hear Polo's words or feel him take the gun. He was too caught up in the effects of taking a life. It was his first kill. He remembered the stories he'd heard in prison about murder. Some people threw up. Others became terrified. And there were a select few that felt empowered by it. Lucky was of the latter class. Killing Draco was a rush, like a surge of unnatural energy pulsing through his body, like Draco's life force had transferred to him, making him stronger. He stared down at the dead body, wanting to kill again. Murder was exhilarating!

"You good, nigga?" Polo asked, touching Lucky's shoulder and pulling him back from the abyss.

Lucky got his focus and the entirety of the situation came roaring back. He had killed a man. Shit!

J-Blunt

CHAPTER 13

He remembered the chunk of building falling on top of him. The cheap structure crumbled when it landed on top of the van. It broke Desmond's left clavicle and shattered his forearm. Metal rods were infused within his radius to replace the pulverized bone. His left eye had also been damaged. A freshly-healed scar went from his eyebrow to upper cheekbone. The vision was blurry, like walking through a blizzard. He could only make out shapes and colors. At night, he might as well had been blind in one eye. He wore a pair of shades to cover the wound.

Only he and Kim had survived the attack. Duke, Carter, and Country were killed on the rooftop. Pictures of their bodies were shown online. The terrorists bragged about killing America's best soldiers. Slayer's body wasn't found. Politics in America had taken over the world stage. A secret military operation failed. Countries were pointing fingers at the United States. Congress demanded answers.

"You hear about the big trade talks going on in the NBA?"

Desmond looked towards the front of the Buick Lacrosse. The driver was a dark-skinned black man. Neatly-trimmed mini fro. Bushy eyebrows. He spoke with a drawl like he was from the South.

"What you say?"

"Talkin' 'bout Kyrie Irving wanna play in Milwaukee. I think it would be a good move. Put him and Giannis together and nobody gon' stop us from winnin' it all," the driver said, eyeing his passenger through the rearview mirror.

Desmond knew who the superstars were, but hadn't kept up with professional basketball in years. "Sorry, brother. Haven't followed sports in a while. But I like the sound of it."

The driver spun in the seat to give Desmond an incredulous look. His eyes showed disbelief. He couldn't understand why a black man from Milwaukee didn't know everything that was happening with the city's basketball team. "Where you been? Another country? It's been all over the news for a week. You don't play?"

"Not in a while. My job kept me busy."

The driver shrugged his shoulders and chuckled. "That cast on your arm tells me you about to have some free time on your hands. We got a good team; check them out. Giannis might win another MVP award."

They continued small talk until the car stopped in front of Melissa and Lucky's house. The price meter said $20.50.

"You can give me a flat twenty if you got cash," the driver said, reaching for the debit card scanner. "I don't got no change. You need help with that bag?"

Desmond leaned over to get the cash from his pocket, giving a look to let the driver know the mistake he made trying to help him with the overnight bag.

"All I need is one arm. I got the bag. Thanks for the ride."

The driver smiled, knowing the "just because I'm hurt don't mean I need help" thinking that afflicted most men. "Alright, brother. Take care of yourself. And get some tickets to see the Buck's. We have a good team, man."

Desmond made a mental note to check out the hometown team as he climbed from the car. The cab driver was right about him having a lot of free time on his hands.

He walked towards the house carrying a strange feeling within. For the first time since joining the army, he wasn't sure of his next move. His goal had been to move up the chain, put in his time and retire with a phat officer's pension. But now that military career looked to be effectively ruined. His team was shredded and his body was bruised and broken. The political firestorm brewing from the blown mission might affect his future in hazardous ways.

The front door opening pulled his thoughts from the military and back to the moment. Lucky stepped onto the porch wearing concern on his face. In his eyes was a little bit of pity from seeing his brother wounded.

"Damn, Des. Fucked up what happened. But you don't look bad. Gimme that bag."

Desmond gave his brother the same look he gave the Uber driver. "I'm good, nigga. I ain't handicapped."

The brother's stood face to face for a moment.

"Take off the glasses. Let me see the eye."

Desmond dropped the bag on the porch and took off the shades. The pinkish-red scar seemed to split his eye in half. The eyeball was a little cloudy.

"Can you still see?"

"A little. Everything is blurry."

Lucky studied it a little more. "Don't look that bad. Scars add character, nigga. Long as you still alive. What they say about the arm?"

Desmond flexed his fingers, making a fist. "Couple rods in my forearm. Be good in a couple weeks. Little rehab after that. Keep this sling on for the shoulder to heal."

Lucky nodded. "You gon' be a'ight, man. We got warrior in our DNA. Everybody in here. Before you go in, let me get a couple words with you. This is important and I didn't want to tell you over the phone."

Lucky's serious tone got Desmond's attention. "What's up?"

"Wacco got a green light on you. They know you killed that nigga on Clarke. We gotta take this serious."

Desmond nodded. "I figured something like that was gon' happen. I just didn't think I would have to come back home and deal with it."

"Lasonya is here and I don't think it would be good to be at her house."

Desmond's face twisted in a mug. "You think I'm stupid? I know Wacco is Quaysha's daddy."

"I'm just making sure. Pussy make niggas do stupid shit and I don't want my li'l brother being stupid."

"I'm Navy SEAL, nigga. I forgot more than you know. I'm staying in a hotel until I figure out my next move."

"No, you ain't. We already got you a room here. You staying with us. And one more thing. I got that nigga that killed Mama."

Hearing that Lucky had killed someone set off alarms in Desmond's body.

When he searched his brother's face, he recognized the look of a first-time kill in Lucky's eyes. He had seen it many times in the war zones of Iraq and Afghanistan. "When? You good? What happened?"

"Polo set it up. Called me to let me know. I went and took care of him."

Polo's name left a sour taste in Desmond's mouth. "You still fuckin' with that nigga after everything you been through?"

"This time was different. I just showed up and did him in. No evidence. And we got rid of the body. It wasn't like what happened with Gutta. Wasn't no robbery."

Desmond was pissed. "Where did you put the body? And where is the gun you used?"

"I gave it to Polo. The body is in a grave. We good."

Desmond didn't think so. Before he could voice any more of his thoughts, Lasonya's voice floated outside.

"Desmond! Oh, man! I'm so glad you're okay!" she yelled, bustling outside to wrap him in a tender hug. "Let me see your eye," she said, grabbing his face in her hands. "It's not that bad. Can you see?"

"Yeah, but it's real blurry."

She kissed his wound. "I think it adds character to your face."

Lucky laughed. "I told him the same thing."

After finally being allowed in the house, he greeted Melissa, Brandy, Brandon, and Quaysha. Then everyone sat around the living room, all eyes and questions directed at Desmond.

"I been seeing all the shit on the news. Trump actin' like it ain't a big deal. How bad is it really?" Lucky asked.

"It's bad." Desmond nodded. "Not going to war bad, but politically bad. Every developed country has spies in other countries. That ain't nothing new. That's how the world works. But to have soldiers killed in an unsanctioned military operation is another thing."

"So, what happened? They showed three pictures in the news. Did you know them?" Melissa asked.

"Yeah. That was my team."

"What was you doing in India?" Lasonya asked.

"Got some Intel that a tier one asset was there. We tried to take him without nobody knowing we was there."

Lucky's eyes were wide with excitement. "I used to watch that Navy SEAL show called *SEAL Team* while I was locked up. They used to do shit like that. Damn, I didn't know it was like that in real life. But y'all had to know everything before y'all went in. That's how it was on TV. What you think went wrong?"

Desmond thought about Slayer vanishing while the team was climbing the fire escape. In his mind, there were two options. Either Slayer was killed, or he had set the team up. But why? And if he was killed, why wasn't his body shown on TV and social media like Country's, Duke's, and Carter's? It didn't make sense. But he couldn't tell his family that. "I don't know, man. All our Intel was on point. We had a guy on the ground. Local assets. This was the first time our team was ambushed during a mission. Got a lotta questions and no answers right now."

"I'm just happy that you made it back safe," Lasonya said, hugging him again. "When Lucky told me you got hurt, I thought the worst. For some reason, I seen you as indestructible. When you knocked out my ex at the gas station, I thought you were the baddest man alive. Hearing about you getting hurt made me realize that you can be hurt too. And it scared me."

Desmond wrapped her in his good arm. "I am still indestructible, baby. I almost got blown up by a rocket and half a building fell on top of me. All I did was break my arm and get poked in the eye. I'm good."

Lucky fist pumped. "Told you us Harrison's got warrior in our DNA. But on what, you got shot at with a rocket?"

"No lie, brah. I had to run and almost jump off the building. I been through a lot during my missions, but this was the first time I had to run away from a nigga with a rocket launcher."

"So, what are you going to do now that you got hurt? Will this affect you going out on missions?" Lasonya asked.

"I don't know. I think my arm will be good in a few months. Don't know about my eye. If it don't get better, it's a wrap."

Lasonya looked apologetic. "I'm sorry this happened to you. I know how much it means to be in the military. Where are you staying? You coming home with me, right?"

Before he left for the mission, he had planned to visit Lasonya's house when he came in town. Now that her baby daddy wanted him dead, that wasn't going to happen. But he didn't know how to tell her that.

"He staying with us," Lucky interjected.

Lasonya looked to Lucky then back to Desmond, questions in her eyes. She didn't understand why he was speaking for Desmond.

"Lucky, I need you to help me in the other room," Melissa spoke up, grabbing his hand and standing. Lucky knew she was trying to give Desmond and Lasonya privacy.

"Be back in a minute." Lucky nodded before following his girl from the room.

"What is Lucky talking about? I thought we agreed that you would come to my house when you came back."

During the distraction created by Melissa, Desmond thought how to respond to Lasonya. He knew he had to keep it real. "Wacco had something to do with what happened to Cookie. That's why I didn't come to your house. His people looking for me. I don't want nobody to get hurt. I'm staying here until I figure out my next move."

Astonishment flashed onto Lasonya's face. "Tony? Quaysha's daddy?" she asked, unable to believe what she just heard.

"Wacco in the streets. He is the streets. Clarke Street Goons run under him. Cookie got caught up in they turf beef. They don't want nobody hustling in they hood and they killin' for it. Cookie was buying some dope when the shootout happened."

She continued to look blown away. "Damn. I knew Tony was big timing, but I didn't know he was that big. I don't understand why they looking for you and not Lucky. He's your brother. Why aren't they looking for him too?"

He thought about what Lucky said on the porch. He had killed Draco. Wacco was going to put the puzzle together and come looking for who did it. "I don't know. But they might be soon."

Lasonya's face changed from surprise to determined. She accepted the problem and moved on with it. "So, what are you going to do?"

"I don't know. I just found all of this out on the porch. I planned on coming back home to recover and decide what I wanted to do with my career. I wasn't expecting all this."

She looked thoughtful. "You're not calling the police, right?" she asked, unsure if he was going to handle it legally or keep it in the streets.

He thought of the deal offered by Detective Perry. "I can't. That could cause even more trouble."

She shrugged her shoulders. "Well, if you kill him, it won't matter to me or Quaysha. I won't ever let her get to know him. I hate him."

Desmond looked taken aback. "Why would you say something like that?"

"I'm not stupid. I know how it goes in the hood. You got trained to kill people."

"I haven't decided what to do yet."

"Well, whatever you decide, I want to help you get through it. I'm talking about Tony and what you decide with your career. I got your back. Before you left, I told you how I felt. I still feel the same way. Do you?"

The question was serious. Now that he was back in town, she put it all on the line. Lasonya wanted to be his woman. Desmond smiled and grabbed her hand. "Yeah. I still feel the same way."

Lasonya smiled sheepishly, getting squeamish inside. "So, can we make it official? Am I your girl?"

Desmond had a lot to figure out with his life. He had a cop offering a deal, a gang trying to kill him, a career choice, and therapy and doctors' appointments to get well. And even with all the storms facing his life, he couldn't stop the way he felt about Lasonya. When he leaned forward, she met him halfway, slurping on his tongue in a wet kiss.

"You really wanna ride or die with me?"

With determination and love in her eyes, she nodded. "We ain't gonna never end."

CHAPTER 14

Wacco didn't like to see his family members in pain, especially his big sister. When a black woman expressed grief, it was different from any other woman's grief. The strength passed down by mothers from hundreds of years of abuse reflected in their eyes, clashing with their desire for a man to lead and protect the black family. To Wacco, his sister was precious, her honor to be defended. Any pain that came her way was to be dished back at the assailant one hundred fold.

"How you doing today?" Wacco asked, embracing his sister.

"I'm doing better." Carmen nodded, the light slowly beginning to return to her eyes. "Trying to get back to normal life. Come in. Vonte was asking about you."

Wacco stepped into the Twenty First Century Cape Cod house. The crib cost upwards of three hundred thousand. Five bedrooms on three levels, two and a half bathrooms, and a two car garage attached. Wacco made sure to take care of his family when he got the bag.

"Where is my li'l nigga? I can't wait to take him to Great America this weekend."

"He with his daddy right now. Went to grab something to eat. What you up to?"

Wacco sat on the black leather couch. "Just came to check up on you. See how you was doing and if you needed anything."

Carmen smiled from the gesture of love. The siblings had a loving relationship. They had been taught by their parents to keep the family love circle tight. "I'm okay. Like I said, it's getting easier every day." She smiled and fought back tears at the same time. "He is my firstborn, so it hurts. I know what happened to him, but I don't want to accept it. It ain't like him to be gone this long without calling nobody. I know he was in the streets. Out there acting crazy. I knew what he did, but he was still my baby."

Wacco reached over and hugged his sister. "We gon' get through this, sis. And I'ma find who did this. That's my word."

Carmen wiped the tears that fell from her eyes. "I wanna know who did it. I wanna be the one to put a bullet in they ass."

Wacco nodded. "And I'ma give you that opportunity. I'm working it out."

"What have you heard?"

"You remember Desmond and Lucky? Grew up on Thirty-Seventh. They mama was Cookie, the cluck."

Carmen thought for a moment, memories of the Harrison brothers as children flashing in her mind. "Yeah. Lucky was your guy. Didn't he go to jail for killing somebody?"

"Yeah. Him and Polo killed Gutta. Lucky took the case and didn't snitch. But he out now. I seen them a li'l while back at Lasonya's house."

Surprise shown in Carmen's eyes. "Quaysha's mother?"

Wacco nodded. "Yeah. Her and Desmond used to have a puppy love back in the day. I went to talk to her about seeing Quaysha and he answered the door. I found out later that he killed one of my li'l niggas on Thirty-Seventh. One of his niggas got hit and now my nephew missing. I know it's them niggas. Got all hands on deck looking for 'em. Polo too. We gon' find them."

The desire for revenge in Carmen's eyes seemed to be momentarily satiated. She believed in her brother. When Wacco spoke on a situation, the situation always worked out the way he intended. That's what made him a boss in the streets, why he had gone from the bottom of the food chain to the top.

"You know this could go bad for you trying to get close to Quaysha? Lasonya won't let you near her if she know you did something to Desmond."

Momentary sadness flashed in Wacco's eyes. "I know. But I can't let nobody violate the family. She a baby. We got time to make it right. But these niggas out of time."

"What about Polo? Why you put him in it?"

"I heard some rumblings in the streets. His name came up. It's only a rumor, but I think all rumors got a level of truth to them. Like I said, I'ma get to the bottom of it. Somebody gon' pay for Draco coming up missing."

***

Two black Chevy Suburbans drove recklessly down the street before stopping in front of the pink and gray house. Both vehicles were loaded with heavily-armed men. Wacco emerged from the lead Suburban followed by two killers. All of the men had bulges in the front or their shirts. They walked towards the house with deter-mination. After opening the screen, Wacco banged on the door like he was trying to knock it off the hinges.

"Who the hell knockin' on my door like that?" a female called from inside the house.

Instead of answering the question, Wacco banged again.

The door was snatched open and Lasonya stood with angry eyes. When she saw Wacco standing on the porch with two goons, the angry look changed to worry and fear. "What are you doing over here? I told you - "

"Where Desmond?" Wacco yelled as he and his niggas pushed past her and into the house.

"Y'all can't be just running in my house! Get out!" Lasonya screamed.

Wacco closed the door and addressed his shooters. "Y'all look around. See if that nigga here."

"No! Don't go looking through my house! Get out!" Lasonya screamed.

It was no use. They had already pulled guns and began search-ing.

"Where Desmond?" Wacco asked.

"He not here. Get them niggas outta my house."

"Where Quaysha?"

Anger blazed in Lasonya's eyes at the mention of her baby. "It's too late to be asking where she at. Don't try to act like you care now. You done already let yo' niggas run in here with guns. If she was here, y'all woulda scared her."

The thought of hurting his daughter pierced through Wacco's anger for a moment. "If you stop keeping her away from me and we could talk like grownups, then I wouldn't have to do this. But this not about her right now. Where the fuck is Desmond?"

Lasonya wouldn't allow him off the hook. "It is about her. It always is. I gotta raise her by myself."

Wacco shook his head. "I told you I would take care of you and Quaysha. You the one keeping me from taking care of her. She my firstborn. My only shorty. You know I wanna be in her life. In yours too."

A deep pain shone in Lasonya's eyes. "Then why did you let them do that to me? I knew you since we was kids. How you let that happen to me?"

The compassion in Wacco's eyes changed to anger. "Why you can't let go of that old shit? I told you I didn't know that shit - "

"He ain't in here," Stink said as he came from the back of the house.

"It's empty," J-Roc confirmed.

Wacco turned back to Lasonya. "Where Desmond? Stop playing with me. I know you know where he at."

"He's not here. He in the military. He left a couple weeks ago. Right after you seen him here last time."

Wacco looked her over, trying to see if she was lying. "What about Lucky? You got his number?"

"No. Can you leave now? You see that he not here."

Wacco nodded to his men. "Y'all go 'head." When they were gone, he moved towards the door. "Sorry 'bout coming in here like this. I gotta holla at Desmond. Next time you see him, tell him to get at me."

***

J-Money didn't mind spending money to have a good time. In fact, the only way to really guarantee to have the best time was to spend that paper. The more you spent, the better. Grind hard to play harder was his motto.

He was currently spending his grind money having a good time at Telly's, a gentleman's club frequented by niggas that were used to spending money. J-Money was known by most of the dancers in the club. He showed his face a couple times a month to blow money fast. His favorite entertainer was back in town, and he showed up to watch her performance. Now that the show was over and money collected, J-Money and Pretty Kitty were downing shots of top shelf Remy Martin.

"You know you gotta stay wit' me tonight." J-Money grinned, squeezing her thick thighs. She wore a sheer black skintight dress, no panties or bra underneath. At the right angle and with the right light, you could see all of her goodies.

"Why I gotta stay with you? Says who?" she sassed, playing hard to get. Pretty Kitty knew she was bad. Redbone. Pretty face. 5'2". A curvy, tattooed body.

J-Money slid his hands higher up her thighs, gripping tighter, knowing she liked a nigga to be aggressive. "Because I said so. I ain't seen you in like two months. I got shot while you was gone. That pussy gon' heal me and make me better."

Surprise lit her eyes. "You got shot, for real? Don't be playing like that."

"I ain't playin', baby. Nigga shot me in the back a couple weeks ago. Tried to take me out the game. Lucky I got this weight on me. But fuck that. I'm talkin' 'bout me and you right now. You know how we do when we do. Baller life, baby. Penthouse suite. I wanna wake up next to you in the morning. Fuck up a check in the mall tomorrow. I seen some thirty pointers that got my name on 'em. Need to be worn by me and I need you standing next to me when I pay for 'em in cash. Baller life, baby!" He grinned, knowing that talking about money was her aphrodisiac.

"Damn, daddy! You know how to get a bitch wet. Know I love living like a queen."

"I know." He nodded. "I'm a emperor, baby. And I want you to fuck me like I'm one. You done in here, right? I'm ready to leave right now."

"Yeah. Let me tell Nay-Nay that leaving with you. I'ma be right back," she said, poking her phatty out as she stood. J-Money gave it a hard slap as she walked away. She came back to the booth a couple minutes later carrying her purse and smiling.

"Let's go, emperor. Tonight I wanna be treated like a goddess. I hope that back ain't still hurt, 'cause I'ma need you to put yo' back into it tonight."

J-Money grabbed her by the hand and led the way to the door. "My back good. Blow yo' back out when I get you to that suite."

"Where yo' truck?" Pretty Kitty asked when she didn't see the maroon Cadillac truck in the parking lot.

"Niggas shot it up. I'm in the Audi." he said, hitting the alarm. Head beams lit up on a brand new white truck with tinted windows.

Kitty smiled like she wanted to fuck the SUV. "Ohh! I love this muthafucka!"

"And it love you, too." J-Money smiled, opening the door for her to get in before going around to the driver's side.

When he got in the truck, Kitty's hands and lips were all over him. "Yo' truck smells new. You know the new smell get my pussy wet."

J-Money smiled, not caring about her love of material things. "Do what you need to do, baby."

Pretty Kitty spun and knelt in the seat, hiking the dress onto her back, her tattooed ass facing him. On one cheek she had a pistol. On the other she had a bag of money.

"What you doing?" he asked, reaching over to grip and rub her ass.

She put her head down, gripping and spreading her cheeks, exposing her shaved ass and pussy. "I told you my pussy wet. Lick my ass. Make me cum right now."

The sight of her ass and pussy got J-Money's dick harder than a nigga in jail watching a fuck flick starring Pinky. He kept one eye on the road and the other on her ass as he leaned over and began licking her sphincter.

"Oh, shit! Yeah, baby! That shit feel so good. Stick your tongue in," Pretty Kitty moaned.

J-Money used his tongue to pierce her rectum, driving her crazy.

"Oh, shit! Oh my God, J-Money! Oh!" she cried, fingering her clit while he licked away. When he stopped at the red light, he slipped two fingers into her pussy and continued licking her ass.

"Oh, J-Money! Nigga, I'm about to cum! Oh shit!"

The hustler was so caught up in the sex show that he didn't realize he was being lamped on until it was too late. Two black Suburbans pulled on either side of the Audi truck, boxing it in. Wacco and J-Roc jumped out of one Suburban. Two more goons jumped out of the other. Everyone was holding heat. Before J-Money knew what was happening, the driver and passenger door of the Audi were ripped open. Wacco pointed a Desert Eagle in his face.

"Get out, nigga. Come take a ride with me."

"C'mon, Wacco, my nigga. What this shit about?" J-Money asked, his eyes wide with terror.

Instead of answering, Wacco swung the pistol like it was a Louisville slugger, catching J-Money on the nose. Blood spewed like someone turned on a faucet. "Grab that nigga, J-Roc!"

The goon jumped in the truck and snatched J-Money out by the collar of his shirt and dragged him to the Suburban.

"Good lookin', Pretty Kitty," Wacco thanked the vixen. "Hit me up later and come collect that."

"Fa sho'. Love you, baby." She grinned, fixing her clothes and climbing from the ride.

Back in the Suburban, J-Money held his nose, trying to stop the bleeding. "What the fuck, Wacco? What I do to you, nigga?"

"Where my nephew at?" Wacco demanded.

"I don't know nothing about what happened to him. You know I ain't no killa. I get money."

Wacco knew J-Money knew something. "How you know he dead? I ain't say nothing about him getting killed."

J-Money paused. In that moment, Wacco convicted him.

"Who did it? Yo' boy Desmond?"

"I don't know nothing 'bout that shit, Wacco. I told you I ain't no killa."

Wacco held his eyes for a moment. "Nah, nigga. You know something. Tell me or I'ma kill you and yo' family. I still know where yo' mama stay. I'll burn that old bitch."

J-Money looked like he wanted to cry. "C'mon, Tony. I told you I don't know nothing 'bout that shit."

Wacco wasn't showing sympathy. "Tell me something, my nigga. You know I don't fuck around and I know you know something. Don't die for them niggas."

J-Money lay back in the seat and closed his eyes.

When he opened them again, he had made up his mind. "Fuck. A'ight, my nigga. I heard something about Polo asking about him. You know Lucky and Polo go way back. Stupid-ass nigga took that charge for him. They know Draco killed Cookie. That's all I'm saying."

Wacco was silent, thinking.

"Am I good?" J-Money asked, ready to get the fuck outta the SUV full of killas.

"Nah. But you ain't gon' be alone. I'ma send yo' niggas to meet you," Wacco said before lifting the Desert Eagle to J-Money's face and squeezing the trigger.

CHAPTER 15

Lucky hoped this was the last time he would ever step foot in a courtroom. Justice had never been in his favor. Being born black in America automatically put him at a disadvantage. And the fact that he was a felon put him deeper in the realm of the underrepresented.

He sat in the open gallery watching The Honorable Judge Bruce Elliott work through the final cases of the morning caseload. The case currently being heard was a pretrial for a domestic violence incident. An oral motion was being made by the defense. While watching the lawyer and district attorney go back and forth, Lucky thought about what he had discussed with his lawyer. Brandon Williams had been highly recommended and was quickly becoming known in the legal world. A couple successful self-defense acquittals skyrocketed his name into the realms of the State's best defense lawyers. He and Lucky had discussed a possible deal: plead guilty to simple battery and pay court costs and the victim's doctor bills in exchange for one year of probation. As much as he didn't want to be on probation in Dodge County, he also didn't want to do any more time in jail or prison. He just hoped his P.O. would be as cool as the one he had in Milwaukee.

"Will all parties with State versus Harrison please step forward?" the court reporter called, slicing through his thoughts.

Lucky gave Melissa a good luck peck on the lips before nodding to his lawyer. Brandon was tall, clean cut, and wore a tailored blue suit. He led the way to the defense table. When he and Lucky were standing at the table side by side, the proceedings began.

"Case number CF2020. State of Wisconsin versus Larry Harrison. All parties present and ready to proceed," the court reporter announced.

"Okay. This was scheduled to be a motion hearing, but I just received notice that the parties have reached a plea agreement. Is this correct?" the judge asked.

"Yes, Your Honor," District Attorney James Rosenberg spoke. "The State has agreed to amend the substantial battery charge to a simple battery for Mr. Harrison's guilty plea. In exchange, the State is recommending Mr. Harrison pay court costs, restitution in the amount of the victim's hospital bills, and one year of probation."

Judge Elliott nodded before looking to Brandon and Lucky. "Okay. Defense, what say you?"

"The Defense agrees to the conditions of the plea agreement and would like to proceed," Brandon spoke up.

"Okay. Mr. Harrison, do you understand the terms of this agreement? That if you admit guilt, the charge will be amended from a felony to misdemeanor?"

Lucky nodded. "Yes, Your Honor."

"Okay. To the charge of misdemeanor battery, how do you plead?"

"Guilty."

"The court accepts the plea of guilt and will pass sentence. One year probation as well as court fines and restitution. Are all parties satisfied with the outcome?"

"The Defense is satisfied," Brandon said.

"The State is satisfied. We will inform the court and defendant of the restitution costs before the day is out."

"Sounds good. Court will take a brief recess before the next proceedings," the judge said before banging his gavel and leaving the bench.

Lucky shook Brandon's hand vigorously, happy with the outcome. "Thanks, man. I like how it turned out."

"It wasn't that hard. I'm going to send you the court and restitution costs as soon as I get them. Take care of yourself. And keep your hands to yourself." Brandon smiled.

When Lucky spun away from Brandon, Melissa was walking towards him with a smile. "Congratulations, baby!"

He gave her another peck on the lips. "Thanks. Now let's get the fuck outta here before these white people try to renege!"

Lucky and Melissa didn't talk much during the one hour drive back to Milwaukee. The lack of communication had been normal in their relationship as of late. They were in an unfamiliar place, and neither knew how to work their way out of the funk. Everything turned into an argument. To avoid a verbal battle, they stopped talking and lived in misery. Lucky listened to SiR sing about Lucy's Love as he drove.

When he got home, Desmond was sitting in the living room waiting.

"How did it go?"

"Probation. Pay a fine. I'm good." He smiled, happy to put the case behind him.

"That's good." Desmond nodded, watching Melissa walk towards the back of the house without speaking. "What's up with her?"

Lucky shook his head. "Man, Des. It ain't working out the way we thought it would. She changed once I came home. Now we stuck."

"Damn. You only been out a month. You making it sound like it's already over."

Lucky sat down on the couch heavily. "I think it is. She insecure. She thinks I'ma leave her. I don't think she can handle my success. It's making her see shit that ain't there. All we do is argue when we talk. So we stopped talking."

"Damn, brah. I like Melissa. I hope y'all can work it out."

"I don't know. We'll see." Lucky breathed. "Where is yo' girl?"

"She went to work," he said as his phone rang. "Matter of fact, this is her calling. Hey, baby," he answered on the speaker.

"Jamar dead," Lasonya blurted out.

Desmond and Lucky looked at each other at the same time.

"What? How you know?" Desmond asked.

"I seen it online. His sister posted a video and said somebody shot him last night."

Desmond hung his head. "Damn."

"Did she say who did it?" Lucky asked.

"No. Said they found his car at a stoplight and he wasn't in it. Found his body a couple blocks away," Lasonya explained.

A funny feeling entered Desmond's gut. "Okay. A'ight. What time you get off work? I'm coming to get you."

"I'm good. You don't have to come. After I pick up Quaysha, I'm coming over there."

"Nah. Tony already came to your house looking for me yesterday. He might've had something to do with J-Money. I'm coming to get you. What time do you get off?" he said, letting her know the conversation wasn't up for debate.

"At four o'clock. You don't have to come. Tony won't do nothing to me."

Desmond checked the time on his phone. It was 1:47 p.m. "I'll be there. I'ma text you when I get outside."

"Okay. Bye."

"You only got one arm, Des. You can't do much," Lucky said, looking at his brother's damaged arm in the cast and sling.

Desmond looked at Lucky like he said something disrespectful. "I can do more with this one arm than most people could do with two."

Lucky saw that he had struck a nerve. "My bad, bro. You trained to go. I forgot. But what you think about J-Money gettin knocked off? You really think it was Wacco?"

"I don't know, brah. But I don't wanna take no chances."

"I hear you. I'ma call Polo and see if he know something."

Hearing the name put a bad taste in Desmond's mouth. "I think you should stay away from that nigga. He bad business. I'm telling you."

"C'mon, brah. Polo is good."

"He a snake, Lucky. I seen it in his eyes. What happened to the pistol you killed Draco with?"

"I gave it to Polo to get rid of."

"So, he knows where Draco's body is buried and he got a pistol with your fingerprints on it?"

Lucky was thoughtful for a moment. "Damn, my nigga. Why you gotta say it like that?

"'Cause that's real. If he get on some bullshit, he got everything he need to get you locked back up. Loyalty is just a word to some niggas. They don't think like you. Nobody wants to trade life in prison for a real nigga badge of honor for not snitching. You should've let me take care of this. I can't believe you trusted this nigga again after he left you on stuck."

Lucky didn't like feeling like a fool and that's exactly how Desmond's words made him feel. So he got mad. "Fuck you, nigga! I ain't stupid. You just being paranoid. He got rid of the burner."

Desmond wasn't fazed by his brother's anger. "Tell me where the body at. I'ma get it and get rid of it."

Lucky stared at his brother for a moment. Even in his anger, he knew Desmond was right. He had put too much trust in Polo. That was dangerous. They had to get to the body and find a way to get the murder weapon. "It's in the cemetery. Buried in a grave. We can go get him tonight. I'ma call Polo and see what he know about J-Money."

***

"I heard about J-Money," Polo said as soon as Lucky walked through Super Fades front door.

The barbershop owner was sitting in a chair getting his beard trimmed. The only people in the shop were the barber, Polo, Scooter the shooter, and Lucky.

"They say who did it?" Lucky asked as he sat in an open chair.

"Nah. But I know it was Wacco. Heard my name being mentioned in some shit about Draco. Did you say something?"

Lucky was taken aback by the question. "What? Nigga, you serious? I just did fourteen years for some shit that I didn't do. You think I'm finna talk about some shit like that."

Polo looked apologetic. "My bad. But I had to ask."

"My nigga, trust that I don't talk about shit that can get me put back in a cell. What else did you hear? Is my name in it?"

"Not that I know, but ain't no telling. The streets is a punk-ass bitch, my nigga. The game is fucked up. Sometimes you don't know what's going on until it shows up at the front door. That's why you gotta have a backup plan for your backup plan. Betta believe I stay two steps ahead of niggas. It's dangerous out here. Gotta be able to work yourself out of the potential jams or bullshit that comes your way."

Polo's words made Lucky remember what Desmond said about niggas not believing in loyalty. "What you do with that heat?"

Polo looked caught off-guard by the question. "I gave it to Scooter to get rid of," he answered before looking to the shooter. "You got rid of that, right?"

Scooter nodded like a yes man. "You know it. That shit at the bottom of the pond in Washington Park."

Polo turned back to Lucky. "It's all good, my nigga. I got you. I'm not gon' let what happened back in the day happen again."

Lucky nodded. "What about li'l dog? You think he good where he at?"

"Only people that know where he at in this room. I know you ain't gon' say nothing. Neither is me and Scooter. I told you I got you, brah. They ain't gon' look for him in a grave. You good. I need niggas like you out here with me to help me get this money. I don't like gettin' money with niggas I don't trust. Speaking of money, tell me about that business plan you was thinking about."

Lucky wanted to talk more about the bad feeling in his gut concerning the pistol, Draco's body, and Wacco killing J-Money. But he didn't feel comfortable talking in front of the barber and Scooter. Plus, Polo had moved on.

"I wrote a business plan while I was on lock about starting my own publishing company. It's easier than I thought. Lotta niggas locked up got talent, but no way to get it out there, so they settle for less than they worth. I did that when I wrote my first book. When you need money, you'll sell your soul to get it."

The barber finished Polo's beard and moved to clean his clippers, allowing Polo and Lucky to speak freely. "Tell me more about this. How can I get involved? It sound like something I'm interested in."

Lucky laughed. "I planned on doing this one on my own. Only cost a couple thousand to get it started. Web designer, book printing service, and an editor is all I really need. Start small and grow it up."

"What if you can start big? I can front you the money for a percent. Fifty or a hunnit G's. Say what you need and I got you."

Lucky was thoughtful for a moment. "If you got money like that, why you need me?"

"'Cause I can't go around spending dope money. That's why I bought this barber shop. And my studio. Got a couple houses too. But I wanna step my game up and I like the idea you proposed. So, can I get in? I know how niggas on lock be reading them hood books. It's some money in that."

Lucky paused to think again. Desmond told him not to trust Polo. But getting a fifty thousand dollar head start on his business plan could allow him to keep his own money and invest in something else. Like his own house.

"Yeah, brah. I think we can do something. I just need to file some papers to start the business and get it registered. Fifty thousand would put us in a good spot."

When Polo smiled, Lucky felt like he was looking in the eyes of a snake. And for the first time since coming home, he regretted running into his oldest friend.

"Okay. I'ma get that to you tomorrow. Cash. You do what you need to do with it. So, what we gonna call the company?"

"Since most of the authors gon' be locked up street niggas, I was thinkin about naming it Chained to the Streets Content."

Polo nodded approvingly. "I like that shit, my nigga. You got something with that."

Lucky smiled. "It's a hit. But before we do business, I need one thing from you."

Polo looked surprised by the last minute request. "What you want?"

"I wanna be the one to put a bullet in Wacco's face. Get me the address."

Polo smiled again, looking like the devil minus the horns. "Say no more, my nigga. I'ma make that happen."

***

Light from the full moon lit up the graveyard like a giant spotlight. Lucky watched his surroundings with wide eyes, like he expected a corpse to rise from the grave and attack him. He clutched the shovel like it was a machine gun, ready to knock the head off a zombie if one came his way.

Desmond walked next to him, a determined mask upon his face, seemingly unfazed being in the graveyard at one o'clock in the morning. His mind was thinking like a Navy SEAL, only focused on the mission: retrieve the body and get the fuck out. With one arm in a sling and the other holding a large mesh bag, he marched on, all of his senses heightened.

"Hold up," he whispered, grabbing Lucky to stop him from taking another step.

"What?" Lucky asked, looking around through wide eyes.

Desmond put a finger go his lips. "I hear something. Voices. Wait right here," he said before ducking low and walking away. He stopped again about a fifty feet away. He saw the head and shoulders of men standing in a grave. They were digging and talking. After a look around, he crept back over to Lucky.

"It's two niggas in the grave. Let me get that shovel."

Lucky looked at him funny. "Fuck you gon' do with a shovel? They might work in the graveyard. Let's get the fuck outta here."

Desmond gave his brother a serious look. "Don't doubt me, my nigga. Gimme the shovel."

Lucky handed it over.

"And I don't think they work here. Why would they be digging up a grave at one o'clock in the morning? They got regular work hours. Did you say something to Polo about the body earlier?"

Lucky thought for a moment. Then a light shone in his eyes. "I did. I asked him if the body was good."

An "I knew it" look flashed on Desmond's face. "Them his niggas. I told you that nigga wasn't shit. He a snake, brah. And I bet he still got that pistol. He using this shit for leverage, brah."

An angry fire lit behind Lucky's eyes. "So how you wanna handle this?"

Desmond smiled. "I got it. I'ma wait for them to finish digging. Let 'em do the work for us."

Lucky looked at Desmond's arm in the sling and wanted to comment.

Desmond saw him look. "I'ma end up having to fuck you up about my arm, ain't I?"

Lucky smiled like he got caught doing something wrong. "My bad, brah. But it's two of them. You sure you got it?"

"I killed a warehouse full of niggas strapped with machine guns with throwing knives. But what else did you talk to Polo about? Anything you ain't telling me?"

"Nah. We talked about doing some business but that shit over now. And about the pistol. He said Scooter got rid of it."

"You believe him?"

"Hell nah. Especially not after this shit."

"What was the business deal?"

"He wanna go in with me on a publishing company, but that shit is over."

Desmond nodded. "Stay right here. I'll be back."

Lucky watched his little brother crouch low and sneak towards the men in the grave. That's when he noticed Desmond's feet didn't make noise as he walked. It was like he was walking on air. When he got near the grave robbers, Desmond disappeared, blending in with the darkness.

It took about twenty minutes for the men to finish digging. They threw their shovels out of the grave and after loud grunts, a large black bag was heaved onto the grass. The first man emerged from the grave and knelt down to help his much shorter partner out.

That's when Desmond struck. He leapt from the spot where he was hiding, moving with a speed Lucky had never seen. The big man didn't make a sound, so the victim never knew what hit him. The shovel sliced through the air and dug so far into the grave robber's head that the metal blade was touching his ear. The man's body froze for a moment before going limp. When Desmond yanked away the shovel, the body fell forward into the grave.

"Ahhhh shit!" the man in grave screamed when his partner fell on top of him. Desmond leapt into the grave holding the shovel high above his head like a javelin. Then everything went silent.

Lucky ran over to the grave to check on his brother. He found Desmond pulling the shovel out of one of the men's heads. Both bodies lay in the dirt unmoving. The sight was gruesome and made Lucky's stomach churn.

"You good, Des?"

"Yeah. I'm coming out now."

Desmond threw the shovel out before reaching a hand up and grabbing the edge of the grave. Then he catapulted himself up, using one arm to pull himself out of the grave. After rolling in the grass, he stood and grabbed the murder weapon. "You gotta carry the body."

Lucky stared at his little brother in amazement. "Man, how the fuck you just do that shit?"

Desmond smiled. "I told you I can do more shit with one hand than most people can do with two."

CHAPTER 16

The sight of Lasonya's naked body caused a charge of electricity to vibrate through Desmond. She was the woman of his dreams and the first girl he ever loved. When puberty and raging hormones came upon his adolescent body, he spilled copious amounts of semen into the toilet while masturbating to thoughts of his childhood crush. Now the dreams he had as a boy were reality.

The bathrobe slipped from Lasonya's shoulders, forming a fabric puddle on the floor as she stood at the foot of the bed in all her buck naked glory. Her beautiful face was topped off by hazel brown eyes, long thick hair, and perfectly kissable lips. Her skin was the color of fine brown sugar. The glorious curves of her body were as amazing as the curves of the Nile River. She had nice 34DD breasts, a flat stomach, wide hips, and a shaved pussy between thick thighs. She had two tattoos: a butterfly on the right side of her ribs and Quaysha's name in cursive on her left shoulder blade.

"You like what you see?" she sang, arching her back, making her body into the shape of an S.

Desmond moved the sheet to the side so she could see the answer. His dick stood erect like the Apollo 13 space rocket on the launch pad. "Get'cho ass over here and let me show you."

Lasonya gave a flirty smile as she walked over to the bed. Desmond didn't like how slowly she moved. He was hungry for her loving and he grabbed her around the waist with his good arm to pull her close. Their lips met in a lustful kiss before he maneuvered on top. His mouth went from her lips to her nipples.

"That feels good!" Lasonya moaned, rubbing his head.

While sucking and nipping her nipples, he moved his good hand between her thighs and rubbed her wet and rapidly swelling pussy lips. His finger slipped easily inside while his thumb gently stroked her clitoris.

"Oh, yes!" she gasped, rocking her head from side to side.

He continued working his fingers in her womb while kissing his way down her belly, stopping when he got to her sweet-tasting twat. After removing his finger, he stuck out his tongue and gave her slit one long pussy-parting lick from top to bottom. Then he moved to her clit, sucking and licking gently while inserting two fingers deep into her love hole.

"Oh shit! Yes! Harder! Suck it harder! I'm cumming!" Lasonya cried, thrusting her hips.

Desmond clamped his lips on her clit and sucked hard while jamming three fingers inside. Lasonya bucked up and seemed to freeze with her ass a foot off the bed as the orgasm passed through her body. When she relaxed enough to lower her hips back to the bed, Desmond crawled up her sweat-covered body and kissed her, making her moan again.

"Damn, you taste good!" Desmond breathed.

Lasonya stared at him for a moment with lust glazed eyes. Then she pushed his chest. "Get up and let me taste you."

Desmond rolled onto his back so Lasonya could roll on top. She started with kisses on his chin then moved down to his neck and chest. Sucked and bit his nipples.

"Ah, shit!" Desmond groaned, liking the pleasure from her lips and pain from her teeth.

Then she moved on, licking down his abs, stopping at the V near his pelvic area. She kissed and licked him there. Desmond began wiggling under her tongue work. Then she moved her lips to the prize. She grabbed him in a fist and admired the package. Her man was long and thick. She pursed her lips against his swollen member, placing a kiss on the head. Then she stuck her tongue out and licked the slit.

"Oh shit!" Desmond shuddered, grabbing the back of her head, wanting to be inside her mouth.

Lasonya gave him what he wanted, taking him as deep as she could. Over and over she bobbed her head up and down, taking a little more of him down her throat. What she couldn't get down her throat, she stroked with one hand while using the other to massage his balls. Desmond closed his eyes, moaning his approval. He didn't want to bust fast, but Lasonya was working magic with her lips and hands.

"Ah, baby! I'm 'bout to bust!" he warned.

168

Lasonya moved her head just in time to watch the white juice gush out of him. She continued pumping her hand up and down, watching the semen spill over her fist and onto his pelvis.

"Okay! Ssss, stop!" he panted, grimacing from the pleasure and pain of her hand on his tender meat.

"That was hot." She smiled, pleased with her work. "Now I need you to finish scratching my itch," she said before climbing on top of his semi-hard stick.

After another round of sweaty sex, the lovers cuddled up, both of them satisfied from the sexcapade.

"I don't ever remember feeling this good being with somebody." Lasonya sighed as she snuggled up next to her man.

"That's because I was made for you and you was made for me. When you put it together, it feel good."

She gave his words some thought. "If anybody but you would've said that, I would've told them to stop because they feeling they self too much. But you might be right," she said before kissing his cheek.

He looked over at her, face twisted in a mug. "Might be right?"

She laughed. "Did I hurt your feelings?"

"I'm a Navy SEAL. We don't have feelings."

"Whatever." Lasonya rolled her eyes. "So, have you decided whether or not you are going to go back to the army after your arm gets better?"

"I don't know yet. It's still a long way away."

"I don't want you to go back. Going to sleep and waking up to you feels good. I don't want it to be over."

"I like it too," Desmond said. "You wanna move in together?"

She sat up to look him in the face. "Are you serious?"

"Yeah. You said you don't want it to be over, right?"

"Yeah. I said it. But we can't go to my house. What about Tony? Are you going to kill him?"

Desmond paused to stare at her. Her dislike for her baby daddy surprised him. "Do you want me to?"

Lasonya looked away for a moment. When she looked at him again, there was hatred in her eyes. "Yes. Will you?"

"What about Quaysha? She needs a daddy, right?"

She shook her head, eyes getting watery. "Not him."

"What happened between y'all? Why don't you like him? What did he do to you?"

Lasonya looked away again. Kept her head turned while she spoke. "He let them violate me."

Desmond reached out and turned her face so he could see her. Tears spilled down her cheeks. "Tell me what happened."

She wiped the tears, gathering strength. The words came out in a whisper. "He let his friends rape me."

The confession hit Desmond in the chest like a 12-gauge slug. "What?"

She nodded. "They drugged me. He put something in my drink. It was my fault. I knew I shouldn't have been messing with him. He wasn't my man, you know? We was just messing around. But I didn't think he would do that to me. I knew him from back in the day. He knew I wasn't a thot. I don't know why he did that to me. I hate him for that. If I was strong enough, I woulda killed him my-self."

A raging fire coursed through Desmond as he digested her words. He couldn't believe Wacco could be so foul. He had already decided to kill Wacco, but knowing what he did to Lasonya made revenge even more necessary.

"Will you kill him for me? For us?" Lasonya's voice broke through his thoughts.

The same fire of hatred that blazed in Lasonya's heart for Wacco was transferred to his. "I'ma bury him next to his nephew," he promised.

***

Desmond lay awake while Lasonya slept next to him. Ever since he had been blown off the building in India, sleep hadn't come easy. The nightmares had been keeping him awake. Visions of the building falling on top of him had scared him awake many nights. Now he slept little more than three or four hours a night.

When his phone began vibrating on the bedside table, he reached for it. The name on the screen made him wish he had fallen asleep. He sat up in bed to answer.

"Yeah?"

"Desmond, how's it going, buddy? I've been looking forward to you calling, but you've been standing me up like a high school jock does an ugly prom date."

"I've been busy saving the world. What's going on, Detective?"

"I need to see you, soldier. Need to talk about our deal."

"I told you I needed time to think about it."

"Your time is up, buddy. I need you to come and see me so we can talk. I've given you almost two months. That's more than enough time. What's it gonna be? Do I have to investigate you for murder or do we have a deal?"

Desmond closed his eyes and let out a breath. Lucky's words about not snitching played in his head. Shit. He needed more time to figure out his next move. But time had run out. He had to make a decision.

"Yeah. We got a deal."

"That's great. Really, really great. It's late, so I'll let you get back to sleep. I'll call you tomorrow to discuss how we'll proceed. See you later, soldier."

Desmond continued to sit up in bed after the call ended. Damn. The last thing he wanted to do was work with the police, but it seemed he didn't have a choice. He needed to figure a way out. Lucky would probably disown him if he helped the police lock up Polo.

"Desmond?" Lasonya called.

He turned and seen her reaching through the dark for him. "Yeah, baby?"

"Where you at? Come back to bed."

He sat the phone on the table and lay down next to his girl. "I got a call."

"Who was it?"

"Nobody. I'm good. Go back to sleep."

***

Desmond walked slowly towards the barber shop, checking his surroundings for anything that seemed out of place or suspicious. When he got to the door, he looked through the floor-to-ceiling storefront windows. There were a few customers inside, some in the chairs getting their hair cut, others waiting for a chair to open so they could get trimmed. He noticed Polo sitting in a chair near the back. Near him stood the tall, skinny shooter.

A bell chimed when the door opened. Polo and the kid looked over when Desmond walked in.

"Desmond, what's good?" Polo smiled.

"What's up, brah?" Desmond nodded as he walked over to shake Polo's hand.

"You know you got it, my nigga," he said, looking at Desmond's arm in the sling and the scar on his eye. "What happened to you? You good?"

"Yeah. I'm solid. Got into some bullshit. Be good in a couple weeks. You got somewhere private we can talk?"

He nodded. "Yeah. Got a office in the back. C'mon."

Desmond followed him into a storage room that was also a break room. Boxes lined the walls on one side of the room, a black three-piece furniture set on the other side.

"Sit down, Des. What's on yo' mind?" Polo asked as he sat down.

"I'm not gon' bullshit you, brah," Desmond began as he sat. "I know about the deal you made with Lucky and I need you to call it off."

Polo's eyes squinted to half slits. "You don't know what you talking about, Desmond. Me and Lucky good. That's my nigga. I'ma help him get Wacco and we gon' make a lot of money. What could be better than that?"

Desmond held his stare, face remaining serious. "If that's yo' nigga, why you send yo' boys to dig up Draco's body?"

If looks could kill, Desmond would have rolled onto the floor and took his last breath. Polo couldn't hide the disdain and hostility he felt towards the trained killer. "What you know about that?"

"I know that you a snake. You got leverage over my brother and I can see through you. That's why I took the body. Take back the deal."

Polo smiled wickedly. "Nah. A deal is a deal. And I don't believe you did that anyway. You didn't kill two niggas with yo' arm like that."

It was Desmond's turn to smile. "I can do more shit with one arm than most people can do with two. I killed both them niggas with the same shovel. You ain't seen shit. I bury mu'fuckas that try to fuck over me and mine. Cancel that deal."

The men had a stare down, neither of them blinking. Both showing they weren't intimidated by the other.

"And if I don't cancel the deal, then what?" Polo taunted. "Lucky knows I got his back. He knows I'ma help him get money. That's my nigga."

"Then you don't know Lucky as good as you think. He knows them was yo' niggas. He knows you a snake. And since I'm being real, I really don't give a fuck about the deal y'all had. That shit is over. I just want the pistol. And I ain't leaving without it."

Even though Desmond didn't say what gun he wanted, the look in Polo's eyes told that he knew. But he played dumb anyway.

"What pistol?"

"The one that killed Draco."

"My nigga got rid of that."

"So, we really gon' sit here and tell lies back and forth? I know you still got it. And I got something that you want, too. Something that you need. I wanna trade."

Interest shone in Polo's eyes. "You don't got shit I want."

"Trust me, Polo. I'm not fucking around. You need what I got."

Polo eyed him again. Decided Desmond knew something. "Okay. What you got that I need?"

"Information," Desmond said smugly.

Polo laughed. "Get the fuck outta my barber shop. I'm done talking to you."

Desmond shook his head. "I'm not leaving without that pistol."

Polo looked towards his shooter. Scooter reached for the pistol in his waist. Desmond was ready and kicked the table into his knees. The youngster fell forward over the table and Desmond leapt from the couch like he was The Flash. A knee to Scooter's face sent him stumbling backwards, his arms flailing while trying to catch his balance. Desmond was upon the shooter before he hit the floor, reaching into his waist, taking the pistol and pointing it at Polo.

"Don't fuck with me, Polo. I'm trained for this shit. I came here for a deal, but if you wanna die, I'll blow yo' shit back right now."

Polo couldn't believe what he had seen. Desmond's display of skill was amazingly quick. If Polo hadn't seen it, he wouldn't have believed a man with only one good arm could be so dangerous. "Damn!" he muttered, looking past the pistol pointed in his face and staring at Desmond like he was a demi god. "That army shit is real, huh? Okay. Put the gun down. Let's talk."

"We done talking. I need that pistol with Lucky prints on it."

Polo looked into Desmond's determined eyes and smiled. "And what you gon' give me?"

"Information. The police looking for you. They wanted my help. I'm not bullshitting about this. Take this serious."

They had another stare off. Scooter tried to get up from the floor but Desmond pointed the gun at him. "Stay right there and keep yo' hands where I can see them."

Scooter remained seated on the floor, keeping his hands visible.

"Okay, Des. I'ma play yo' game. But I need something from you, too. In exchange for that pistol, I'ma need you to tell me what you know about this muthafucka that's investigating me. And I'ma need three favors."

Desmond laughed. "This ain't a negotiation, nigga. I'ma tell you what I know in exchange for that pistol. That's it."

Polo looked unfazed. "Nah, Desmond. You don't got the leverage here. If that pistol gets in the wrong hands, Lucky won't ever see the streets again. You can shoot me, Scooter, and everybody in the barbershop, but that won't get you that pistol. Only I know where it's at. So, how you wanna play this? I just need three favors, baby. Do we got a deal?"

Desmond mugged Polo. The snake knew he had Desmond in a bind. And the Navy SEAL couldn't leave without that pistol. "A'ight. We got a deal. What's the three favors?"

Polo smiled like he won a hundred million dollar lottery jackpot. "Three kills. I'ma let you know when I want 'em done," he said before turning to his shooter. "Scooter, go get that burner and bring it to Desmond."

Scooter looked at the pistol in Desmond's hand. "I need that back."

Desmond shook his head. No way was he about to give him a weapon after he just whipped his ass. "Nah. Finder's keepers. Go get that pistol."

Scooter mugged Desmond as he got up and left the room.

Polo got up from the couch with his arm outstretched. "Let's shake on that deal while you tell me about this investigation."

After tucking the pistol, the men shook hands. "The cop's name is Detective Perry. I met with him earlier today. He wants me to set you up in exchange for making a possible charge on me disappear."

J-Blunt

CHAPTER 17

Being in prison was easier than being free.

That's what Lucky thought as he stood at the sink, wrapped in a bath towel, staring at his reflection in the bathroom mirror. In prison, he had no one to think about but himself. Even though he had been surrounded by a thousand people, he felt alone. Only had to fend for himself. As long as he was respectful to others, they were respectful to him. Most of the time. The rules were simple. Stay out of the guards' way and they stayed out of yours. Stand for count. Try not to get caught for anything that could send you to the hole. Clean up after yourself. And most importantly, mind your own business. For fourteen years that had been his schedule. His life.

And now everything was different. He had a family that he was responsible for. Kids that he loved but weren't his. And was locked in a passionless relationship. Last night he jacked off while watching porn on his phone because Melissa didn't want to give him some pussy. While he was in prison, he often lay in his bunk at night, dreaming of a loving wife and family when he was freed. He had planned trips. Vacations. Wanted to take pictures and videos so the moments could be etched into history forever. But nothing worked out the way he planned and now he was weighing whether or not being free was better than being in prison.

"I'm tripping." He laughed to himself before hanging the face towel on the rack. His worst day of freedom was ten times better than his best day in prison.

A knock on the door interrupted the moment with himself.

"I'm in here."

"Can you hand me some tissue," Melissa called from the other side of the door.

He grabbed the roll and handed it out the door. They locked eyes for a moment. Her empathetic eyes reflected true emotions. She had grown to resent the man she once loved. The look in her brown irises stabbed Lucky in the chest like a steak knife. He held onto her hand when she grabbed the roll of tissue. Confusion wrinkled her eyebrows.

"What?"

"Is this how it's gon' be?"

At first she didn't know what he was talking about. She stared blankly until she recognized the message in his eyes. "I don't know," she mumbled, looking away. When she looked at him again, there was an accusation in her angry eyes. "You the one that changed."

Lucky continued to hold her hand, wanting to feel her touch. Not wanting to argue. "I didn't change, Melissa. I'm still the same man you met five years ago. I don't want to argue. Can we talk for once without arguing? I want us to figure this out."

Melissa looked down at his hand holding hers and then into his pleading eyes. Slowly the fire in her eyes dimmed. "Okay."

Lucky pulled her into the bathroom, and leaned against the sink. Melissa a couple feet away with her back on the wall. An awkward silence passed between them as one waited on the other to speak.

"I still love you," Lucky began.

Melissa stared into his eyes for a moment, gauging the truth behind his words. Then she looked away. "Sometimes I don't feel like you want to be with me anymore."

Lucky frowned. "Why? What am I doing to make you feel like that?"

She continued to avoid looking at him. "One of the reasons is the way you look at other women. I've seen you trying to be slick when you check them out. You think I'm not looking but I am. I know I'm old and fat. I have stretch marks. I don't have the kind of booty like the young girls out there. I've seen the way you looked at them. You are attracted to them."

Lucky took a moment to think before responding. And that slight pause was all it took for Melissa to convict him.

"See! I knew it!" she spat, the angry fire reigniting in her eyes.

Lucky reached out and grabbed her wide hips, closing the distance between them. "Wait, baby. Let me talk before you get mad. We talking not arguing, right?"

She squinted her eyes at him, temporarily curbing her desire to start a fight. Then she nodded. "Okay. Talk."

"I honestly don't know what you see when you say I check out other females. I didn't realize I was doing that."

She let out a long angry breath and mugged him.

"I'm serious, baby. But I need you to know that they don't matter to me. Even if I do check them out, I don't love them or want them. I want you. I want your stretch marks. I want your thirty-six-year old ass with the dimples in it."

She tried to hide the smile that was creeping onto her face as he continued.

"Everything we built is real, baby. I'm in this with you for the long haul. Them girls didn't spend the last five years building the relationship we have, and I'm not giving them your spot. They wasn't struggling with me. They wasn't with me shooting in the gym. I love you, for real. I'm in love with you. I'm attracted to you. You are my woman and I'm your man. I didn't mean to make you feel the way you do and I'm sorry. I want my best friend back. I miss you so much."

Melissa tried to hold onto the tough exterior, but Lucky's words made a crack. And that crack shattered the walls she built between them. Her eyes softened as tears spilled down her cheeks. "I miss you too!" she cried.

Lucky wrapped his arms around her waist and pulled her body into his. Melissa let out a satisfied sigh as their bodies melted together. The hug was warm and filled with love.

"I love you," Lucky mumbled into her ear.

"I love you, too." Melissa smiled, staring at their hugging reflection in the mirror. She had her man back and it felt good. Damn good.

Lucky leaned back and stared into her eyes for a moment before going in for a kiss. Melissa received his lips like an alcoholic does a morning sip from a bottle of liquor. She wanted it all. Their tongues danced against each other's like two freaks on the dance floor in a packed club. Moans escaped their throats as they pawed at one another's body. Lucky's dick grew under the towel, pressing into Melissa's gut. Melissa's pussy grew moist in her pajama bottoms. Then she broke the kiss.

"Wait. The kids. I have to make breakfast and take them to school."

Lucky's eyes reflected the deep hunger he had for his woman's flesh. "You woke them up already, right?"

She nodded. "Yeah."

"They can eat cereal. Right now I need you," he mumbled before kissing her again and dropping the towel.

"Wait, Lucky," she protested, breaking the kiss again. "What if they come in?"

Lucky kicked the bathroom door closed. "We good. We in our bedroom."

"But, what if - "

"Stop talking!" Lucky snapped, grabbing her throat aggressively.

Melissa's eyes grew wide with fear and excitement, her breathing rapid. Then she nodded. Lucky smiled at the compliance, kissing her lips before dropping to his knees. He pulled her pajama bottoms down as he knelt. When Melissa stepped out of them, he guided her to the sink and helped her sit on it. She wasn't wearing any panties. He remained kneeling, moving his face between her thighs and taking a sniff. She smelled like flowers and musk, heat emanating from her pussy in waves. When Lucky kissed her lips, a shiver went through Melissa's body as a moan escaped her lips.

"Oh, baby!"

He used two fingers to spread her labia, exposing her swollen pink clitoris. He blew on it before flicking his tongue across it.

"Oh, my God! That feels so good, baby." Melissa grabbed the back of his head in both hands.

Lucky went from licking her clit to sucking it, then back to licking. Kept alternating until Melissa was screaming in pleasure.

"Oh shit! Aaaahhhh, Lucky! Aaaahhhh!"

After she came, Lucky stood between her legs and slipped his meat inside. She was hot, wet, and tight. He hadn't had pussy in two weeks. Her insides were like a warm blanket to a homeless man in the winter. He pushed all the way in until they were pelvis to pussy.

"Oh, bae!" Melissa cried, grabbing his shoulders.

Lucky's lips found hers in a greedy kiss while his hips moved slowly back and forth. Moments later he had to break the kiss to gain leverage because Melissa was trying to close her legs to stop him from going so deep. He pried her thighs apart and thrust his hips forward, pile driving the pussy.

"Oh, shit! Ahh, baby! Ah shit!" Melissa moaned, lifting her head toward the ceiling and crying out in pleasure.

Lucky could feel his nut getting close so he slowed down and pulled out, holding his juice-slick dick like it was a dangerous weapon. "Turn around."

Melissa slid off the sink, spinning around and bending over. Lucky spread her wide ass cheeks apart and watched her face in the mirror as he pushed deep inside her pussy.

"Mmmhhh! Shit!" Melissa moaned, meeting his eyes in the mirror.

Lucky attacked her pussy from behind, gritting his teeth as he held onto her hips. Melissa held onto the sink, loving being able to see her man fuck her from behind. The way his muscles rippled, jaw clenched, and the way his eyes held hers. Her second orgasm came on strong.

"Oh gawd! Oh my gawd!" she cried as the orgasm rocked her body, making her knees weak.

Seeing his woman's pleasure and feeling her pussy spasm as she came sucked the nut right out of Lucky's dick. His body went stiff while his dick coughed up semen. When his dick stopped pulsing, he leaned forward and kissed the back if Melissa's head.

"I missed you so much, baby."

***

At seven o'clock, Melissa walked out the front door with the kids, a big smile on her face and extra sway in her wide hips. Lucky also had an extra glide in his stride as he saw them off and ducked back inside the house.

Today he had to go to the Department of Motor Vehicles to finish the paper work on the 2016 Ford Mustang he had bought yesterday. He had just locked the front door when his phone rang. Anger surged through his body like he had been hit by a lightning bolt when he looked at the screen.

Polo had called and sent several texts over the last couple of days. Lucky ignored every attempt at communication. His nigga from way back was a snake. Loyalty meant nothing. It was all about self-preservation at any cost. Getting leverage over everyone. Having a way out of every situation, even if it meant sacrificing someone you claimed to love. Self-preservation meant more than keeping it real. Freedom meant more than anything. And despite these feelings, Lucky answered the call.

"I thought we was niggas, brah. I thought you fucked with me," Lucky said accusingly.

"C'mon, Luck. You know you my nigga. We go way back. That's why I'm calling. I wanna make sure we good."

"Nah, we ain't good, nigga. You tried to fuck me over. I was loyal to you, nigga. I took that bid with no problem, nigga. I did that time for you and this how you do? Kept the pistol and tried to take the body. You a snake, brah, and I don't fuck with yo' kind."

Polo's end of the phone went quiet. For a moment, Lucky thought the call was over.

"It's a different game out here, Lucky. You gotta be two steps ahead of niggas that's already two steps ahead. A word to the wise: loyalty will get you fucked over out here. Fuck loyalty. It's all about royalty. The game changed since you been gone and you need to catch up. It's harsh, but that's how it is now. I know I was wrong for keeping that burner and tryna take the body. But I was just playing the game. I see you don't wanna fuck wit' me no more, and I'ma respect that. I was just calling because Sharday was tryna get at you. She said call her. It's important. 444-6573. Catch up with the game, my nigga. Niggas playin' for keeps."

Lucky stood in the middle of the living room and thought on the call. Polo knew he was doing something wrong and did it anyway. The game had changed and he adapted to the current tide to stay ahead. What he did wasn't personal. Just the way the game went. And for that reason, Lucky couldn't be around niggas who played a game without rules.

After deciding that he no longer wanted to fuck with his supposed day one, he thought about Sharday. What the fuck did she want and why was it so important? Things between him and Melissa were finally getting better. He even got some pussy this morning. Was calling Sharday worth possibly fucking that up? And did she really have something important to talk to him about, or was she just trying to kick it with him again? He wasn't sure about any of the answers to his questions so he decided to make the call. She answered quickly.

"Hello?"

"Hey, Sharday. This Lucky. Polo said you needed to holla at me about something important."

"Hey, Lucky. Um… Yeah. We need to talk," she stuttered.

Her uneasiness made Lucky apprehensive. "Okay. What up?"

"Shit, Lucky. I don't know how to tell you this." She paused. "I think you might be Laronda's daddy."

Even though she spoke clearly, the words registered in Lucky's mind as mumble jumble. For a moment it sounded like she said he was Laronda's daddy. "What you just say?"

She took a breath before repeating herself. "I think you might be my daughter's father."

He heard her clearly the second time. His mind went numb for a moment as the words registered. But it still didn't make sense. How? He had stopped messing with her before he got locked up. It was impossible. Why didn't she tell him before? "What do you mean? I thought you said Ricky was her daddy?"

"Shit, I thought he was, too. But he's not. I think you is?"

"But why me? We stopped messing around before I got locked up. You sure about this? And how you know it ain't Ricky all of a sudden?"

"She had to do a bone marrow match. He got leukemia. She was supposed to donate some marrow, but wasn't a match."

Lucky sat down heavily upon the couch as the enormity of the situation dropped onto his chest like a heavy-ass weight. "You sure it ain't nobody else? This shit sound crazy. You mean to tell me that I might have a teenage daughter?"

"Look, Lucky. I'ma tell you the truth because I think you a good nigga and I wanna be real. I was messing with you and Ricky at the same time when I got pregnant. I knew you couldn't take care of no baby. Shit, you could barely take care of yourself back then. Ricky seemed like a better choice at the time. That's why I stopped coming around and calling you. Ricky was gon' take care of me and Laronda and I needed that at the time."

If hearing he might be a father was the most shocking news of the day, her truth upped the ante. It pissed Lucky off and left him speechless for a moment. When he was able to find his voice again, it was filled with hurt and anger. "Seriously? How, bitch, how? You knew I might've been her daddy since day one and you never told me? What kinda bullshit is that?"

"I was young. I thought I was making a good choice at the time. I'm sorry."

Lucky stood again, pacing the living room as an angry fire shot up through his bones. "Fuck sorry, nigga! That shit don't help. I can't believe you did some bitch ass shit like that. Shit, you sure you was only fucking me and Ricky? How I know you not lying about that too?"

"Because I don't got no reason to lie, nigga," she said, copping an attitude. "I'm not trying to play you. I didn't think no shit like this would happen. I'm just as surprised as you is. I apologized but I ain't about to kiss yo ass."

Silence filled the line for a few moments as Lucky gathered his thoughts. He might be a daddy. Laronda was a grown-ass teenage street walker that was raised up thinking another man was her daddy. Shit. "So, what now? What you wanna do?" he asked, unsure how to move forward.

"We can take a DNA test to make sure."

"A'ight. I don't know how to set that up so I need you to do it. Set it up as soon as possible. I'll pay for it. I need to know."

"I got you. I'ma text you the information and date. I'm sorry."

Lucky ended the call without another word. Fuck sorry. Sorry wasn't going to help their situation at all. She didn't even tell him about the possibility of him being the father while she was pregnant. And he thought they were in love. Thought she was his girl. But she was a trick.

"What's good, brah?" Desmond asked, walking into the living room.

"I think I might have a daughter."

Desmond stopped in his tracks and eyed his big brother. When he saw the crestfallen look on Lucky's face, he knew the situation was serious. "You got Melissa pregnant already? How you know so fast?"

"It ain't Melissa. It's Sharday. She got a fifteen-year-old daughter that might be mine."

Desmond looked confused. "What the fuck you talkin' 'bout, brah? This shit ain't making so sense."

"Sharday was pregnant before I got locked up. She was fuckin' me and some other nigga at the same time and chose him. They just found out Ricky ain't the daddy."

Desmond's eyes grew three times their normal size. "Shit, brah! That's some scandalous-ass shit. Damn. So what now?"

"Gotta take a DNA test. Sharday making the appointment."

Both brothers flopped down on the couch wearing similar looks. In Lucky's mind he repeated the thoughts he had while in the bathroom.

Being in prison was easier than being free.

J-Blunt

CHAPTER 18

Mario thought of himself as a made nigga. In fact, that's what they called him in the streets. Made Nigga Mario. He wasn't a made man like the old school Italian mobsters. He didn't have to kill to get the made title. He got the name because he was known for making things happen in the streets. And when he accomplished whatever the task was, he confirmed it with his catch phrase "Mario made that happen", thus the name Made Nigga Mario. In the streets, he was one of the few at the top of the food chain. In Wisconsin, he was revered and worshipped like the great hustlers of yesteryear. Frank Lucas. Rick Ross. Turnpike Ike. Big Meech.

Made Nigga Mario had an unassuming look. Dark skin. A couple inches over five feet tall. Light in the ass with skinny twigs for arms and legs. Uncombed afro with a taper and crisp lining. Clean shaven with a light mustache. Twenty-five years in the game gave him the swag of a man with confidence that was used to having money. At thirty-three years old, he felt like he was in the prime years of his life.

"I bet all the money in my pocket right now that Giannis don't make both these free throws," he blurted out, staring at the group of hustlers seated at the table before him while digging into the pocket of his Balmain jeans.

They were in a suite at the Fiserv Forum watching the Milwaukee Bucks play the Los Angeles Lakers. There were two minutes left in the fourth quarter. The NBA's current MVP was on the free throw line trying to give the home team a hard fought win.

"I'ma take yo' money and raise you," Amir spoke up.

He and Mario were good friends. Amir was also a diehard Milwaukee Buck's fan. He bet big on his team any time he could. Most of the time he walked away a winner. "I bet my Audemar with the diamond bezel against yo' platinum bracelet, too."

Made Nigga Mario lifted his wrist to show the iced-out bracelet flooded with forty carats of ice. He had paid seventy-five thousand for the wrist wear. Then he looked to the watch on Amir's wrist. The eighteen carat white gold time piece had sixty carats of Asscher cut diamonds crushed in the face. It was worth a little more than one hundred fifty thousand. While he paused to consider the bet, the four other ballers waited with baited breath to see outcome, their eyes going back and forth from the Greek Freak readying to shoot the free throws to Mario.

"My bitch Fantasia needs a new watch." Mario smiled, turning his attention to the game.

After taking a few dribbles, Giannis shot the first free throw. The net swished. Amir smiled.

Made Nigga Mario lifted a finger in the air. "I put my platinum cross on it too. Against yo' bitch Priscilla's phone number. You know she wanna gimme that pussy."

Amir laughed. "When I win, I wanna fuck Fantasia. Bet."

"Bet," Mario affirmed.

Giannis took his time releasing the ball. It floated through the air, hit the iron, and danced around the rim. When it rolled off, Anthony Davis grabbed the rebound.

"Mario made that happen." The made nigga laughed.

After the Buck's one point win, Mario walked towards his Bentley GT with his security in tow, showing off the new watch while Facetiming his new girl. "C'mon, Priscilla. You know I ain't one of them thirsty-ass niggas that back bite and dirty mack. That's petty. I told Amir what the move is and he told me it was cool to get at you. We bosses, love. We do what we want. Ain't no rules sayin' you can't have a good time with me because Amir is my nigga."

The brown-skinned beauty looked skeptical. "I don't know, man. I mean, you cool and all, but I ain't tryna get in no drama. Amir is my nigga and I fuck wit' him the long way."

Mario laughed. "Amir is yo' nigga, not yo' man. You married to gettin' a bag, baby. Stop playin'. Fuck wit' me, you know I got it. I told you I ain't no playa hata, so check this out. Call Amir and do what you need to do to make sure everything cool. I'm on my way to yo' house. Make sure you got on something sexy by the time I get there."

Priscilla smiled, liking the thought of having another baller on her line. "Okay, nigga. Talk that boss-ass shit to me then. I'ma see you when you get here."

"See if she got a friend?" the shooter asked.

"Ay, I'm bringing my nigga, Mobster, with me. You got a roommate he can kick it with?"

"Yeah. My bitch Toiya in the other room. She down."

"Bet. We on our way."

"You really gon' fuck yo' nigga's bitch?" Mobster asked as he walked to the passenger side of the Bentley. He was a big man, 6'4" and 260 pounds, and he carried a big gun, usually two fifty caliber Desert Eagles. He also had some military training, having served four years in the Army National Guard.

"Why not? You know these hoes ain't shit. Get that paper and they line up to give that pussy to you. Amir ain't wifing that bitch. He know what she is. I know you remember Kenya's bad ass? We shared that bitch, too."

Mobster nodded as the locks clicked. "That was one bad bitch, Kenya. I woulda sucked shit outta her ass for a shot of that pussy. What ever happened to her?"

Mario stopped to mug his big homie over the roof of the car. "Check this out, my nigga. That shit sounded nasty as fuck. Don't ever talk about eatin' a bitch's shit for a shot of pussy when you with me. If anything, them hoes gon' eat our ass to get the privilege of tasting our shit, you feel me? It's a thousand of them hoes, but only one you."

The big man nodded. "I hear you, boss."

Priscilla lived in a blue two-story house on Milwaukee's East side. By the time the Bentley parked at the curb, Made Nigga Mario had already gotten a text confirming their rendezvous was a green light. The men walked towards the house with the strut of niggas that knew they were about to get some pussy.

After ringing the doorbell, they waited. But not for long. Priscilla opened the door wearing a red and gold kimono, looking like a night with her would be the best of your life. Standing six feet tall with the slim build of a runway model, she was best known for

189

her long brown legs, blue hair, and pretty face. The woman was also an entertainer and knew how to please a man.

"Damn, you bad!" Mario nodded.

"Not as bad as you. Come on in."

The made nigga brushed up against Priscilla, taking a big sniff of her sweet-smelling perfume as he walked into the house. "You smell good as a mu'fucka. You did that for me, right?"

She gave him a sexy look as she closed and locked the door. "Yeah, baby. You know I gotta be on point for you. You made that happen."

Mario smiled, loving how she stroked his ego. "I did, didn't I?"

She nodded. "You come with me. Yo' friend can chill. Toiya still getting ready. She'll be out in a minute."

Made Nigga Mario followed the swaying of her hips up a flight of stairs and into a bedroom. After he sat on the bed, she took off the robe, exposing a naked body toned to perfection. Perky 36C's sat up nicely, the five thousand dollar investment a gift from a trick that kept on giving. Flat stomach. Slim waist and thighs. Shaved pussy. She struck a sexy pose, confident that the sight of her naked body had Mario's dick hard as a brick.

"Lemme see yo' birthday suit." She grinned.

Mario stood and slipped out of the designer threads, making sure to leave all of his ice on. He knew hoes stole niggas jewelry on a regular.

"You not gon' take that off?" she asked.

"Nah," he said, throwing his wrists up to show off the new watch and diamond bracelet. "I like to fuck with my ice on. Now show me why a made nigga need you on the team."

A challenge flashed in her eyes as she closed the distance between them, towering over Mario by almost a foot. She pushed him onto the bed and crawled beside him, spinning around and tooting her ass up so that he could see her asshole and pussy. She dipped her head and spit on the tip of his dick, using her had to coat most of him with saliva. Then she licked the tip of his penis before sucking him into her mouth slowly. Mario reached a hand towards her pussy and slipped a finger inside. Priscilla moaned her approval as she took more of him into her mouth and down her throat. They both were enjoying the moment when a loud noise sounded downstairs.

"What the fuck was that?" Mario flinched.

Priscilla stopped sucking him, also concerned about the noise. "I don't know. What's up with yo' nigga? He don't be on no bullshit, do he?"

Mario reached for his pants, a sinking feeling in his gut. "I don't know?"

When Toiya screamed, Priscilla jumped up from the bed, grabbing the kimono from the floor and slipping it on as she ran from the bedroom. Mario threw on his pants and followed close behind. The living room was empty. They turned towards the dimly-lit hallway and saw the cause of the screams.

Mobster lay in the middle of the hallway on his back, his head turned to the side at an unnatural angle like his neck was broken. There were also two bullet holes in his chest. The sight sent a chill of terror through Made Nigga Mario's slight frame. It was a set-up! He had fallen for the oldest trick in the book, allowing the stripper to get him alone. He turned to confront Priscilla when a tall black shadow emerged from a corner in the hallway. Made Nigga Mario thought it was a ghost and almost pissed in his pants.

He didn't realize the shadow was human until he saw the pistol with the silencer.

Clap, clap, clap!

***

Desmond could feel the danger in the air as he climbed out of the car. It was a familiar feeling. He felt similar when he went on secret missions. Nervous energy and excitement flooding his body, heightening his senses. Lasonya wanted to go home to grab some things for her and Quaysha. Being the protector that he was, Desmond didn't want her to go alone. Knowing that Wacco could pull up at any moment, Desmond stayed ready. His head moved on a swivel, checking their surroundings, his good eye alert and constantly searching.

"We're fine, baby." Lasonya laughed as she put the key in the door and unlocked it.

"We can't take no chances," he mumbled, pushing her into the house and locking the door. "We need to be out of her in five. Let's get it," he said, looking out the curtains to make sure no one was creeping upon the house.

Lasonya didn't understand his paranoia. She felt he was overdoing it. "C'mon, Des. You don't have to do all that. We came here twice already and nothing happened. We're fine," she said, walking up to him and running a hand over his pectoral. "Plus, we alone. You don't think we should make good use of our time together?" she flirted.

Desmond wrapped an arm around her waist and grinned. "I like the way you think," he said before pecking her lips. Then he shoved her towards the bedroom. "But we gon' worry 'bout that later. Go grab what you need."

"Aw, man," Lasonya whined as she went to pack.

It took fifteen minutes to fill two suitcases with everything needed for the extended stay at Lucky and Melissa's house. Desmond moved to the window to peek outside and make sure everything was cool. When he saw the white 750 Mercedes Benz parked behind Lasonya's Camry, a flash of battle energy surged through his body. There was also a Yukon truck behind the Benz. Wacco and three men were walking up the walkway. Lasonya was reaching for the lock on the front door when he grabbed her hand.

"Desmond, what - "

He stretched his damaged arm and pursed an index finger to her lips. "Shhh! Wacco out there," he whispered.

Fear shown in the white of her eyes. "Shit, Des! What we gon' do?"

Desmond pulled a pistol from his waist and pushed Lasonya towards the back door. "We gon' run out the back."

They had just reached the back door when knocking started at the front door. They paused and stared at one another. Waiting. Then Wacco spoke.

"Open the door, Lasonya. I know you in there. I seen the curtain move."

There was a small window on the back door and Desmond ducked just as one of Wacco's niggas approached.

"Shit," he cursed, hoping he hadn't been seen. "It's one outside."

Lasonya's eyes grew even wider as the fear engulfed her body and crept into her bones. "What we gon' do?" she whispered, on the verge of tears.

The knob twisted as the goon tried the locked door.

Desmond's heart was thumping in his chest like a kick drum. If he was alone or with someone that knew how to fight, he might consider taking Wacco and his niggas out. But he didn't want to risk Lasonya being hurt.

"Open the door, Lasonya! Is Desmond in there?" Wacco called, banging on the front door again.

Desmond knew he had to act. If Wacco and his niggas got in the house, they would be trapped. And he couldn't let that happen. "When I tell you to, I need you to snatch the door open," he told Lasonya.

She looked hysterical. "What? You wanna let him in!?"

"Nah. We going out," he said, twisting the lock slowly, trying not to make any noise.

"Desmond, I'm scared," Lasonya whined.

"I'ma get us out of here, baby. But we can't stay in this house. If they come in here - "

Boom!

The front door being kicked in forced Desmond into action. "Now!" he screamed.

Lasonya snatched open the door as Desmond lifted the pistol. The nigga outside was caught off guard. All he could do was flinch as Desmond fired.

Pop!

The single gunshot hit him in the chest, knocking him out of their way. Desmond stepped over the felled body with Lasonya close behind and ran towards the back of the house. They made it to the garage when someone began yelling.

"They running down the alley!"

"Keep running. I'ma catch up," Desmond told Lasonya before taking cover behind the garage and taking aim at their pursuers.

Pop, pop, pop, pop, pop, pop pop!

He wasn't able to shoot anyone, but he succeeded in making them pause and get out of the way of the bullets. Then he ran and caught up to Lasonya.

"We need to find a car."

"My friend lives on the next block. She got a car."

CHAPTER 19

Lucky watched the clock on his phone with great angst, doing a countdown in his head with every minute that ticked by. He had learned a lot about time while in prison. That it could play tricks on you. And when you were anticipating something, like a visit, or release, or meeting, time always moved slower. Like it was for Lucky right now. He was awaiting the sound of Melissa's key being inserted into the lock on the front door. And at 12:27 a.m., he heard the unmistakable sound of metal sliding against metal. The door opened a heartbeat later. Melissa walked in the house looking tired from working eight extra hours at the cheese factory. She looked surprised to see Lucky sitting on the couch.

"Hey, baby. Why you still woke?"

"I couldn't sleep. How was your day?" he asked courteously, wanting to get the pleasantries out the way before dropping the bomb.

"It was okay. I'm tired. I hate working overtime," she said before plopping down on the couch next to him and pecking his lips. "Are the kids asleep? How was your day?"

He let out a breath. "Yeah. They went to sleep a couple hours ago. But I ain't doing too good."

She gave him her undivided attention. "What happened?"

He dropped the nuke. "I got a daughter."

Melissa looked as if she couldn't comprehend what he said. Like he just told her to find the square root of two hundred seventy five million. "What you just say?"

"I have a daughter. I found out earlier today."

She blinked away the confusion caused by his words and stared at him for a moment. "What do you mean you have a daughter? How?" she asked, wondering how a man fresh out of prison could have a child.

"With my ex, Sharday. Her name is Laronda. She's fifteen. Sharday got pregnant before I got locked up but didn't tell me. Thought a nigga name Ricky was her father until he needed some type of blood transplant a couple days ago."

Even though he fully explained the situation, Melissa still had a hard time understanding it. "How do you know she's yours? You already took a DNA test?"

He nodded. "Earlier today. It was one of the cheap ones from the store. We take the official one next week."

Melissa's face went blank and she sat for a couple of moments staring at an invisible spot on the wall. By her breathing, Lucky could tell she was getting mad.

"When did you find out she might be yours?" The question sounded like a charge.

"Yesterday."

She mugged him. "And why didn't you tell me yesterday when you found out?"

"I don't know. I guess I didn't want to bring a problem into our relationship if it wasn't necessary. And because I didn't really think she was mine."

"So everything you told me in the bathroom was all bullshit? You talked all that lovey dovey shit, then turned around and hid something important from me."

Lucky's face twisted into a frown. "What the fuck are you talking about? My daughter don't got nothing to do with what I said in the bathroom. I'm not talking about our relationship right now. And I didn't lie about shit."

Melissa's eyes squinted in anger, her top lip curling, finger pointing in his face. "Yes, you did. You talking to your ex behind my back. How long has that shit been going on? You probably fucked while I was at work too. Didn't you?"

For the briefest moment, Lucky had a vision of choking Melissa until she passed out. He didn't understand how telling her he had a daughter could turn to him having to defend himself against accusations of cheating. And the longer he sat and thought about the situation, the more he realized that Melissa was fucked up in the head and arguing with her or trying to reason with her wouldn't work.

"You know what? I'm good, Melissa," he said as he stood. "I just tried to talk to you about some serious shit going on in my life and you turned it into an argument. That's all the fuck you wanna do is argue, but I'm good. I don't know how to talk to you no more. I tried. If you wanna be miserable, you can do that shit by yo'self," he said before turning towards the basement.

Melissa got up and stormed towards the stairway leading to their bedroom. Before either could make their escape from the living room, the front door was pushed open. Lasonya walked in the house looking like the sky was falling outside. Desmond walked in behind her with a tight face. Melissa and Lucky stopped to eye the suspicious-looking couple.

"Y'all good?" Lucky asked.

They answered simultaneously.

"No," Lasonya said.

"Yeah," Desmond nodded.

Lucky and Melissa looked at each other before making their way back into the living room.

"What happened?" Melissa asked.

"Tony came - " Lasonya began before Desmond cut her off.

"Nothing. We good," he said, silencing Lasonya with a serious look. Then he turned to Lucky. "I need to holla at you."

Lucky nodded towards the basement. "Come downstairs."

Desmond nodded to Lasonya. "C'mon, baby."

"Wait. What happened?" Melissa asked, not wanting to be left out.

"I'ma come up and talk to you later," Lucky said as everyone walked down stairs.

When they were standing in the middle of the furnished basement, Desmond spoke. "Wacco came by the house. We barely got away."

"And he shot somebody," Lasonya said like she was reliving the incident. "I think he dead."

Lucky looked from Lasonya back to his brother. "Shit! You shot Wacco?"

"Nah." Desmond shook his head. "He had a nigga guarding the back door. Only way to get out the house was through him."

Lucky looked blown away. His brother was a certified killer. Since he had come home, Desmond had killed four people. Only needed one hand and a shovel to kill two of them in the graveyard. "Damn, Des. Did anybody see you?"

"I don't know. But it happened at the house, so the police gon' start asking questions and looking for Lasonya."

Lucky looked worried. "Fuck. What do you wanna do?"

Desmond shook his head again. "I ain't sure, brah. I'm in a jam and don't got many options."

"Can't we just say it was self-defense? What about the police that you talked to about Cookie getting killed? You think he can help?"

Lucky gave Desmond a questioning look. "What she talking about?"

Desmond looked thoughtful for a moment. Then he looked almost relieved. "She might've just gave me an ally."

***

"What's so damn important that you stopped me from taking my ass home and getting some shut eye?" Detective Perry asked, rubbing his bloodshot eyes. He had just finished a two day shift on eight hours sleep. "And what the hell happened to your eye and arm."

"This is why I'm back on leave. Battles scars. But fuck my injuries, I need your help. Actually, we need your help," Desmond said, gesturing towards Lasonya.

Detective Perry looked at Lasonya and noticed the fear of uncertainty on her face. Then he looked to Lucky. The ex-con stood tall and straight-faced. They were meeting outside of a grocery store. The parking lot mostly empty because of the late hour.

"Okay. What happened? You shoot somebody?" he cracked.

When nobody laughed, he blanched at Desmond. "Shit. You killed somebody else?"

Desmond nodded. "A couple hours ago. I'm not sure if he died, but I shot him in the chest."

"Upper northwest side? Near Carmen?" the detective asked.

Desmond nodded. "Yeah. That's her house."

"Yeah, he died. I heard it on the radio. Damn, soldier. Even with one good arm you're keeping us busy." Perry laughed and shook his head. "Tell me what happened. Why did you kill him?"

"They were looking for me for what happened on Clarke with Big Man. He was CSG."

Detective Perry looked very interested. "How do you know it was CSG?"

"Because he was with Wacco. This is the second time they came to her house looking for me."

The detective looked to Lasonya. "Who is she? How is she connected to all of this?"

"I have a daughter with Tony."

The detective looked surprised. "Tony Everson, a.k.a. Wacco?" he asked.

"Yes, I have a daughter by him," she confirmed.

Something shone in the cop's eyes before he looked to Lucky. "And you? What's your deal with this situation?"

"I don't have a deal. Desmond is my brother."

Perry's interest in Lucky disappeared quickly and he turned back to Desmond, pulling out a pad and pen. "Okay. So Wacco comes to his baby's mother's house looking for you and you killed one of his people. Is this the gist of it?"

"Yeah. Wacco and about three or four people broke in the house through the front door. The guy I shot was guarding the back door. I fired a couple more shots at them from the alley before we got away."

"Okay. You still have the gun?"

"Yeah. It's mine. Registered to me."

He nodded. "Okay. Make sure you don't lose that. I'll need it eventually, but I won't take it now because it sounds like you still need it. I need to make some calls and see what I can find out. I'll be in touch."

"So, are you going to help us?" Lasonya asked.

The detective looked at her and smiled before looking to Desmond. "Oh yeah. Desmond is a good man. Great soldier fighting for our country who comes home to clean up the streets. Yes. I'm going to help. And I'm going to need a little something back from all of you."

"Like what?" Lucky asked, not liking the gleam in the detective's eyes or the implications in his tone.

"Maybe a few statements against Wacco. I've wanted his ass for so long. Dammit, Desmond. You are the gift that keeps on giving."

"I don't do no snitching," Lucky said seriously.

The comment made the detective a little uneasy. "The guy is trying to kill your brother and you don't want to do anything about it?"

"I didn't say I didn't want to do anything about it. I said I didn't want to snitch."

Detective Perry looked at Lucky, his expression showing disbelief. "Is this guy serious? Nobody believes in that no snitching shit anymore. Do yourself a favor and stop being stupid."

"Stupid?" Lucky mugged him, offended by the slight. "How about you try to stop getting people to do yo' job for you. Do some real investigating instead of always trying to get people to snitch. Fuck you and yo' statements, pig."

The detective looked like he wanted to shoot Lucky, or at least arrest him on a bullshit charge so he could spend the night in jail. "You better watch your tone."

"Chill, Lucky," Desmond intervened. "We need his help, man. This shit serious."

Lucky mugged Desmond. "Nah, I ain't chilling shit. I told you about that snitching shit with Polo. I ain't gon' be a part of this. I'm good," Lucky said before climbing in the car.

"Fuck is his problem?" Perry asked, glaring angrily in Lucky's direction.

"A lot of shit. Mainly that he went to prison for Polo and didn't snitch. He's serious about that."

Surprise lit Perry's eyes as he nodded. "Makes sense now. Funny how you're all connected to the biggest criminals in the city. I meant it when I said you're the gift that keeps on giving. Are you two going to cooperate?"

Desmond and Lasonya nodded.

"Okay. I'll be in touch. Stay off the street. Do you have somewhere to lay low?"

"Yeah. We'll be at my brother's."

"Okay. I'll be in touch."

Lasonya and Desmond stood next to each other in the parking lot and watched the detective drive away. Then she reached out to hug him. "I'm scared."

"I know. But we got the police on our side, so that's gonna help."

"What about Lucky? He seem serious about us not working with the police."

"I don't know. But what other choice do I got? I'm not going to prison. But you don't got nothing to worry about. All this gon' fall back on me if it go sour."

She cut her eyes at him and took a step back, folding her arms across her chest. "That's how you feel, for real?" she asked, looking and sounding hurt.

"What did I do?" Desmond asked, not understanding why she got mad.

"You think you the only one that got something to worry about? You don't think something happening to you will affect me too? I told you I was in this with you. Plus, Tony knows I'm with you. My life might be in danger too."

Desmond recognized his mistake. "My bad. I didn't think before I said that. I know you down with me. I apologize," he said opening his arm to get a make-up hug.

She kept her arms crossed but moved close enough for him to wrap her in a hug. "You are not alone no more. I'm in this with you, for real. I'm your girl."

Desmond stared into her brown eyes for a moment, reading the look of love and devotion. "Okay, Bonnie. It's me and you 'til the end."

She smiled like he just recited poetry and kissed him.

Lucky blew the horn and lifted his arms. "Can we go now? Y'all done?"

After another kiss, the love birds hopped in the car. Desmond the passenger, Lasonya in the back. Lucky drove.

"Fuck working with the police, Des. That's some bullshit," Lucky vented.

"What else do you want me to do? Go to jail?"

"If that's what it takes, hell yeah. I seen too many niggas do fuck shit while I was locked down. Niggas need to stand up and be held accountable."

Desmond blew him off. "You sound crazy."

"You not seriously telling your brother to go to jail, are you? Especially after you just got out from doing fourteen years," Lasonya asked incredulously.

"Yes, I am. I don't like rats."

"What else do you expect me to do, Lucky? I ain't got no other options."

"I say we go kill Wacco and figure out the rest as we go."

"Do you know where Wacco live? 'Cause I don't," Desmond said. "What about you, Lasonya?"

She shook her head.

"Even though I don't like the nigga, Polo plugged out here. I know he can find him," Lucky offered.

Desmond thought for a moment before pulling out his phone and sending a text. A couple minutes later, the phone rang.

"What's good, Desmond?" Polo asked.

"I need to holla at you. It's important."

"I'm not moving around right now and it's late. Can it wait 'til tomorrow?"

"Nah. Life or death."

Polo let out an unsatisfied breath. "Okay. I need a few minutes to get ready. Where you at?"

"I'm riding with Lucky. We coming to you."

"Lucky with you, for real?"

"Yeah. I told you it was life or death."

There was a slight pause. "Okay. Meet me at the barbershop."

It only took Lucky five minutes to get to the barbershop. After parking in back, they waited.

"I took the blood test today. Laronda is my daughter," Lucky said.

Desmond turned to look at him. "Shit. You got a daughter and I'm a uncle. Hell of a surprise, ain't it?"

"Who you telling. And she a li'l thot."

"Wait. What? You have a daughter?" Lasonya asked.

Lucky nodded. "Yeah. Sharday got pregnant before I got locked up, but didn't tell me. Thought it was some other nigga baby until he needed some type of blood transplant."

"Damn. Well, congratulations, I think," she mumbled.

"Tell that shit to Melissa. She found a way to argue with me about it and accuse me of cheating when I told her."

Desmond laughed. "You bullshitting?"

Lucky mugged him. "I'm glad you think it's funny, because I'm serious. I think I'ma leave her. I don't got time for all the bullshit. I can't do it no more. I been miserable since I came home. The only time I feel good is when I'm not around her. She draining me."

"Damn, bro. I'm sorry to hear that. But you know what I'ma say. You gotta do what makes you happy," Desmond said.

"I feel the same way, Lucky. Don't force yourself to be miserable. You just got out. You have to live your best life," Lasonya echoed.

"Yeah. I agree," Lucky said, looking towards the headlights of the car pulling into the parking lot. "Here go this snake-ass nigga right here."

Desmond, Lucky, and Lasonya got out of the car and waited for Polo to exit his. He wasn't alone. Scooter got out first and mugged Desmond. Desmond laughed.

"Got the whole gang here, huh?" Polo smiled as he got out the car. "What's good, Lucky? Tell me what's so important that y'all got me outta some good-ass pussy"

Lucky nodded but didn't speak.

"I need to find out where Wacco lives," Desmond said.

Polo looked at Lasonya. "You didn't ask his baby mama?"

"She don't know."

"Neither do I."

"But you can find out," Lucky spoke up.

"Maybe. But what's in it for me?"

"I'ma finish those other two favors," Desmond said.

"You was gon' pay that anyways. You a man of yo' word. I kept my end of the bargain; now keep yours. By the way, that was good work you did with Made Nigga Mario. Getting his security out the way was an added bonus. I hated that big ole bitch-ass nigga."

"What you talking 'bout?" Lucky asked.

Polo smiled. "Oh, you don't know? Desmond is my shotta. That nigga loves you, Lucky."

Lucky looked to Desmond. "Fuck is he talking about?"

"I owe him three bodies for the burner."

Lucky mugged Polo. "You ain't shit, my nigga. You gon' do me like this, huh? After I kept my mouth closed and did that time for you?"

Polo shrugged. "Cold game, my nigga. I told you, the rules changed. You gotta get in where you fit in. And since we standing here talking, I already decided who I want you to hit next. Get that bitch-ass fag that's investigating me. I need him out the way."

Desmond shook his head. "I need him around a little longer. He's helping me with something."

"C'mon now, Desmond. A deal is a deal, my nigga."

"I hear you. But I can't do it right now. I need Wacco's info. He came looking for me today and I need to put an end to that shit."

Polo took a moment to think. "I tell you what. Gimme what I want and I'll give you what you want. Meet me in the middle."

CHAPTER 20

The interrogation room stank.

That's what Mickey thought as he sat on the small concrete slab handcuffed to the wall. Chlorine bleach and piss burned the hairs inside his nostrils leaving an acidic taste in his mouth. Thirty minutes of breathing the toxic fumes made his throat numb. Mickey knew the police put him in the room on purpose. It was all a part of their tactics, a game he knew all too well.

When the door opened, a tall white man in his mid-forties walked into the room. Salt and pepper hair was ruffled atop his head like he hadn't groomed in days. The whites of his brown eyes were red like he hadn't slept either. The off white dress shirt tucked into blue slacks told that he was a detective before Mickey's eyes went to the badge on his belt loop and empty gun holster on his hip.

"Mickey, my main man! How's it going?" the detective asked, smiling like he had known the twenty-five year old drug dealer all of his life.

"I wanna call my lawyer." Mickey mugged him. He knew the drill. Don't say shit, they don't know shit.

The cop looked offended by the response. "C'mon, man. I'm being cordial. Seeing what's up. Why you gotta bring in the legal jargon? Let's talk," he said, sitting a cell phone on the table and copping a squat on the concrete slab opposite Mickey.

"We ain't got nothin' to talk about. I ain't makin' no statements and I want a lawyer."

The detective leaned against the wall and stared the young black male in his eyes like he was trying to read his life story. The stare on went on for about ten seconds until Mickey looked away.

"Okay. Since you want to get down to business, let's do it. I'm Detective Perry. Homicide. Only time I come around is when I'm about to bust someone's ass. And even though you're a little on the skinny side, I'm about to get in your ass. Now, you got two options. You can keep playing the tough guy role and I can tell the officers outside to book you for murder and you can fight the system that loves to lock up black men at an unprecedented rate. The heroin that my officers found in your car is the same stuff that killed a man in Brookfield. By the way, he was white, and I'm sure you know how unfair it is for a black man accused of killing a white man. And this is a case that will stick. Your number was in Steven's phone. Now, I love to help people that help me. If you want, we can have a conversation about option two and maybe work out a deal that can stop you from being charged with murder. So, what do you want to do? Twenty to forty years or have a conversation? It's up to you."

The veteran detective continued to act nonchalant, leaning against the wall acting as if he didn't care about Mickey's decision. Mickey didn't have the luxury of acting aloof. He had already done eighteen months in prison. Going back was terrifying. Doing twenty years up north seemed impossible. If he could find a way out of the jam the bad dope had gotten him in, he would be foolish not to take the deal.

"What you wanna talk about?"

Detective Perry leaned forward, resting elbows on his knees, keeping strong eye contact with his perp. "I heard you know a guy named Polo."

"Yeah. I know him a little bit. Not that much."

Perry smiled. "I'm investigating him on several crimes. If you help me get him, I'll make sure you don't get charged with murder."

For the first time since stepping foot in the interrogation room, Mickey felt relieved. "Can I speak to the district attorney and get that in writing?"

"Yes, you can. But first, tell me what you know. You don't have to say details yet, but give me something so I know you're not blowing smoke up my ass."

Mickey thought for a couple moments. "I know that he sells dope. I can set up a buy."

The detective didn't look interested in a drug bust. "I'm not into narcotics. Can you give me something more serious? Like a murder?"

Mickey thought again. "I heard he had something to do with Mario gettin' knocked off."

The detective's ears perked up. "You talking about Made Mario?"

Mickey saw the gleam of hunger in the white man's eyes and knew that deal was his. "Yeah."

"What do you know?"

"They got into it because Mario tried to take Polo's connect. They used to be boys, but I guess Mario got greedy. Polo is one of them shiesty muthafuckas that don't ever forget when somebody try to fuck him over."

Perry was damn near drooling from the information. "How do you know this? And who actually killed Mario and his bodyguard? Was it Polo?"

"I know his shooter, Scooter. That's my nigga. He told me about the whole move. Polo didn't actually kill Made Nigga Mario. He said they got a army nigga that's putting in work. Nigga supposed to be like a ninja or some shit. Scooter wanna clap him up because he did some of that karate shit on him and took his pistol."

Even though Perry had been a cop for twenty years and had seen it all, this information rocked his world. "Okay. Okay. Wait one second. You're saying that an army guy is going around killing people for Polo?"

"Yeah."

"Have you ever seen him?"

"Nah. Only thing I know is that he supposed to only have one arm or some shit like that. I thought Scooter was lying. Ain't no army ninjas with one arm running around Milwaukee killin' niggas."

"I wouldn't be so sure about that," the detective mumbled. "Okay. I'm going to make a phone call to the district attorney. I'll see if he can get down here within the hour so we can record your statement and work out a deal. You've been a big help, and I'll do my best to stop you from being charged with murder," the detective said, extending his hand.

Mickey shook his hand. "A'ight. Thanks."

As soon as he stepped foot in the hallway, Perry called District Attorney Mitchell Sellers.

"Hey, Detective."

"Mitch, I got a big one!" The cop beamed. "I need you to come down to the station. I think we got what we need to get Polo."

"Don't bullshit me, Mark. You know how bad I want Polo."

"I'm not bullshitting. A kid named Mickey got picked up a couple hours ago for selling bad dope that killed a guy. Turns out he is a friend of Polo's friend. Knows some shit that blew my mind, and you know how hard that is. We got a rogue Navy SEAL involved in murders for Polo. This is going to be big."

"Holy shit, Mark! I have a debriefing in about ten minutes. I'll be by the station within the hour. I can't believe you got him."

***

Detective Perry left the police station at 9:57 p.m., preparing to head home and get a full night's sleep. He needed all the energy he could muster for the next couple of days.

The interview with Mickey had gone better than expected. The snitch was a well of valuable information. Every time he was asked a question, Mickey answered with more than enough information. Polo was done, his days in the streets numbered. And so was Desmond. The detective no longer needed the soldier's services now that he was connected to Polo, unless he would be able to give intimate details of the murders he did for Polo in exchange for a lighter sentence.

What Perry didn't understand was why Desmond attempted to play both sides. He couldn't understand why Desmond would agree to work with the police to investigate someone he already worked for. It didn't make sense. But once he got Desmond in an interrogation room, he would find out. Which is why he needed sleep. He would have to be sharp. Tomorrow was a big day.

He was walking across the parking lot, heading for his unmarked blue sedan, when he got a strange feeling in his gut. Like he was being watched. He took a long look around the dark parking lot. There wasn't much going on. A few cops coming or going. Nothing jumped out at him, but the feeling didn't leave. Figuring he must be overacting to the upcoming investigation and lack of sleep, he hopped in the car.

During the drive home the detective decided to have a night cap and detoured to one of his favorite watering holes. During the drive, he glanced in the rearview mirror a few times just to make sure he wasn't being watched or followed. Twenty minutes later, he pulled into the parking lot of The Baked Clam. The pub was owned and operated by a thirty year vet of the police force. Fellow badge holders that were on or off duty frequented the joint.

When he climbed from the car, he took a cautionary glance around before entering the bar. Three beers and thirty minutes later, Detective Perry left the bar with a good buzz. He was relaxed and at ease. He envisioned himself going home, falling into bed, and going right to sleep. He whistled Jason Aldean's song "Dirt Road Anthem" on the way to his unmarked car.

He had just opened the door when the feeling of being watched overcame him again. He went for the service pistol while spinning around. Then something hit him in the throat, making him stumble. He crashed into the car, the blinding pain in his neck making him drop the gun and reach for his throat. Blood coated his hand when he touched the knife handle. Then another sharp pain pierced his chest. A knife handle was sticking out of the left side. It only took a moment for him to realize he was about to die. He began sinking to the ground, his eyes fluttering around, trying to find his killer. He spotted the black shadow a little more than a hundred feet away before everything went black.

***

"Uncle Polo, I wanna be a ballerina when I grow up."

Polo looked down at his niece lovingly. Mariah was the prettiest and smartest seven-year-old he'd ever seen. She was skipping alongside him, her shoulder length pigtails bouncing with her up and down motions. He loved the child like he'd given her life. She was truly the apple of his eye.

"That's good, baby. Did you tell your mother to take you to classes so you can start practicing?"

"Not yet. I just decided it now. I'ma tell her when we get home."

"I like the sound of it. And I bet you gonna be the best ballerina in the whole world."

"I am, uncle. I'ma practice all the time so I can be the bestest."

Polo barely heard his niece's response. He was too focused on the two niggas walking past him giving mean looks. They looked familiar, and the way they were looking at him told that he looked familiar to them as well.

"You know them?" Polo asked Scooter, turning his head to watch the men some more.

"I think the tall nigga is CSG. His name Weeble or Weezy or some shit like that," Scooter said, turning around and watching the men continue to watch them.

"Keep yo eyes open." Polo said before turning his attention back to his niece. "We in the mall so I don't think they gonna try it."

"Try what, Uncle?" Mariah asked, straining her neck to see what her uncle was staring at.

"Nothing, baby girl. Let's go in here so you can pick out your first pair of custom red bottoms. You gotta show up to yo' birthday party on fleek. Make sure that when you start liking boys, if he can't afford to buy you the best, you don't give him no play. You special. Make sure everybody treat you like the rare gem you are."

After getting his niece her first pair of designer heels, Polo and Scooter led the little one back to the silver Benz in the parking lot. He had just popped the locks when an engine revved and tires screeched. A black SUV slid to a stop near the Benz. The passenger door sprang open and out jumped Weezy with a chopper. He fired shots at Polo and company, not caring that a child was in their midst.

Polo shoved his niece to the ground and took cover while Scooter pulled a pistol from his waist and shot back. The gun fight only lasted about ten seconds before the chopper wielder jumped back in the SUV. Scooter continued shooting at the fleeing vehicle until his pistol was empty.

"You good, Polo?"

Polo didn't respond. He couldn't talk. The worst pain that he ever felt gripped his body, twisting his heart in his chest. He lay on the ground, his eyes focused on Mariah. The little one wasn't moving. Her limbs were twisted at unnatural angles. Blood was beginning to pool around her head.

"Mariah!" he screamed when he found his voice.

She didn't move. Polo scrambled up from the ground over to her lifeless body and tried to shake her awake. "Mariah! Baby, wake up! Mariah!"

J-Blunt

CHAPTER 21

Desmond lay awake, listening to Lasonya's light breathing as she slept. Next to the sleeping beauty was Quaysha, also fast asleep. Unfortunately, sleep had been escaping him as of late. Visions of the building falling on top of him continued to keep him awake most nights. Add to that his uncertain legal situation and he would probably never sleep again. He had killed the only ally that could possibly make the murder charges he might be faced with disappear.

He could still see the shock on Detective Perry's face when death came and got him. He regretted the kill. In truth, he had done it for Lucky. To keep Polo honest. And now he was probably fucked in the game. He wasn't sure how he would get out of the jam he was in. He hoped he hadn't saved his brother's life only to trade his.

The sound of the doorbell ringing pulled him from thoughts on the outcome of his life. He checked his phone for the time. It was late. Almost one a.m. Nothing good happened after midnight, especially at Melissa and Lucky's house. They didn't get late night visitors. He threw on a pair of shorts, grabbed his gun, and left the room. Lucky was already in the hallway.

"You expecting somebody?" Desmond asked.

"Hell nah," Lucky growled.

Desmond took the lead. "Let me answer."

Lucky didn't argue. He'd seen his little brother kill two people with a shovel with one arm. If somebody outside wanted trouble, they were going to get it.

"Who is it?" Desmond called, turning on the porch light and checking the peephole. It looked like Polo was on the porch.

"Polo."

Desmond and Lucky shared a look. Lucky nodded. Desmond opened the door. On the porch was Polo, Scooter, and another man the brother's hadn't seen before. What caught Desmond's eye were the assault rifles held by the shooters and the bloodstains on Polo's shirt.

"What's going on? You good?" Desmond asked, keeping the pistol in plain view.

"Come outside. We need to talk," Polo said, his voice serious.

Lucky and Desmond stepped out together.

"What's goin' on, Polo? Is that blood?" Lucky asked.

Polo spoke to Desmond, not even acknowledging Lucky's presence. "You still owe me a favor."

"It's kinda late for that shit, ain't it?" Desmond asked, noticing the hostile looks from the unwanted guests.

"Wacco's niggas got at me. They killed my niece. I need to get back."

"Damn," Lucky mumbled, feeling Polo's pain.

"Okay. If you got Wacco's address, give it to me and I'll take care of it," Desmond said.

Polo shook his head. "I don't got it, but I got my niggas looking."

Confusion spread across Lucky's face. "A'ight. So why y'all come over here?"

Polo continued to ignore Lucky, keeping his eyes on Desmond. "You still owe me, and I came to collect. I need Wacco's daughter up outta there. He took my niece and I gotta take from him," he said ominously.

The silence that followed his words was thick, and the fear in the room reeked, as the severity of Polo's statement pounded in the other's ears.

To Be Continued...
Chained to the Streets 2
Coming Soon

Submission Guideline

Submit the first three chapters of your completed manuscript to ldpsubmissions@gmail.com, subject line: Your book's title. The manuscript must be in a .doc file and sent as an attachment. Document should be in Times New Roman, double spaced and in size 12 font. Also, provide your synopsis and full contact information. If sending multiple submissions, they must each be in a separate email.

Have a story but no way to send it electronically? You can still submit to LDP/Ca$h Presents. Send in the first three chapters, written or typed, of your completed manuscript to:

LDP: Submissions Dept
Po Box 870494
Mesquite, Tx 75187

DO NOT send original manuscript. Must be a duplicate.

Provide your synopsis and a cover letter containing your full contact information.

Thanks for considering LDP and Ca$h Presents.

Coming Soon from Lock Down Publications/Ca$h Presents

BOW DOWN TO MY GANGSTA

By **Ca$h**

TORN BETWEEN TWO

By **Coffee**

STEADY MOBBIN **III**

By **Marcellus Allen**

BLOOD OF A BOSS **VI**

SHADOWS OF THE GAME II

By **Askari**

LOYAL TO THE GAME **IV**

By **T.J. & Jelissa**

A DOPEBOY'S PRAYER **II**

By **Eddie "Wolf" Lee**

IF LOVING YOU IS WRONG… **III**

By **Jelissa**

TRUE SAVAGE **VII**

MIDNIGHT CARTEL

DOPE BOY MAGIC II

By **Chris Green**

BLAST FOR ME **III**

DUFFLE BAG CARTEL **IV**

HEARTLESS GOON **IV**

A SAVAGE DOPEBOY II

DRUG LORDS III

By **Ghost**

A HUSTLER'S DECEIT III

KILL ZONE **II**

BAE BELONGS TO ME III

Chained to the Streets

SOUL OF A MONSTER III

By **Aryanna**

THE COST OF LOYALTY **III**

By **Kweli**

THE SAVAGE LIFE III

CHAINED TO THE STREETS II

By **J-Blunt**

KING OF NEW YORK V

COKE KINGS IV

BORN HEARTLESS III

By **T.J. Edwards**

GORILLAZ IN THE BAY V

De'Kari

THE STREETS ARE CALLING II

Duquie Wilson

KINGPIN KILLAZ IV

STREET KINGS III

PAID IN BLOOD III

CARTEL KILLAZ IV

Hood Rich

SINS OF A HUSTLA II

ASAD

TRIGGADALE III

Elijah R. Freeman

KINGZ OF THE GAME V

Playa Ray

SLAUGHTER GANG IV

RUTHLESS HEART II

By Willie Slaughter

THE HEART OF A SAVAGE II

J-Blunt

By Jibril Williams

FUK SHYT II

By Blakk Diamond

THE DOPEMAN'S BODYGAURD II

By Tranay Adams

TRAP GOD II

By Troublesome

YAYO II

A SHOOTER'S AMBITION II

By S. Allen

GHOST MOB

Stilloan Robinson

KINGPIN DREAMS II

By Paper Boi Rari

CREAM

By Yolanda Moore

SON OF A DOPE FIEND II

By Renta

FOREVER GANGSTA II

By Adrian Dulan

LOYALTY AIN'T PROMISED

By Keith Williams

THE PRICE YOU PAY FOR LOVE II

By Destiny Skai

THE LIFE OF A HOOD STAR

By Rashia Wilson

TOE TAGZ II

By Ah'Million

CONFESSIONS OF A GANGSTA II

By Nicholas Lock

Chained to the Streets

Available Now

RESTRAINING ORDER **I & II**

By **CA$H & Coffee**

LOVE KNOWS NO BOUNDARIES **I II & III**

By **Coffee**

RAISED AS A GOON I, II, III & IV

BRED BY THE SLUMS I, II, III

BLAST FOR ME I & II

ROTTEN TO THE CORE I II III

A BRONX TALE I, II, III

DUFFEL BAG CARTEL I II III

HEARTLESS GOON

A SAVAGE DOPEBOY

HEARTLESS GOON I II III

DRUG LORDS I II

By **Ghost**

LAY IT DOWN **I & II**

LAST OF A DYING BREED

BLOOD STAINS OF A SHOTTA I & II III

By **Jamaica**

LOYAL TO THE GAME

LOYAL TO THE GAME II

LOYAL TO THE GAME III

LIFE OF SIN I, II III

By **TJ & Jelissa**

BLOODY COMMAS I & II

SKI MASK CARTEL I II & III

KING OF NEW YORK I II,III IV

J-Blunt

RISE TO POWER I II III

COKE KINGS I II III

BORN HEARTLESS I II

By **T.J. Edwards**

IF LOVING HIM IS WRONG…I & II

LOVE ME EVEN WHEN IT HURTS I II III

By **Jelissa**

WHEN THE STREETS CLAP BACK I & II III

By **Jibril Williams**

A DISTINGUISHED THUG STOLE MY HEART I II & III

LOVE SHOULDN'T HURT I II III IV

RENEGADE BOYS I II III IV

By **Meesha**

A GANGSTER'S CODE I &, II III

A GANGSTER'S SYN I II III

THE SAVAGE LIFE I II

CHAINED TO THE STREETS

By J-Blunt

PUSH IT TO THE LIMIT

By **Bre' Hayes**

BLOOD OF A BOSS **I, II, III, IV, V**

SHADOWS OF THE GAME

By **Askari**

THE STREETS BLEED MURDER **I, II & III**

THE HEART OF A GANGSTA I II& III

By **Jerry Jackson**

CUM FOR ME

CUM FOR ME 2

CUM FOR ME 3

CUM FOR ME 4

Chained to the Streets

CUM FOR ME 5

An **LDP Erotica Collaboration**

BRIDE OF A HUSTLA **I II & II**

THE FETTI GIRLS **I, II& III**

CORRUPTED BY A GANGSTA I, II III, IV

BLINDED BY HIS LOVE

THE PRICE YOU PAY FOR LOVE

By **Destiny Skai**

WHEN A GOOD GIRL GOES BAD

By **Adrienne**

THE COST OF LOYALTY I II

By Kweli

A GANGSTER'S REVENGE **I II III & IV**

THE BOSS MAN'S DAUGHTERS

THE BOSS MAN'S DAUGHTERS II

THE BOSSMAN'S DAUGHTERS III

THE BOSSMAN'S DAUGHTERS IV

THE BOSS MAN'S DAUGHTERS **V**

A SAVAGE LOVE **I & II**

BAE BELONGS TO ME I II

A HUSTLER'S DECEIT I, II, III

WHAT BAD BITCHES DO I, II, III

SOUL OF A MONSTER I II

KILL ZONE

By **Aryanna**

A KINGPIN'S AMBITON

A KINGPIN'S AMBITION **II**

I MURDER FOR THE DOUGH

By **Ambitious**

TRUE SAVAGE

TRUE SAVAGE II

TRUE SAVAGE **III**

TRUE SAVAGE **IV**

TRUE SAVAGE **V**

TRUE SAVAGE **VI**

DOPE BOY MAGIC

MIDNIGHT CARTEL

By **Chris Green**

A DOPEBOY'S PRAYER

By **Eddie "Wolf" Lee**

THE KING CARTEL **I, II & III**

By **Frank Gresham**

THESE NIGGAS AIN'T LOYAL **I, II & III**

By **Nikki Tee**

GANGSTA SHYT **I II &III**

By **CATO**

THE ULTIMATE BETRAYAL

By **Phoenix**

BOSS'N UP **I , II & III**

By **Royal Nicole**

I LOVE YOU TO DEATH

By Destiny J

I RIDE FOR MY HITTA

I STILL RIDE FOR MY HITTA

By **Misty Holt**

LOVE & CHASIN' PAPER

By **Qay Crockett**

TO DIE IN VAIN

SINS OF A HUSTLA

By **ASAD**

Chained to the Streets

BROOKLYN HUSTLAZ
By **Boogsy Morina**
BROOKLYN ON LOCK I & II
By **Sonovia**
GANGSTA CITY
By **Teddy Duke**
A DRUG KING AND HIS DIAMOND I & II III
A DOPEMAN'S RICHES
HER MAN, MINE'S TOO I, II
CASH MONEY HO'S
By Nicole Goosby
TRAPHOUSE KING **I II & III**
KINGPIN KILLAZ I II III
STREET KINGS I II
PAID IN BLOOD **I II**
CARTEL KILLAZ I II III
By **Hood Rich**
LIPSTICK KILLAH **I, II, III**
CRIME OF PASSION I II & III
By **Mimi**
STEADY MOBBN' **I, II, III**
By **Marcellus Allen**
WHO SHOT YA **I, II, III**
SON OF A DOPE FIEND
Renta
GORILLAZ IN THE BAY **I II III IV**
DE'KARI
TRIGGADALE I II
Elijah R. Freeman
GOD BLESS THE TRAPPERS I, II, III

J-Blunt

THESE SCANDALOUS STREETS I, II, III

FEAR MY GANGSTA I, II, III

THESE STREETS DON'T LOVE NOBODY I, II

BURY ME A G I, II, III, IV, V

A GANGSTA'S EMPIRE I, II, III, IV

THE DOPEMAN'S BODYGAURD

Tranay Adams

THE STREETS ARE CALLING

Duquie Wilson

MARRIED TO A BOSS... I II III

By Destiny Skai & Chris Green

KINGZ OF THE GAME I II III IV

Playa Ray

SLAUGHTER GANG I II III

RUTHLESS HEART

By Willie Slaughter

THE HEART OF A SAVAGE

By Jibril Williams

FUK SHYT

By Blakk Diamond

DON'T F#CK WITH MY HEART I II

By Linnea

ADDICTED TO THE DRAMA I II III

By Jamila

YAYO

A SHOOTER'S AMBITION

By S. Allen

TRAP GOD

By Troublesome

FOREVER GANGSTA

224

Chained to the Streets

By Adrian Dulan

TOE TAGZ

By Ah'Million

KINGPIN DREAMS

By Paper Boi Rari

CONFESSIONS OF A GANGSTA

By Nicholas Lock

<u>BOOKS BY LDP'S CEO, CA$H</u>

<u>TRUST IN NO MAN</u>

<u>TRUST IN NO MAN 2</u>

<u>TRUST IN NO MAN 3</u>

<u>BONDED BY BLOOD</u>

<u>SHORTY GOT A THUG</u>

<u>THUGS CRY</u>

<u>THUGS CRY 2</u>

<u>THUGS CRY 3</u>

<u>TRUST NO BITCH</u>

<u>TRUST NO BITCH 2</u>

<u>TRUST NO BITCH 3</u>

<u>TIL MY CASKET DROPS</u>

<u>RESTRAINING ORDER</u>

<u>RESTRAINING ORDER 2</u>

<u>IN LOVE WITH A CONVICT</u>

<u>Coming Soon</u>

BONDED BY BLOOD 2

BOW DOWN TO MY GANGSTA

Chained to the Streets

CPSIA information can be obtained
at www.ICGtesting.com
Printed in the USA
LVHW021949290321
682891LV00023B/815